CAMELOT & VINE

Petrea Burchard

*Diana —
I can't thank you enough —
Petrea Burchard*

Boz Books

Camelot & Vine

✠

Published by
Boz Books
BozBooks.net

978-0-9858837-1-3

for
John,
Boz,
and our Camelot

"It is all true, or it ought to be;

and more and better besides."

— *Winston Churchill*

"If you tell the truth,

you don't have to remember anything."

— *Mark Twain*

CAMELOT & VINE

ONE

The day before my fortieth birthday was my last day as Mrs. Gone. For nine years, every American who turned on a television knew me as the wacky neighbor with the solution to their household cleaning problems. They're *Gone!* That's right! *Gone!* cleans everything! Which it didn't. I bought it once (not that the *Gone!* company would give me a free bottle) and never bought it again. That didn't mean I wouldn't endorse it on national television for a cut above union scale.

Being a product spokesperson was good work. I owned a sunny condo in the fashionable Los Angeles suburb of Toluca Lake. I drove a relatively new BMW coupe. The cleaning lady came on Tuesdays. I ate take-out and never cooked. I went to yoga occasionally, and occasionally showed up at acting class. I auditioned for and sometimes got parts in low-budget films.

I thought of it as an acting career until the day before my fortieth birthday when, on the set of my latest *Gone!* commercial, the director shouted, "That's a wrap!"

As usual, I handed over the empty product bottle to the props guy, returned my earrings to the costume girl and, avoiding the candy bowl at the craft services table, strode directly out the studio doors.

The director followed me to my trailer. "Casey," he said. "Bill. What?"

He dug his Nike toe into the asphalt of the studio lot. I waited. He

1

cleared his throat and stared at his feet, like a kid who's afraid to tell his mom he got a bad report card. Finally he looked me in the eye and squinted, moving his scalp and making his lonely forehead hairs sprout like weeds.

"This is our last spot. They fired us."

"Wow. What'd you do?"

"All of us. The client's 're-thinking' the campaign."

My empty stomach flinched. "Can we talk to them?"

"They left already. Whaddaya gonna do, call 'em?"

Actors don't call clients. Actors call their agents, agents call casting directors, casting directors call producers and producers call clients. Or nobody calls anybody.

"I'll work for scale."

"It's not about money, Casey. They want to appeal to a new demographic." He looked away and rubbed his temples. "You gonna be all right?"

"Sure," I lied, the acid level building in my stomach inch by inch. "I've got irons in the fire."

"Yeah, irons," he grumbled. "I feed my family on irons." He slumped away.

I gripped the handrail alongside the trailer's metal steps. I knew what it meant to re-think a campaign. I knew what a "new demographic" was. It was younger. I lied about my age but it didn't matter. Hollywood had discovered the truth and lost interest in me. Actually, no. Hollywood had never been interested in the first place.

Inside the trailer my hands shook while I changed from Mrs. Gone's flowered, cotton blouse and pressed khakis into my long-sleeved T-shirt and jeans. I zipped on my gorgeous, high-heeled boots (a Rodeo Drive splurge), slung my giant, lime green purse/bag thing over my shoulder and stepped out into the Hollywood sun, hoping to get off the lot without talking to anyone.

The props guy wheeled a cart across the tarmac. "Have a good Fourth!" he called after me. Obviously, he hadn't gotten the word. Another voice, I think it was the makeup woman, said, "Happy birthday, Casey!"

It would have been nice of me to respond. But I was in a hurry to get lost.

I turned the BMW north on Cahuenga Boulevard, blasting the air conditioner. Traffic was heavy so I cut east on Fountain to take Vine Street to the freeway. A bad idea. That route took me past the Motion Picture Academy's Pickford Center, a nicely-timed reminder that I would never win an Oscar.

Vine wasn't much better than Cahuenga. Forced to wait at light after light, I gazed out of my tinted windows at billboards advertising Hollywood blockbusters to the trapped traffic. A hapless beggar pirouetted amidst the cars, singing and shaking his 7-11 cup of coins. For a backdrop he had an old pawn shop, an empty book store and a brand new Schwab's Pharmacy, two miles east of where the famous original had been demolished long before I moved to Los Angeles.

I inched the car uphill past Sunset toward Hollywood Boulevard. Out-of-towners cruised the streets, hoping to spot a movie star. It amused my cynical side that among the tourists a girl (always a girl) teetered in high heels and tight pants, glancing from side to side to see who was seeing her. Girls like her paraded through Hollywood every day, hoping to be discovered.

I had not been prey on the streets of Hollywood. I'd been smart. Being born on Independence Day was significant to me only in that I depended on no one. But Hollywood was a business and my only current credit was Mrs. Gone. It wasn't exactly awards show material but it was what I had, and even that would soon be as valid as last year's box office flop. If nothing else came up I'd eventually have to get a real job. I didn't know how to do anything except act and I'd proven to be less than stellar at that. Could I make mortgage payments waiting tables? People would recognize me, and the thought of Mrs. Gone saying, "Would you like fresh ground pepper on that?" was too horrible to contemplate.

My nose tingled as the BMW finally burst onto the freeway. Would a normal person cry? I wouldn't. In less than two hours, Mike was returning from the set of his reality show in Mexico City. He might stop by on his way home from the airport. A forty-year-old woman whose boyfriend thinks she's thirty-seven doesn't need puffy eyes.

I grabbed a tissue from the box on the console and blew my nose. Then I had a great idea: surprise Mike at the airport! Even if he couldn't get away that evening, we'd have a few minutes together. I hadn't seen him in a week. I'd just lost my job. I deserved a dose of comfort before he went home to his wife.

"Aren't you on TV?"
"Nope."

Inside the international terminal at LAX I scowled into the restroom mirror and tried to run my fingers through my bottle-blonde hair. Nothing doing. Too much hairspray from the day's shoot. The makeup itched, too, but I resisted the impulse to plunge my head under the tap and wash it off. Mike liked me in makeup.

"I reconnize you. You're Mrs. Gone. From the commercial." The woman splashed water but no soap on her French manicure. A tiny thing, she teetered on precariously high heels. Her bleached grin sparkled from between shiny, pink lips. "If you wanna be incognito, I won't tell." She winked.

I'd bought an iPod just for the earphones so I could avoid such conversations, but the skinny, white cord was buried somewhere in my huge, green purse. I nodded to the woman and slung the purse over my shoulder. I almost hit her with it but it would have been an accident.

Back in the terminal I found Mike's Aeromexico flight number on the screen. His flight had already landed. Security didn't allow me in the terminal or anywhere near the baggage claim, so I positioned myself where I'd be able to see him when he came through the passageway. He'd have to go through customs so I figured I had time to wait.

There was a café, but I wasn't hungry. I could have grabbed a newspaper, but I've never cared about current events. So I found a seat (high-heeled Rodeo Drive boots are beautiful, but not practical for standing around) and daydreamed. By the time Mike sauntered out of the terminal, I was hoping he'd have time for an afternoon wrangle in my bed.

Mike strode at the head of the crowd, as usual, his bag slung carelessly over his shoulder, his dark jacket swinging open, his tie loose. A quiver tickled my chest at how his faded jeans molded to his shape and his Mexican tan set off his blond curls. He wore his hair long, in what I imagined was a gesture of defiance to all things corporate, even though he was destined to be a network executive. He was handsome enough to be a movie star but smart enough to know from where the money flowed. The show he produced (shot in Mexico because production costs were cheaper there) was a competition between sexy couples to see who could get pregnant first, with adultery thrown in for spice. I hadn't told him I wasn't crazy about it.

I stood and stepped forward when I saw Mike, then stopped when his eyes lit on something. I followed their beams to his wife. Damn. I recognized her because the two had been photographed together for the tabloids. She wasn't what I expected. The photos had made her out to be a pudgy woman with no fashion sense. In person she was cute, if mousy, with a shy smile. She was also very young and very pregnant.

I ducked behind a sign for Budget Rent-A-Car.

At the sight of his wife, Mike's cheeks went pink and his eyes brightened. When the two met beneath the enormous video screens he held her—tenderly, so as not to squish her baby bulge. She threw her arms around him, and her cubic zirconium ring flashed in the fluorescent light. For a moment I wondered if he'd lied to me about the ring and it was really a diamond.

Mike kissed his wife in a way he'd never kissed me, his whole body relieved to be in her arms. His lips moved. I think he said, "I missed you." He had told me the marriage wasn't working and he was thinking of divorcing her. He hadn't bothered to mention the pregnancy, or the exquisite tenderness he obviously felt for her.

When he opened his eyes and saw me, his expression soured. I wasn't happy about the situation either. He turned away and picked up his suitcase. The lovebirds walked past me with their arms around each other. I buried my nose in a rental car brochure.

I'd bought the purse because it was fashionable and roomy. The phone had to be in there because the purse was ringing. I finally found the phone at the bottom under a couple of headshots, amid loose change and old lipsticks. It was stuck inside my passport, which was still there from my last trip to Mexico to the set of Mike's show. I'd had to pretend I was his assistant. The head of Wardrobe had hated me.

"Hello."

"She's in the john. She's *always* in the john." He sighed.

"I guess she would be."

"I'm sorry. I didn't tell you she was pregnant because—"

"It doesn't matter."

He purred. "Hey girl."

I'd once thought he reserved the "Hey girl" purr for me. It meant things were going to be all right. I'd fooled myself into believing he was going to divorce his wife and that made it okay for us to be together. But in that moment, "Hey girl" sounded like what it most likely was, an empty phrase he purred to all the women he slept with. I figured he used it on whoever he was sleeping with in Mexico. Probably the head of Wardrobe.

I didn't answer.

"It was sweet of you to come, but you should have called."

Smug bastard. "I didn't come to see you, silly. I'm going to—" (a travel poster glowed on the wall and I went with it) "—London. I've got a job."

"Really?"

I took the surprise in his voice as an insult. "Yeah. Indie film. The lead." I was a professional. I made my living at stretching the truth.

"That's great. When will you be back?"

"I don't know. A few weeks."

We waited for one of us to say "I'll call you," but neither of us did. At least that part of the conversation was honest.

I returned the phone to the depths of my purse.

Lies had never bothered me before. I had dated other men while seeing Mike and without telling him about them. But I hadn't married those men or told them I loved them. And judging from the protuberance his wife sported, Mike had started telling me the love lie at about the time his wife became pregnant. I wondered how it could be worth it for what must have been, to him, plain old extramarital sex.

But I had lied, too, and not just about my age. While I stood behind the rental car sign and dug in my purse for my headphones, I came up with the truth: my whole life was a lie. My job, which wasn't my job anymore, consisted of pretending to be someone I wasn't in order to sell a product I didn't use to people who didn't need it so I could pay for my fake blonde, fake smile, fake everything. I had dabbled in acting classes but never worked hard enough to become the artist I didn't really care to be. I wasn't a real actor. I wasn't even a real person.

So what was I without my spokesperson job and my married, TV producer boyfriend? Casey Clemens was a name printed on a headshot. My real name was Cassandra, but there was no Cassandra in that picture.

The woman from the bathroom tottered by my rent-a-car sign on her way out the door. She winked, and flashed her shiny grin. "Bye-bye, Mrs. Gone," she said.

TWO

In the departure area I stopped at a drinking fountain to give the acid in my stomach something to churn. Crowd chatter and intercom drone echoed up and down between glistening floors and high ceilings, creating a hollow buzz. I stepped into a line that turned out to be the British Airways ticket counter.

I hadn't planned on flying anywhere. I hadn't planned on a mid-life crisis, either, but I was gripped by the urge to run. I was supposed to be in London anyway, shooting my fabricated film. England had romance and castles, where a runaway didn't have to learn another language to hide out and brood. In England, no one but American tourists would recognize me as a has-been, and they wouldn't know that right away.

England also had King Arthur. When I was small enough to fit in my dad's lap, he and I would sit together in his recliner while he read to me from a picture book about King Arthur and his brave Knights of the Round Table. By the time I graduated kindergarten I was in love with the king of chivalry. It probably soured me on real men. No one had ever come close.

Nothing tied me to Los Angeles. Nobody cared where I went. I could suffer atop the ramparts of a medieval castle as well as anywhere else. I'd tour every castle England had to offer. I'd speak to no one but the staff at my hotel, who'd wonder about the sad but glamorous American woman who tipped so well. I'd meet a rich and titled Brit who'd fall desperately in love with me. I'd marry him and live with him at his country estate and never have to work again.

I stepped out of line. Fantasy would get me nowhere. I'd stay in L.A., face my problems and swear off handsome men who lied to get what they wanted.

Not that I hadn't done the same. Not that anyone wanted me anymore.

I stepped back into line.

As soon as the plane took off I knew I'd made a mistake. I dug out my wallet: two ones and a ten. I carried more credit cards than pieces of legal tender. Fighting panic, I began to count the change in the depths of my gargantuan purse.

The pilot chattered away over the intercom. It would take something like nine hours to get to London. Nine hours of panic in economy class was just plain impractical. I took a breath and tried to relax. The credit cards would serve. When we landed I'd turn around and immediately fly home to LA. I'd call my agent, drum up a few auditions, get some TV work. It would take time but I knew how to fend for myself. I'd been doing it most of my life. It was either that or fresh ground pepper.

I asked the flight attendant for magazines and a scotch—with water— it was going to be a long flight. On the bright side, I had a few hours to relax and the seat beside me was empty. I put on the headphones, leaned back and closed my eyes.

People lost jobs every day, and boyfriends, even sanity. I was still in possession of one of those things, I reminded myself, and I refused to lose it. I knew how to take charge of my life and protect myself. I'd been doing it for a long time.

"Your drink, ma'am." I opened my eyes. I wasn't supposed to be "ma'am" until my birthday. Still, the English accent took the edge off it. The flight attendant dropped a couple of magazines on the empty seat next to me and leaned across with my scotch poised in her purple-tipped fingers.

I took the cup and raised it to her. "Cheers. Might as well bring another."

Below her perfect, brown bangs the attendant's eyebrows went up just a little when she smiled. "Surely." She disappeared.

I took a soothing sip, recalling the smell of straight scotch on my father's breath. Our Camelot storybook lay hidden in the drawer of the sleek, white nightstand chosen by the interior decorator for my Toluca Lake condo. I hadn't read much else about the Knights of the Round

Table, but I had loved my little book about the Arthur/Guinevere/ Lancelot love triangle so voraciously that its cloth-bound corners were worn like a well-cuddled teddy bear.

As a historian, my dad sought facts, but I preferred the drama of the legends. There may never have been a real Arthur, but the legendary one had achieved eternal greatness. The British had admired him down through the ages. Yet in one way it didn't matter how great he was. He never got the love he deserved from his wife. If a great man loved me like that, I'd cherish him.

Mike wasn't a great man. He wasn't even a good one. His wife was probably sweet. He'd cheat on her again. She'd be true to him regardless. Her heart would break, her child would suffer and people would admire her principles or her fortitude or something. Such admiration would be no comfort to her whatsoever.

I swallowed the rest of the scotch. My nose tingled, a signal of tears on the way.

"Here's your drink."

"Thanks." I pulled down the tray table.

The attendant's purple-tipped fingers placed the plastic cup and airline logo napkin in the indented spot. "Would you perhaps like something to eat?" Her prim smile indicated corporate kindness. Still, it was a good idea.

"Okay," I said. "What've you got?"

"There's vegetable pasta, beef curry, or lemon chick—"

"Pasta. And can you bring me another drink?"

She looked away. "Are you sure?"

"I'm sure," I snapped.

She sniffed and disappeared again.

Mike was a bastard. I should have known that going in. From now on I would choose differently. Never again would I date an unavailable man. Never again would I accept second best. Never again would I *be* second best. And no more lies. Not from a man, not from anyone. Especially not from myself.

"Excuse me." A businessman leaned across the aisle. "Are you reading those magazines?"

"Yes." I grabbed them, slapped them down on my tray table and opened the top one to a random page. It turned out to be a print ad for *Gone!* with an air-brushed picture of me gazing lovingly at the product bottle. I flipped the page so fast I tore it. My eyes clouded. The scotch wasn't working fast enough.

The attendant reappeared and cleared my empty cup to make way for the third scotch. She placed a miniscule bag of airline-logo peanuts on the tray table. "Just in case, while the meals are being heated."

"Thanks."

"And...let me know if there's anything I can do." This time the shy smile was her own, not the one the airlines paid her for.

Guilty and grateful, I gave a weak nod, embarrassed that my distress was visible. When she was gone I tossed the peanuts onto the seat next to mine, locked my tray table and curled up with my magazines and my drink. The plane cruised above the flat, green center of America, the part I'd grown up in. My father was buried there. My mother still lived there, preying on younger men and fantasizing about a life that would never exist for her.

Maybe I wouldn't go back to Hollywood right away. Maybe I wouldn't go back at all. Maybe I'd spend a week or two or more in England. It would be fun to shop in London, and I could visit the Arthurian sites my father and I had once talked of exploring together. I'd find a quiet place to stay. I'd relax, maybe even read a book. Hell, I could walk the moors like a character out of Brontë. Wear a wide-brimmed hat. Carry a basket. Pick some heather, whatever the hell that was.

But that was acting. I didn't want to pretend anymore.

The tears came. The cocktail napkin was insufficient. My T-shirt had long sleeves.

I was staring out the window when the meal service cart rolled down the aisle. I closed my eyes and faked sleep. The attendant hesitated. I heard her open the tray table next to mine and place something on it before moving on. I waited until she'd passed before glancing over. She'd thought to leave a packet of tissues beside the tray. It was the nicest thing anyone had ever done for me.

THREE

The hangover that followed me through customs and into Heathrow's Terminal Five came with nausea and a pounding headache. I squinted at the overhead signs. A huge clock read 11:30. It felt like night, but sunlight filtered through the windows and blared the morning news. I followed the crowd to the exit and stepped outside to gulp the relatively fresh air. Overcast, but warm, with a touch of exhaust.

Now what? I should make a call, let someone know where I was. Not Mike. Not Mother.

I dug in the purse for my mobile phone and soon discovered I didn't have service in England. I remembered a bank of pay phones in the terminal and stepped back inside, only to find my American coins were useless in them. My brain was barely functional but I finally figured out how to dial my agent using a credit card. I had no idea what time it was in Los Angeles and I was relieved to get her voice mail as opposed to her actual voice.

"Hi Liz, it's Casey. I had to fly to London...for a family emergency. I don't know how long I'll be gone. A few weeks maybe. I'll call as soon as I get back." I hung up. I couldn't bring myself to mention I'd lost the *Gone!* gig. She probably already knew.

It didn't matter. Liz didn't need me. Nobody needed me. Not Liz, not Mike, not Mother, not Hollywood. Exhausted and unable to think, I slumped against the phone booth, my brain the mental equivalent of four empty plastic scotch tumblers and an untouched tray of airline pasta.

I had no one else to call. Nobody needed me. I had constructed my life to make certain of it. I'd remained aloof in acting class, been too cool to give my phone number to people I met on the set. I hadn't wanted the complications of being nice. I had made acquaintances, not friends.

No one cared where I was. In England I had no phone number or address. I could die and no one would know. The possibilities were endless.

✠

Adjacent to the phone bank stood a tourist information booth. A pimpled girl slouched behind the counter in a drab uniform. I thumbed through a dumbfounding array of brochures, without the slightest inkling of which charming spot to choose for my quiet stay in Olde England.

A handsome man with wavy blond hair reached for a brochure, bumping into me without excusing himself. He reminded me of Mike. When I moved out of his way I saw a travel brochure tucked in a slot at the side of the booth. It showed a photo of an ancient stone ruin overlooking a sunny, windswept sea. "Tour King Arthur's Britain," said the medieval lettering.

"Excuse me," I said to the counter girl. "Where can I get a King Arthur tour?"

She shrugged. "Anywhere."

"How about a place where tourists don't go?"

That made her giggle.

"Really," I said.

"You mean like…Slough?"

That got a laugh from the rude man, who found his train schedule and breezed away.

"I don't know. I mean a pretty village. With cottages. A bed and breakfast. Someplace with not a lot going on."

"Sounds like where my auntie lives."

"All right."

The girl frowned. "They don't have a cinema. They don't even have a Starbucks."

"Perfect."

She cocked her chin, like someone who's about to say "I told you so" while they tell you so. "You'll have to alight at Salisbury and take a taxi because the bus doesn't go to Small Common." She gathered brochures for me and put them in a paper bag. "It's the only village within miles of Stonehenge that doesn't cater to tourists."

That sounded like a slogan to me. I thanked her profusely, stuffed the brochures into my purse and shuffled off to the restroom.

The sight in the mirror sobered me, though it did nothing to improve my headache. My hair was stiff with hairspray from the previous day's shoot, and it had formed itself into a square where I'd slept on it. My jeans felt slimy and my T-shirt hung on me as though I'd fought with it during the flight, which I probably had. I'd never bothered to wipe off yesterday's makeup. Tears and mascara had painted gaudy streaks across my face. I'd been in public. People had seen me.

I shoved the purse onto the floor between my feet. Ignoring the glances of more put-together travelers, I washed my face and hair in the sink with dispenser soap. Still dripping, I dragged myself into a stall, locked the door, hung my purse on the hook and cried while I peed.

Blue-black clouds rumbled over Salisbury, like dust kicked up by galloping, skyborne horses. I loped off the train and followed the tourist traffic along a main road that led into a warren of narrow, cobbled streets. Salisbury had everything: stationers, bakeries, souvenir shops and name brand stores, the latter being at least expedient if not quaint. At a chain store I bought a gray, hooded sweater—acrylic, because wool itches. The loose knit resembled chain mail, which I thought charmingly appropriate. I bought the matching cargo pants, too. It was the secret, interior Velcro front pocket that sold me. With pockets in front, back, and even on the legs I might never have to lug that lime green horror again.

A belted pack would relieve me of the purse entirely. It wasn't exactly a fashion accessory, but that no longer mattered. Nobody knew me and I was rabid to be free of things that weighed on me. When I asked for a fanny pack the store clerk appeared to be either confused or insulted. She pursed her lips as though she smelled something offensive and said, "Bum bag," instructing me in the proper terminology in the same way she might correct an irritating four-year-old.

Loaded with shopping bags, I retraced my steps along the cobbled streets to the queue of taxis at the train station. Trotting to beat the rain, I cursed myself for not buying an umbrella. But the day was ending, I was hungry, and I needed to get a room.

Two cabbies chatted at the head of the line. Their eyebrows arched to their hairlines when I asked for a ride to Small Common.

"Alex'll go," said the bald one.

"Got relatives there?" asked Alex. He stroked his clean-shaven double chin with his thumb.

"No, just looking for a quiet place."

"Small Common's quiet all right," he said, sizing me up with beady eyes.

"My money's on North Tidworth for quiet." The bald man scratched his pate. "It's positively tedious."

"Winterbourne Dauntsey's a bit dull as well," said Alex.

They both nodded, considering the dullness of Winterbourne Dauntsey.

At last the bald man folded his arms across his chest and, with a definitive lift of his chin, proclaimed, "Middle Wallop."

"Ah!" said Alex, shaking his fists. "You win."

In Alex's rickety cab I dozed to the steady rhythm of the windshield wipers, snapping awake when the car slowed. "Are we here?"

"Amesbury. Only just a corner of it, then I'll have us on the highway again."

I sat back and watched the impossible green. After years of southern California's dry climate it was a shock to see all that water flying around, as if it didn't know where to go. The cab picked up speed for a few minutes, slowing again when we caught up to traffic.

"There it is," said Alex, jabbing his thumb at the driver's side window.

I scooted across the seat to wipe the fog from the window behind him. I couldn't make out what he meant so I let the window down, allowing in a few raindrops. Then I drew in a breath that I didn't let out.

I hadn't expected to see Stonehenge squatting alongside the highway like a roadside zoo. My image had been of proud stones standing aloof on the wide, open plain. But like captive animals on display, the stones did not stand so much as hulk. With umbrellas open against the rain, well-behaved tourists filed past them on roped-off walkways. I closed my window. The windshield wipers beat fast and steady.

"Going to be a full moon tonight if it clears up," said Alex. "The loonies are out. Want to stop while it's light?"

"No thanks."

"You have to see Stonehenge while you're here."

"I'll wait for a day when it's not so busy."

"No such day," he said.

Alex soon turned north, delivering us from the main highway to the quiet countryside via a twisted, two-lane road lined with farmland. The entire drive from Salisbury to Small Common, even through the Stonehenge traffic, took a little over half an hour. By the time we arrived in the village the rain had stopped, and late-day sun broke through the clouds. Golden drops glistened on every drooping rose petal and thatched roof. A mist hovered above the lane like steam on a swimming pool when the water's warmer than the air. In my heart I thanked the brochure girl and her auntie.

Alex rolled the taxi to a stop on the gravel driveway in front of a two-story brick house that looked like it might be haunted. "Suggestion for jet lag, if I may," he said.

Apparently it was obvious. "Sure."

"Stay awake until a normal hour tonight, say, ten o'clock. Then don't sleep more than eight hours. You'll be on local time quick."

"I'll try." I didn't question why Alex should be an expert on jet lag. I only doubted I could stay awake much longer, and I had no idea what time it was. Although my headache persisted, the nausea was gone. My stomach's growl had progressed to a roar.

Alex retrieved my bags from the trunk. I paid him the exorbitant sum he requested and tipped him ten percent.

"Coo," he said under his breath. Or something like that. "Full moon." He tucked himself behind the wheel and drove off in the direction from which we'd come.

I gazed up at the house, which leaned a tad sideways and managed to loom even in the sun. A sign propped against the front steps said "Langhorne Bed and Breakfast." I dragged myself up the stone steps and knocked. When no answer came I opened the creaking door and stepped into a dark, low-ceilinged hallway. The faint smell of curry arrived at my nose, making my mouth water. A Persian runner ran the length of a hardwood hallway so dark it was almost black. Lugging my shopping bags, I followed the banter of television news to a doorway at the end of the hall.

"Hello?"

"Oh!" came the response, then a little crash of dishes. "Ah, well." A thin, fortyish man with dark eyes and delicate features peeked out the door, dabbing a linen napkin at a spot on his crisp, white shirt. "Hello. Do you need a room?"

"Yes."

"Lucky you, I've got one." His socks slid across the floor. I followed him into a dining room wallpapered with faded toile, where he gestured for me to sit at the huge table.

"The attic room's all I have. A hundred and twenty quid if that suits you. Sorry you've missed dinner. Where're you from?"

"Los Angeles." I tried to smile. I was too proud to ask what a hundred and twenty quid might equal in dollars, too tired to return his sociability.

He ran my credit card through a device attached to the wall phone. We waited for the beep. "How long will you be staying..." he glanced at my card as he handed it back, "...Ms. Clemens?"

"Uh, a week?"

"Lovely." His smile was genuine, his teeth naturally white. He extended his hand to shake. "I'm Ajay."

"I'm Casey."

"A pleasure. The loo's one flight up. Your room's at the top of the second staircase." He lifted a small, old-fashioned brass key from a peg on the wall and gave it to me. "Bags?"

"Just these." I held up my shopping bags.

"Oh." His voice registered slight surprise, but he didn't pursue it.

Outside my dormer window, the last of the sun still gilded the rooftops. The peanuts I'd eaten on the plane were long gone and I regretted skipping the pasta. Food would have to come before sleep, even before a shower.

After more than twenty-four hours of stress, my long-sleeved T-shirt was no longer white. I pulled the chain mail sweater on over it and changed into my new cargo pants. Sick of carrying my lime green albatross, I dumped its contents onto the yellow coverlet of the single bed.

Lipstick, makeup, note pad, sunglasses, the tissues the flight attendant had given me, a purse-sized container of Vaseline, a plastic sample jar of ibuprofen and that grainy, linty stuff that ends up at the bottoms of purses. Business cards with my picture on them. Post cards with my picture on them: dyed blonde hair, makeup and cheesy grin. I turned all the pictures face down and dug through the pile for my wallet. Beneath the mess my fingers found a plastic flashlight keychain with the *Gone!* lightning logo stamped on it in bright red. The keychain was a giveaway premium, a trinket, a piece of junk forgotten in the bowels of my purse. I clicked the end and the flashlight shone in my eyes. Like a pinch, it served as a reminder of my misery. I threw it into the tin trash can next to the little wooden desk by the window.

I considered taking my iPod but decided against it. I never used the thing for listening to music and nobody was going to bug me. Passport, credit cards and cash went into the fanny pack/bum bag (both misnomers for a small, black, canvas pack I wore belted around my belly, for easy access). I zipped it closed, clipped it around my waist and reached for the glass doorknob.

At the last second I remembered the brass room key by the lamp on the nightstand. The key was small, easy to lose. The *Gone!* keychain would have to do. I had earned that stupid keychain. I retrieved it from the trash, attached it to the key and tucked it into the hidden Velcro pocket of my new pants.

Later, I regretted not bringing the tissues.

FOUR

Ajay appeared at the bottom of the stairs with a steaming cup of tea.

I felt my face relax into a smile. I must have been frowning for hours. "That's so nice of you."

"I wasn't sure you'd be coming down. You do seem tired."

"The cab driver suggested I stay up 'til ten. I don't know what time it is."

"It's just coming on eight. Come sit for a second."

I followed him into the dining room, where he placed the china cup and saucer on the table before me. "It's still so light out."

"Northern latitude. You get used to it."

My hands shook when I raised the cup. The tea was hot but not too; I drank it down and returned the cup to its saucer. "I guess I should head out."

"Fancy a taste of our night life, do you?"

"I'm pretty hungry."

"There's just the one pub. Tom'll fix you something."

"Can you give me directions?"

He laughed softly. "You're in Small Common, dearie. It's *small.*" He leaned forward in his chair. "Ms. Clemens, are you all right?"

The polite concern in his bright eyes reminded me of the flight attendant. Strangers could be so kind. People in my own life—people I'd slept with, even—hadn't shown me as much consideration. I had a knack for gathering the ungenerous into my inner circle. Perhaps like attracts like.

"It's only jet lag. I'll be fine."

"Okay," he said, sitting back.

"And." I had a sudden urge to tell him I'd lost my job, my boyfriend and my hold on life. Tears welled in my eyes.

He saw, and waited.

"I'm, um. Looking forward to a rest."

He nodded. "Shall I walk you to the pub?"

"No. Thanks." I blinked back the tears. I'd be fine.

The six or eight streets that made up Small Common had never been gussied up for tourists. Shadows draped across thatched roofs of the same stone cottages they'd been dressing for hundreds of years. There, a shaded lane drew my eye toward the private space behind a stone house to glimpse a bright, blue wheelbarrow. Here, climbing pink roses framed a garden gate in need of a fresh coat of paint. Beyond, an empty cottage awaited care in the midst of a yard gone wild with the lack of it. I allowed myself to imagine the cottage as mine. I would put glass in the windows but perhaps not paint the gate. I'd see about the yard.

Most of Small Common was well tended. Attractive window boxes, overloaded with flowers, lined a row of stone houses. Clean, cobblestone streets invited me to wander along them. I took each turn to sweet scents and sights: a green painted door, the steeple of an old stone church, a distant hill. The few people I encountered nodded or said a quiet "hello." I strolled without aim, glad to know no one, momentarily forgetting my hunger and imagining life in obscurity. What if that cottage were mine? Could I live there? What did people do in Small Common? Did they garden, read books, make art? Or just commute to someplace else?

At the southern edge of the village, the street curled away from civilization out into the misty countryside. A hand-painted sign named the route Old Wigley Road. I'd missed Tom's pub and would have to turn back. If I kept walking I might find a castle, or faeries, or a handsome prince.

A piercing neigh broke the calm.

"You here to ride?"

An elfish boy of about eleven leaned against an unobtrusive, single-story structure. I must have passed the building without noticing. It was set back from the street amid overgrown bushes next to a gnarled apple tree, its stone walls camouflaged green with moss. A sign hanging from a branch said "Livery Stable."

"It's fourteen pounds fifty an hour and that's cheap," the boy said. He blew a puff of air upwards, lifting long, brown bangs from his dirty face.

"What kind of horses do you have?"

"All kinds." He jerked a thumb toward a gray mare who stuck her head out of an open window. "Lucy's a good horse."

"May I ride out that way?" I pointed to my imaginary castle in the mist.

"Yeah. But you have to be back in one hour because we're closing."

I assured him I wouldn't be nearly that long.

As an ingénue I had learned to ride horseback for the role of "The Blonde" in a low-budget Western that shall remain nameless. Riding Lucy was different. The sleek, English saddle offered fewer things to hold onto than the Western one with its protruding horn. But though the faded blacktop of Old Wigley Road was uneven, I soon eased into the rhythm of Lucy's comfortable gait. She knew the way, so I let her drive while I enjoyed the scenery. Crumbling stone walls ambled across acres of green, serving as fences just as they had for hundreds of years. A ruined barn slumped alongside a new one in a field dotted with grazing sheep. A light appeared in the window of a cottage just as we ambled by the cozy grove in which it snuggled. The world smelled fresh after the rain.

How long had I been awake? My exhaustion was so supreme I felt exalted. At last I let myself cry, softly, allowing my shoulders to settle on my back. Being alone was safe. Everything about the ride was relief: Lucy's shoulders rocking smoothly beneath my knees, the disorientation of being in a new place, the sun's final blink. I sensed I'd escaped something dangerous at the last minute.

With the dusk came big drops of rain, one at a time. Lightning crackled above a faraway hill, then a closer one. Lucy hopped sideways and tossed her head. I patted her big shoulder and she responded, calming. I didn't mind a bit of rain. Astride a strange horse on a strange road in a strange country, I felt safe for the first time in as long as I could remember. Running away from everything I knew wasn't the smartest thing I'd ever done but it wasn't the dumbest, either. Disappearing might be good for me.

Mind it or not, the rain became heavier and I finally turned Lucy around. It was time to get back anyway. The big gray trotted and snorted, straining against the bit. I loosened the reins a little so she could canter. That gave her enough lead to run, and she took off.

I gripped the front of the saddle (where the damned horn should have been) barely in time to keep from flying off of it. "Whoa, girl!" I shouted, trying to show her who was boss. But she already knew who was in charge. I had no authority to slow her down, and in the increasing darkness and downpour I couldn't see to guide her. My only option was to hang on where I could, and trust Lucy to know the way. She picked up speed on the slippery pavement. I yanked the reins and told myself if she slid it would mean only broken bones, not death. That did not comfort me. She did not slow down. Lucy's pounding speed increased, along with her determination to return to the stable regardless of my pitiful commands. I gave up because I had to, allowing the onrushing rain to cleanse my face of tears. There's nothing like a twilight ride on a runaway horse in blinding rain to make you forget your troubles.

The headlights appeared from nowhere. "Lucy!" I screamed, jerking the reins. Brakes screeched. Tires turned on gravel. Lightning struck a sign post beyond the car, turning sight into a photo negative and illuminating the silhouette of a man behind the wheel.

Lucy bent her head, trying to dig her hooves into the asphalt. Her steel shoes skidded on slick pavement. She couldn't stop. I lost my grip and flew forward over Lucy's broad neck into the wide, black gap in the bushes.

FIVE

At the other side of the gap crouched a muscled, grizzled man, not at all like the flock of frightened sheep I expected. Surrounded by moonlit forest, the man gripped a gleaming sword with both hands. The bare muscles of his upper arms shone with sweat in the soft light of night, and his eyes were wide with surprise.

I must have looked as shocked to see him as he did to see me. I didn't want to run into him but I had no idea how to control my flight and I was hurtling toward him like a terrified spear.

A shadowed figure stepped between us. I rammed into it head first, crash-landing in a thicket of thorny brambles. Groaning, I rolled onto my back. Above me, the full moon wobbled. Something wet splattered my sweater, which I regretted. The T-shirt was already ruined anyway. A body landed beside me with a thud. I tried to sit up. A dead arm flopped across my chest, knocking me backward. I scrambled away in revulsion, thorns grabbing at my clothes, my head throbbing. The moon, which had ceased to wobble, lit the dead man's armor.

Before I could scream, the grizzled man yanked my arm and pulled me to my feet. We stood face to face (or face to chest) and I looked up into his wild eyes. He seemed amazed by me, or maybe just curious: brows lifted, lips ajar, square jaw gaping in awe.

"Os ta sabrin?" His hushed voice scraped like sand on gravel. The sword he raised dripped fresh blood. I didn't understand his question but I wanted very much to give him the right answer. He waited. The rain had ceased, leaving a fine mist shimmering on the darkness.

In a moment the forest resounded with shouts, and our silence was broken. My assailant looked to the trees, drew in a breath, and threw me aside like a fistful of leaves. Another dead body broke my fall but not softly; the chain mail it wore made for a rough landing.

Footfalls thundered toward us and the grizzled man shouted out more jargon I didn't understand. He might have been talking to me but I couldn't be sure. Either I was no longer in the Wiltshire countryside or his dialect was one I hadn't come across before. I scrambled behind a giant tree and peeked out.

A huge man leapt from the forest and bounded over a third body, brandishing a sword and shield. His empty eyes gazed out from the darkness of his brass helmet, searching the clearing until they found the grizzled, square-jawed man. With a roar, the bigger man attacked. Grizzle was agile, but his opponent had the advantage of size. Grizzle wore no helmet nor did he carry a shield, and the other man wasn't above using his to smash and bang at Grizzle at every opportunity. This was no gentleman's parry and thrust, no Hollywood choreographed sword fight. They kicked. They elbowed. They sliced each other's flesh.

My heart whammed while they grunted and stomped, clanking their swords in the moonlit clearing. I had never seen a real sword fight before and couldn't imagine why I was seeing one then. Were they performers in a Renaissance fair? Did they even have those in England? Was I a wench to be fought over? Why was their hair so long? Was there no barber in town? But no, no, the cut on Grizzle's arm dripped real blood. The bodies already lying dead in the clearing did not stand up to fight again.

Grizzle stumbled, exhausted. The big guy towered over him and raised his sword to strike the final blow. No amateur, Grizzle leapt aside, avoiding death in a second, and thrusting his blade under his adversary's shield. The man staggered. Grizzle shouted his triumph and jerked his sword free, pushing off the dying man's thigh with one well-worn, leather boot. Again, with rage in his roar and in the whites of his eyes, he shoved the blade into his enemy's bleeding torso. The man fell helpless to his knees and again, needlessly, Grizzle stabbed him. The big man toppled against my tree, shaking the trunk and splattering me with warm blood.

I ducked behind the trunk and squatted, gulping bile and tears. In all directions, the blue-black trees raised their twisted branches in horror. All paths of escape led only to the deep oblivion of the woods.

Grizzle's steps came close. His heavy breathing slowed. He waited.

I could not look at him, so afraid was I of what he would do. "I don't know anyone here," I managed to sputter. "I won't tell." My ragged sniffling shrank my voice to mewling.

Grizzle squatted beside me. I turned to him at last because his waiting demanded it. The savagery had disappeared from his face, leaving a gaze that was intense and at the same time tender. His straight hair, the color of mud dusted with snow, hung loose about his weary eyes. Close up he looked fifty, though he'd fought with the vigor of a young man. He reached out his open palm, startling me. He wanted something.

I gave him my hand, not daring to disobey. His callused grip squeezed my manicured fingers in reassurance. *"Kowetha,"* he said, nodding. He held out his other hand. I placed my other in his and he gripped them, lifting me to my feet.

Around us the shouting had stopped. Grizzle dropped my hands, grunting as he bent to retrieve the corpse's helmet with a twist and a pull. It was a plain iron cap with eyeholes, a face guard and hinged flaps like giant sideburns. Grizzle plopped it on his head and grinned, then shouted to the trees more words I didn't understand.

Within seconds, a helmeted soldier sauntered into the clearing leading an unsaddled horse. Grizzle mounted in a leap. *"An benyn biri me yn Cadebir,"* Grizzle commanded the soldier. With a nod toward me he continued, *"Thew hy nos-godhvos."* He reined the horse around and cantered off into the woods, his long hair flapping from beneath his newly-acquired headgear.

Trapped between tree and corpse, I faced the soldier.

The soldier made no move. He was bigger than Grizzle, or at least his armor made him appear to be. His eyes were slits, his mouth a grill of eerie, grinning holes. He stood opposite me in the clearing, staring silently from behind his helmet.

I wanted to be brave but I couldn't stop my shaking or my uneven whimpers. My heart continued its incessant banging, out of my control.

At last the warrior leaned against a tree and removed his helmet, freeing long, golden curls to shine in the moonlight. He ran his fingers through his hair to pull it away from his eyes, assessing me with a gaze so direct I sensed a different kind of danger.

His slow smile told me he knew I had never seen a more gorgeous man.

SIX

"Pandra nos-godhvos?"

The handsome soldier's smile was no comfort. Why couldn't I understand him? I must have hit my head pretty hard. My forehead throbbed where I'd hit the dark thing and crash-landed. Something wet trickled into my eye. It was either my own blood or spray from the murdered man. And I was confused. It wasn't as if I'd escaped Hollywood for Mongolia or Burma or the Amazon jungle. I was in England. I'd been riding a rented horse on a country road in Wiltshire. I got caught in the rain. Then...what? Lightning, tires screeching, flight. Flight was the part I hadn't figured out yet. One of the parts.

Footsteps crunched on soft underbrush. A stocky man stepped into the clearing, moonlight glinting blue on his blond braids as he moved. He spoke to the gorgeous one and they conspired, watching me like a couple of horse trainers might watch a mare they were thinking of buying. They needn't have whispered because I didn't understand them.

Another man trudged into the clearing and the two greeted him in their odd language, grabbing his arms and patting him on the back. Then came another and another, most of them carrying their helmets and clinking as they stepped over the dead bodies to meet in the middle. Along with their mail they wore bits of dented armor: a chest protector here, shin guards there. Some carried bloody axes and swords. Knives and scabbards dangled from their belts. Sweating, scarred and splattered with blood, they looked like a Dark Ages film crew after a hellish shoot.

Across the clearing from where I clung to my tree they formed a group and gaped at me, murmuring to each other, puzzled.

The stocky man with the braids crossed the open space and approached me, frowning. As tall as he was wide and built like a Jeep, his cautious steps made his blond braids swing back and forth from under his helmet. I anticipated every horror—rape, dismemberment, torture—culminating in slow, anonymous death.

He opened his mouth to speak.

I cringed and breathed hard.

"Matir—" His glance shot past me in alarm. I stiffened.

Something behind me, unfamiliar and damp, fondled my arm. The warriors remained silent, though their mouths and eyes opened wide. The moist touch crept up my sleeve and along my neck to my ear, where a soft nibble set off a static tingling. For a long while or for a second, ocean waves pounded in my ears. I shivered so hard my muscles gave way and I clung to the tree to stay on my feet.

When the static and rushing dissipated, the Jeep man was talking.

"That your horse?" he asked, his voice emerging from the noise. His language still sounded foreign and odd, but I understood it.

I dared a glance over my shoulder. The rental horse, the one I'd been riding in the rain before whatever happened happened, browsed the underbrush behind me. Lucy, her name was—a plain, gray mare. I grabbed her reins and cleared my throat. "Yes," I said. It came out breathy and clipped.

"Grand beast," said Jeep.

"Unusual saddle," said a broad, tall man in the crowd. His shoulders drooped as though the whole thing made him sad. A mumble of agreement arose from the men. Lucy was grand. Her saddle was unusual.

I reached to wipe blood away from my eye. Several soldiers flinched, emitting a collective "huh!"

"Do not move!"

I froze.

"Arms to your sides! Slowly."

In slow motion, I brought my bloody fingers away from my face and lowered my hands to my sides.

The group had grown to about a dozen men. The gorgeous one stepped out from the rear. In an accent stiffer than that of the others he said, "The king ordered me to deliver you to him." He sounded French, but his speech was more guttural than the French accents I knew from Los Angeles waiters.

"Do you go willingly?" asked Jeep.

"It is not her choice," said Gorgeous. "Chain her."

The men shifted uneasily.

"I'll go." I figured my other options were to run and be caught, or fight and fail.

"She'll go," said Jeep.

"We cannot chance it, Bedwyr," said Gorgeous.

Jeep nodded in acquiescence, so I guessed that made him Bedwyr.

"Let us finish then," Gorgeous ordered.

Let us finish? What did that mean? Upon hearing his ominous proclamation I clutched Lucy's reins and clung to my tree with all my strength, which wasn't much. How had I ended up in that forest? Why had I run away from Hollywood? Who were these creeps? If they were some sort of medieval warfare aficionados they were taking the game too far.

Jeep/Bedwyr called to the broad, sad one, "Help me, Sagramore."

Someone pulled my fingers open one by one, taking Lucy's reins and leading her off into the blue-black woods. The warriors shuffled after her. Bedwyr gripped my left arm. His nose came only to my chin, but what he lacked in height he made up for in daunting presence. Sad Sagramore joined us and, taking solid hold of my right arm, sighed a breath that stunk of something dead. They unstuck me from the tree like a child from her mother's leg. I had no power to resist either of them.

We waited for the line of soldiers to pass, then the two men ushered me into the woods, them marching, me stumbling. Moonlight found its way through the upper leaves, dusting a silver glow onto ghostly trunks. Already frightened into hiding by the chaos of battle, not one animal chirped or scrambled. I heard, more than saw, soldiers fanning out among the trees. When I tripped over a body lying sprawled against a tree, I jumped and gasped. My captors gripped harder.

"Sorry," I whispered.

I tried staring at my feet but it was too late. I'd already seen what I didn't want to see: the aftermath of a blood riot, tinted blue with moonglow. In the shadows away from the path, soldiers labored over corpses in the underbrush, making soft, clinking sounds while stripping the dead of their weapons. Torn muscle and viscera dripped purple from between armor plates and shreds of cloth.

Perhaps I was safe until they delivered me to their leader. Then they'd have to kill me, because I'd seen. I had to do something, and fast. My mind raced in all directions. Birds must have sung. Twigs must have cracked beneath my silly boots. Surely the air smelled of oak or underbrush or blood. But I was aware only of the fear ringing in my ears, drowning out the questions. My head pounded from where I'd struck the dark thing, but the fear was worse. It gripped me like a hand, clutching my heart and squeezing the blood from it.

At the forest's limit we climbed a short rise to an unpaved country lane where men loaded booty onto a pair of wooden wagons parked near the trees. Late fog clouded the dark lane. No street-lamp lit the way, no farmhouse slept alongside the road where it snaked off through the mist, no cars came, their low beams searching for a way through the earth-borne cloud.

"Climb up," said Bedwyr, offering me a seat in the nearest wagon, the bed of which was so full of booty it didn't rock with my weight. If I wanted the piled swords to point away from me, my only option was to sit behind the driver facing the rear, between a row of shields and a heap of mail.

As if it were as light as a T-shirt, Bedwyr removed his chain mail and laid it in the wagon bed. He climbed aboard after me and squatted at my side. Chains clanked against the outside of the cart as Sagramore took them down from their hooks and handed them over the edge to Bedwyr.

"What do you call yourself?" Bedwyr asked, taking the chains in his big hands.

"Casey."

He began wrapping the heavy iron around my ankles. "Mistress Casey," he said, "I regret the chains, but we can't have you flying away. Wrists."

I extended my hands.

Bedwyr exhaled a surprised "Oh!"

"What is it?" Sagramore peeked into the wagon.

"Nothing."

Another soldier came to line up more shields with the others in the wagon bed, making two rows: one of round, plain shields, the other of oblong ones, with bronze plating and jeweled designs.

Bedwyr collected himself and continued looping my wrists, which fell into my lap with the weight. He finished by attaching my leg chain to the cart with an old-fashioned padlock and a flat key, which he pocketed in a pouch at his belt. He cleared his throat.

"Your pack." He pointed to my new fanny pack, belted at my waist. "I'll take it."

"All right." I could barely hear myself.

Sagramore peeked over the wagon's side once more, this time to witness the removal of the pack.

I turned as far as I could to give Bedwyr access to the plastic clasp at my hip. Its mechanism must have been unfamiliar to him. He worked on it for half a minute before giving up and reaching for his knife. I froze. With an expedient motion, Bedwyr slashed the belt without even grazing my sweater. He then offered the pack to Sagramore, raising it between two fingers as though it were toxic waste. Sagramore waved it off, refusing to touch it.

Bedwyr raised the pack to the moon's light, gazing at it as though trying to guess what it was made of or what it held inside. He finally tucked it into his belt without opening it. "Now," he said, "give me your word you won't try to escape."

Even under the circumstances I had to bite my lip. My ankles were piled so heavily with iron that I couldn't move my legs. Chains weighted my hands, making it impossible to lift them from my lap. No savior came along the road.

"You have my word."

It seemed to satisfy him. How my word could assure him any more than iron chains I didn't know, but I'd say whatever he wanted to hear. Just the day before I had sworn off lying, but honesty was not useful in the situation. And unless the circumstances changed, what I told him was the truth.

The moon veiled itself behind a bank of clouds, lending barely enough light to separate Bedwyr's silhouette from the wagon's. Breathing heavily, he climbed down and trudged off with Sagramore to where the horses grazed a few yards away in the mist alongside the road. Even in dark and fog, Lucy was easy to spot among the animals because she was a full hand taller than the others. Though she wasn't really mine, it was a relief to see her.

Considering I was so weighted with chains that I could anchor a ship, I didn't understand why two men guarded me. But although they stayed by the horses, Bedwyr and Sagramore were my personal sentinels. While we waited what felt like hours for the others to finish their bloody work, the sky faded from black to purple and the mist began to dissipate. An occasional shout floated up from the woods when a soldier made a discovery—a bit of money, a fine knife—but mostly the looting was a methodical business. The men did not sneak, nor did they hide. They'd killed everyone within earshot except me.

I shivered in the early morning cold. The loose-weave sweater I'd bought the day before was just another mistake on a long list.

Stepping out from among the trees, two young warriors carried a blanket-shrouded body toward the road. Without speaking, they settled it into the bed of the cart next to mine. After tucking it in, they stomped back to the forest and soon returned with another wrapped corpse. This they placed on the wagon bed next to the first, alternating feet and heads like gift-wrapped goblets. One of the warriors took off his helmet and sighed. The second man removed his helmet as well and rested his hand on the other's shoulder. He looked to be the younger of the two. With their dark hair and matching mustaches, they could have been brothers. Not looking at each other, they left their helmets on the wagon and returned to the woods.

I had nothing else to do but watch them. The third body was the last. When they finished loading the wagon, the older one sat by the side of the road and hung his head. The younger strode by my cart and gave me a gentle smile, the only person besides Grizzle to have done so.

The young soldier's smile did not, could not, make me feel safe. The previous night I'd thought a ride would bring me quiet time to think about why my life had fallen apart. I'd gotten about as far as I could get from Hollywood and I needed to figure out what to do next. It had never occurred to me that a lonesome ride on a rental horse could place me in the hands of a gang of sword-wielding barbarians.

I didn't remember closing my eyes.

"...examine the saddle," Sagramore was saying. "I'd like to copy it."

"The woman is harmless then?" a younger voice asked.

They hovered next to my wagon but I couldn't see them over the side.

"Don't know," whispered Bedwyr. "She's odd. Her mail's forged of gossamer. Her fingertips are painted blood red."

"I wonder why the king wants her," said Sagramore.

"Lancelot said—"

"Oh, *Lancelot.*"

Someone spat.

"He wouldn't lie about this, Sagramore," said Bedwyr.

"Hmph."

"The woman wears trousers," the young man whispered. "She's brazen."

"Indeed," said Bedwyr, "everything about her is strange."

"If she wasn't important she'd be dead," said the young one.

The cart rocked slightly when someone leaned against it.

"Yes," said Bedwyr. "The king would have killed her, sure."

SEVEN

"Leave the rest." Gorgeous, in command astride a white stallion, tightened his hand on the reins of his skittish mount.

The purple sky had turned to lilac and still no police car came to my rescue. The warriors led their horses out of the forest and gathered on the road, where the night-time fog had diminished to a fine mist at the animals' hooves.

"If others are about," said Gorgeous, loudly enough for those others to hear, "let them come upon their dead once the vermin have at them. Let them know what happens to a Saxon inside British borders. Let them learn not to come this far again."

"They're not known for their brains, Lancelot," Bedwyr said under his breath.

Of course. Gorgeous rode a white stallion and lorded it over everyone. He would be the one who called himself Lancelot.

The horses neighed and strained at their bits, breath rolling from their nostrils like locomotive steam. The warriors mounted with a running jump and a pull on the withers. I thought saddles with stirrups would have made more sense than the animal hides they used.

With a churning of wagon wheels and a chaos of pounding hooves, our small band headed away from the forest. I pretty much gave up on the cops.

I didn't hear the name of the red-haired, freckled boy who drove my cart. From the looks of his pimpled peach fuzz he was too young to be a soldier. I was wondering if he was even in his teens when a more mature rider sidled alongside us to have a leer at me. He was as broad and muscular as Lancelot but not as pretty. Where Lancelot was golden, this man was a ruddy brown. He might have been handsome, but his looks were marred by a serious scar across his left cheek.

"Ah, good," said Lancelot. "Lyonel, help us watch the prisoner."

"Gladly." Lyonel leered some more, as though I were dressed in nothing but my panties instead of my ensemble of mud, blood and chains.

As if those chains weren't enough to keep me, Lyonel and Lancelot flanked my wagon, while Bedwyr rode behind. Behind Bedwyr came the wagon carrying the gift-wrapped bodies. The driver of that wagon stared ahead without speaking and although his line of vision seemed to lead directly to me he never looked at me. The young soldier who had smiled at me rode alongside him and even gave me a reassuring grin. I meant to smile back but I couldn't get the corners of my mouth to turn up. It had been a long time since I'd slept or eaten or had anything to drink. I needed to pee. I didn't know who the king was or whether or not he was going to kill me or why, or why I was even there. Wherever I was.

The denizens of Small Common couldn't have ignored the clopping of dozens of hooves on stone. But inexplicably, Small Common was not there. The night before, Lucy and I had cantered past neat hedgerows and cozy farms. That was all gone, replaced by jagged stones, giant cairns and mounds of grassy earth looming in the dawn. I must have ridden too far in the wrong direction, although I was confused about that and afraid to ask. Fear made me quiet on the outside but inside my ears rang, my head hammered and my mind shouted question after regret after curse. Who was this "king?" How did he know about me? What did he want me for? How had I ended up where I was, and where the hell was I? If only I hadn't lost my job. If only Mike's wife hadn't been at the airport. If only I hadn't boarded that plane. Damn Mike. Damn his wife. Mostly, damn me.

No longer protected by the cover of the forest, the men watched the countryside, alert in their exhaustion. Bedwyr's every muscle pulled taut in vigilance as we rode across the wide, grassy plains. Though not a tall man, he could likely take down ten TV producers and never break a sweat, and he was probably pushing fifty. I had witnessed kindness in him, though he was hardened enough to be fearsome.

Lancelot, the handsome thug whose idea it had been to chain me, was easily twenty years Bedwyr's junior and not hardened in the same way, but I knew to be wary of him. He swaggered, even on horseback, which annoyed me. I'd seen it in Hollywood. I'd seen it with Mike. A person that beautiful becomes accustomed to being watched. Posing becomes second nature. So does mistrust.

I ducked down inside the cart as much as I could. Lancelot's scarred friend, Lyonel, continued to ogle me whenever he took his eyes off the road. A crust of blood had dried on my face. My chains tore at my clothes. I couldn't move my arms to cover myself and I didn't appreciate the way Lyonel made me feel like I wasn't even wearing a sweater.

All that, and no breakfast. Nothing to eat for more time than I could figure out.

In less than an hour after we left the woods, the riding rhythm slowed, then stopped. No one had spoken since we'd gotten clear of the forest. I stayed low in the cart to listen.

"The horses won't make Cadebir today," said Bedwyr.

"Yes," said Lancelot. "I invite you and your men to refresh at Poste Perdu. It is better to make the trip tomorrow, after rest."

Lucy sighed. Tied by a rope and trudging along behind the wagon, she must have been as tired as I was. I tried to sit up. Over my right shoulder, an infinity of tall grass waved in peaceful unity. The sun rose over endless plains, burning off the last of the mist and telling me we headed south. I turned as far as I could to the left and caught my breath.

A few feet off the road stood Stonehenge.

When I'd ridden by it in a taxicab the previous day the stones had reminded me of tamed beasts in a decrepit zoo. But in the morning sun the monument stood proud. The grass grew high and wild enough to sway in the breeze. Stonehenge was wanton with weeds.

We were so close to the stones they dwarfed us. How had we gotten inside the fence? They don't let you just walk right up to the monument. You pay at the visitor center across the road. You wait in line with the other tourists. You circle around on the sidewalk.

We were the only ones there. No tourists. No traffic. No visitor center.

No fence.

Things were not just bad. They were *wrong*.

EIGHT

From my position on the hard floor I attempted to comprehend my predicament. The armor should have been my first clue. Then the odd language, the bloody swords, the names.

We had continued south for a short while, that much I knew. At a crossroads we'd gone east. I remembered some sort of stone marker, but by that time I was beyond jet lag, beyond hunger. Such relatively minor deprivations would have made me woozy enough without the added confusion of having landed in the wrong century. As it was, I'd swooned in and out of consciousness, for how long, I didn't know.

"They'll come indeed, and with vengeance." Bedwyr sounded worried.

"We should have burned the bodies." That was the big one, Sagramore.

At his mention of burning, I smelled smoke. My chains kept me from rolling over. About ten feet away across scuffed mosaic tile, the road-dusted, lace-up leather boots of four men faced each other around a table.

"Cremation sends the message that we respect their dead," came Lancelot's stilted accent. "It is the wrong message. I assure you the border is tight. I do not know how they got in but if any are yet alive they will not get out."

"Still, we should go back and be certain."

Steel rang against steel. Shouts against shouts.

"Lyonel, hold!" Lancelot sounded almost scolding.

"He dares to doubt you—"

"Put up your sword, cousin." Lancelot again, the voice of reason. "You too, my friends. Bedwyr is only being cautious, are you not, Bedwyr? Let us respect his wisdom."

After a quiet moment, where strained breathing was all I heard, swords slid back into scabbards. At least I thought so, from the slip-stop noise of steel on steel.

Then silence.

"What about her?" said Bedwyr, sending my heart on a whole new race.

"There is a cell near the north gate with bars strong enough to hold a giant." said Lancelot.

"Don't like it." Bedwyr's low whisper wafted to me along with the scent of wood smoke.

"Again, cousin, this one doubts you."

"Bedwyr and I are friends, Lyonel," said Lancelot. "Friends may disagree. But Bedwyr, while we remain at Poste Perdu I must do as I see fit."

After a short pause, Bedwyr answered, "We'll comply. Arthur's grateful for your hospitality."

"It would be easier to kill her," said Lyonel.

"*Mais non*, Lancelot said, "Arthur wants her."

"She may be important."

"*Oui, je comprends.*"

I could not shift my position.

"She is awake."

One man stood, took deliberate steps to my side and squatted, blocking my view of the others.

Lancelot's symmetrical face loomed sideways above me in shadow. "I am sorry for your discomfort, my lady," he said. "We are not barbarians. But as I cannot be certain you will not use your powers against us, I will take no chances."

My powers.

He rose and moved out of my field of vision. "Would you like to sit?"

"Mmmhmm."

"Agravain. Gareth." Lancelot had only to say their names and the matching brother guards came to lift me. My chains made me heavy and the process wrenched my shoulders. It was only pain on top of the pain I already felt. If these are the not the barbarians, I thought, I hope I never meet them.

The brothers seated me in a leather-bound chair and took positions beside me with ready hands on the hilts of their swords. From my seat I had an opportunity to get my bearings. Across the long, low room a single torch flickered, braced in an iron wall-bracket like a medieval sconce. In the jagged shadows beneath it, Bedwyr and Sagramore sat at a wooden table, watching me. A legion of axes leaned against the wall in the dark corner behind the two men; beyond that an archway led I knew not where. A stand of spears lined another corner. At either end of the room the doors stood open, allowing small streaks of daylight to enter while letting out the smoke. Whatever the building's original use, it was now an armory. I didn't see Lyonel and I hoped he was gone.

Lancelot faced me across a pit in the floor in which burned a small fire that perhaps warmed the inches nearest its embers but not those near me.

"*Bienvenue à Poste Perdu. C'est ma petite garde joyeuse,*" said Lancelot, his tongue somewhere in his cheek, "my happy little outpost. We are not far from the border I share with King Arthur."

"Um, *merci.*" My voice came out ragged.

"You speak the Gallic?" he asked, abruptly leaning forward in his chair, as if my knowing French made me dangerous.

I didn't remember much from high school, except we didn't call it 'the Gallic.' "Just a couple of words."

"Have you had dealings with the Belgae before?"

"I...don't think so. What is the Bell-gee?"

A laugh thundered from the dark, somewhere behind me. Lyonel was not gone.

"I am Belgae," said Lancelot, "as are my men." I looked beside me, to the brothers. "Not them. Agravain and Gareth are Britons. The Britons and Belgae are allies." He leaned back in his chair. "But I sense you know this. From where do you hail and whom do you serve?"

I didn't want to lie. But if my father's theories about King Arthur were right, I was in the Dark Ages and America didn't exist yet. "I come from across the water to the west. And I serve no master."

"You are a Scot!" Lyonel's voice sounded more incredulous than accusing. Almost.

"Patience, Lyonel," said Lancelot. "You must forgive my cousin, mistress. Many enemies are abroad." He considered me. The room's daytime shadows softened the angle of his high cheekbones and the highlights in his hair. "You do not sound like a Scot, nor do you look like one. You look like a Saxon."

Sagramore sucked in a sharp breath. Bedwyr's chair groaned when he leaned forward, his face lit more by interest than by torch light. The older brother, whether Gareth or Agravain I didn't know, fingered the hilt of his sword. To be a Saxon was bad news.

Lancelot continued. "You appeared during a Saxon raid. You lived through it, without a weapon. If I were not under orders to deliver you to King Arthur I would have left you behind, or killed you, as you might pose a problem." His beatific smile came across as surprisingly warm. "But it is for the king to decide if you live or die. You are fortunate. He is a great man, Count of the Britons, *Dux Bellorum,* Leader of Wars."

He waited.

"You may speak," he said.

Upon his permission, the question foremost in my mind popped from my lips. "Do mean the *real* King Arthur?"

Lancelot gripped the arms of his chair. "There is an impostor?"

The warriors at my sides shifted their feet.

"No," I said quickly. My headache had intensified since my sojourn on the floor, and it was becoming difficult to look at Lancelot without blinking. I struggled to cover what could be a deadly error. Smoke and body odor filled my nostrils along with the air I had to have. "It's just... amazing...to think I'm going to see him."

Lancelot relaxed back into his chair. "You shall. Tomorrow. If you cooperate."

My father had believed the Arthurian legends were fiction and much of the real story was unknown. I wished I'd paid more attention to my dad's academic studies than my storybook. It would have been nice to know what year it was, for example, or how much time had passed since the Roman occupation. I knew the Saxons had invaded Britain some time after the Romans left. Saxons were the enemy and Lancelot thought I looked like one. I wasn't about to tell him I'd probably descended from them.

My handsome interrogator contemplated me. The smoke between us forced me to squint. To look him in the eye was too defiant, so I rested my gaze on a row of helmets lining the floor like neatly planted posies, their empty eyes staring. Above them, too high on the wall for me to see myself in it, a bronze mirror reflected smoke and torch light. I must have looked half dead by then.

Bedwyr spoke into the silence. "The lady is unwell. I will take her to her cell, if I may."

"Very well. I will send men to guard her while she sleeps. *If* she sleeps." Lancelot rose and ambled toward the rear door where Lyonel emerged, like smoke from the shadows, to follow him.

"I may trust you to walk with me as far as the north gate, may I not?"

Bedwyr said to me.

"Yes."

With the key from his pouch he unlocked the chains that bound my legs. The rusted iron links fell away, revealing the ruin of my cute, expensive boots. The brothers helped me to my feet, which was useful because with my wrists still chained I couldn't use my hands to leverage myself from the chair. My legs didn't want to unbend at first but apparently the men were familiar with the process and they waited while I got myself straightened out. Though my ankles were sore my legs felt light, no longer anchored to the planet.

Halfway to the door, Lancelot's husky accent stopped us. "If I hear the prisoner has been molested in any way, the transgressor shall answer to me," he said. "The lady belongs to the king."

PETREA BURCHARD

NINE

After an awkward episode at a drainage gutter where I was allowed to relieve myself behind a wall in broad daylight, the brothers Agravain and Gareth led me across a courtyard into a decrepit cement barracks missing a large portion of its tile roof. Bedwyr followed, carrying my chains.

"The prisoner has no privileges," he told the four guards who waited at the end of a dark hallway. Where the roof was still intact, two more guards stood in the daytime shadows.

Bedwyr dismissed the brothers, then led me through an archway into a small cell with a haphazard pile of furs on the floor and floor-to-ceiling barred window overlooking a sunny expanse of dirt.

"Sit there," said Bedwyr, pointing to the furs.

I sat. He squatted beside me, his corn-silk braids dangling, and got busy chaining my ankles.

"When I'm finished I'll find you something to eat."

"Thank you, Bedwyr—may I call you Bedwyr?"

"You must, for I have no other name."

No 'Sir,' then. No knight in shining armor. I was starving for the food he promised but even more hungry for answers. "Bedwyr, what does it mean to belong to the king?"

He squinted at his work. "Means you're his property."

My stomach rolled. "Will I be a slave?"

"Better slave to a good king than prisoner to a bad one. There." He

43

finished, locked the chains, and stood. "I'll be back."

"Bedwyr, why so many guards? Why all the chains?"

"It's working, then?"

"One guard would be plenty."

He laughed. His smile made him almost jolly. "One guard overpowered by a single spell and off you go." His smile disappeared. "I won't be fooled so easily, my lady, not while Lancelot's in charge."

My powers again. Maybe their fear of me would come in handy.

"Will the king kill me?"

"Doubt we'd be going to such trouble if he wanted you dead." He shrugged and started for the door. "But perhaps he wants the pleasure for himself."

TEN

"Medraut! We've not seen you in a fortnight!"

My chains made it impossible for me to roll over, so I turned my pounding head to the light. Sun heated the pile of furs on which I lay, releasing a sharp, rancid scent.

The barred window opposite the cell door looked out across the sunny, dirt yard, where the younger brother guard admitted two men at the gate, closing it behind them as they passed under a stone archway. The older brother acknowledged the men with a wave then returned to cleaning his horse's hooves with a pick.

"It's fine to see you, Gareth."

The slimmer of the two riders addressed the young brother. To the older one he simply nodded. At least I finally knew which brother was which.

"How fares our brother Gawain?" asked Gareth, which disconcerted me. I really didn't need them to have more brothers.

The skinny man dismounted in a fluid movement. "Gawain is well," he said. "All's well at Beran Byrig. So well that though the harvest is not finished the granaries are quite full." His chubby companion remained on his horse, unable to sit still, adjusting and readjusting himself.

"Your news is good, Medraut!" Gareth seemed incapable of cynicism. "Did you find any Saxons afoot? Two nights ago we killed seventeen not far from the Giant's Ring."

Medraut's mouth opened. He backed up to support his skeletal

45

frame against the gate. "Seventeen? At the Giant's Ring?"

"Well, in the woods. But nearby, nonetheless."

The thin man's thin lips remained open but he didn't speak. His chubby friend dismounted with a wriggle. "You must have killed them all," he said. "That or they spared us, as we've just come that way."

Gareth laughed. "It would be unlike them to spare a British soul."

Their conversation was drowned out by the clink of marching chain mail approaching in the hallway. A jagged chill trickled up my spine. Four guards entered my cell, refusing to make eye contact, their faces blank to me. I could have saved them so much bother if they had only unchained me, but they went to the trouble to lift me, chains and all, and lug me down the hall.

We emerged in an overgrown courtyard where the guards deposited me in the bed of a waiting wagon, the same one in which I'd ridden the day before. I landed in a semi-seated position, with my back against a pile of chain mail. The guards gave no thought to the fact that, thus trussed, it was nearly impossible for me to right myself. Surrounded by armed men and the rubble of deteriorating buildings, I had no time to think of my morning ablutions or to rejoice that my jet lag was finally gone.

The red-haired boy from the previous day climbed aboard to drive, glancing over his shoulder to make sure I was securely fastened and unable to do him mischief. He clucked to the horses. The cart jerked forward to rumble along the uneven streets of the walled, ruined fort Lancelot called Poste Perdu. Armed men watched us from the doorways of cement barracks. In the drying mud of the streets, soldiers ceased their dice games to witness our rolling passage. The few women seated at the well stopped washing, allowing their braceleted arms to soak their laps while they gazed at me.

I wanted to pull my blood-crusted hair away from my eyes, but my wrists were chained and it was too late to attend to beauty. I gazed back at the women, making a conscious attempt to appear to be at peace but not placid, confident but not indifferent, brave but not defiant. Eyes open wide. Not too much blinking. No smiling, but no frowning either.

Lancelot, Bedwyr and the rest of the previous day's party awaited us on horseback at the end of a walled street. Together we exited the fort by a southern gate. Although I feared what the day would bring, I wished Poste Perdu good riddance.

Our band of travelers was much the same as before, augmented by about two dozen of Lancelot's men and the pair of soldiers who'd arrived that morning: lean Medraut and the tubby sidekick he called Pawly. The only other difference I noted was the laurel branches with which the brothers Agravain and Gareth had freshened the hearse wagon, and the three horses, probably those of the dead soldiers, plodding behind, tethered by their reins.

Retracing our steps, we headed west. Within a couple of miles we came to a crossroads indicated by a giant stone marker and lined with leafy trees. I had seen the marker on the previous day's ride but had been too delirious to recall it in detail. Cut into the stone, taller than a man, was a weathered cross inside a circle, carved with symbols and festooned with bird droppings.

Our choices at the crossroads were south, north, or west. Without lingering, we continued west. In the early miles the men scoured the hillsides and groves, wary as our wagons rolled through open country, wheels groaning against the stone road. I watched, too, but saw no threat, only wildflowers and tilled fields. The few people we passed labored amid crops in the open. Each ceased his work to salute us as we went by, with a hand raised to a ruddy cheek.

If not for the iron rubbing against my skin, if not for the ache in my muscles from lack of movement, if not for fear of where I was and knowledge that I couldn't possibly be there, I might have thought I was in paradise. A picture from my storybook had come to life: the one of the road winding through watercolor green meadows and rising in the distance to a castle in the clouds. Grassy lumps, sprinkled with flowers and too small to be hills, dotted the landscape on either side of the road. They might have been graves, but not recent ones. Some were marked by giant stones that had long since fallen, allowing waving grasses to grow across their pocked shoulders. Small groves of trees peeked around this lump or that hill, and the sun gloated over everything.

My fate would soon be in King Arthur's hands. All morning my heart hurtled between wonder and despair, terror and romance. The thought of dying out of time chilled me even in sunshine. My presence in that wagon on that road was a scientific impossibility, but when we hit a bump and I tensed to balance myself, the weight of the shackles was real, the clang of jostled chains was loud enough to draw attention from the mounted guards, and the bump on the back of my head when it hit the driver's seat was perhaps a small thing but painful enough, real enough.

I tried to remember what I'd learned, in the yoga classes I'd bothered to attend, about holding a pose. The lack of movement gets tiresome but you *are* moving; you hold the pose because you're working in that pose, you're stretching or feeling a muscle. You're becoming stronger. You know that. You aren't supposed to take pride in yoga but you do, or at least I did, when I did it well. But I was too impatient for it. I couldn't see the point. Why sit there for so long doing nothing? What was I going to need that skill for? When was I ever going to have to sit for any more than a few minutes in the same position?

Hours in the wagon, chained and unable to move, did not give me a sense of pride or achievement. The pain deadened itself. I grew blessedly numb and less blessedly bored. Keeping the larger dread at bay, little things occupied my mind: how Bedwyr's braids bounced against his back when he bounced on his horse; how Sagramore was in ways Bedwyr's opposite: so large and broad it was inconceivable for him to bounce and I pitied his horse; Medraut's dark eyes poking in every direction as though he thought he was watched, yet always watching, too; Pawly a constant at Medraut's side, rarely saying a word; and Lancelot, shining and fine as I had always imagined he would be though not quite, with that strange shadow of mistrust between us I wished I could shatter; not to mention his shadow of a cousin Lyonel, whom I wished would disappear.

When the land flattened we stopped by a stream in the heat of mid-day. The men took their rations and sat by the water, and the horses were allowed to graze. By their joking and laughter I assumed the allied warriors were on friendly terms, though Lancelot's men tended to stick together and speak "the Gallic" among themselves.

Bedwyr and Gareth came to attend to me. By then I was vulnerable to baking in the sun and I was relieved not to be forgotten. My chain mail sweater was damp with sweat and my chains were heating up like little irons.

"We're within Arthur's borders," Bedwyr said, unlocking them. "As the king's lieutenant I'm now in command." He began slowly unwinding the chains at my wrists. Gareth worked at my ankles. "This will hurt," said Bedwyr, his tone matter-of-fact.

A few yards away, seated beside the stream, the men shared a leather flask, passing it around in a circle. Their voices wafted to us. Lancelot and his cousin spoke to each other and glanced our way. A murmur came from among the men, then laughter.

The chafing iron had scabbed in places and my wounds opened again when Bedwyr pulled the chains away. I sucked in my breath and held it. I would not let Lancelot hear me cry out. The wounds were small, I told myself.

"Can you walk?"

"I think so."

With the grace of a drunken sheep I crawled around the piled shields to climb out of the wagon. The two soldiers helped me to the ground, allowing time for my aching legs to unbend. I was weak, but my wounds would heal. Eventually I'd have little white scars on my wrists and ankles. While Gareth rummaged among the supplies, Bedwyr ushered me to a shady spot near the stream, away from the others.

"I'm releasing you against Lancelot's wishes," he grumbled under his breath. "Unless you can fly, any one of these men can kill you in seconds. Don't make me a fool."

"I won't." I wouldn't. Where would I go?

"Here we are." Gareth stomped over with an armload of bread and dried meat, which he dropped on the ground without concern for germs. Bedwyr took his food a few feet away and, with a middle-aged groan, lowered his bulk to sit with his back against the wagon wheel in a spot of shade.

Gareth motioned me to sit on a clump of earth beneath the branches of a willow by the stream. He joined me there, dipped a brass cup in the water and offered it to me. My thirst overcame any concern I might have had over the little floating bits of algae and dirt in the cup. The cold water tasted thick. Gareth was already eating.

"What kind of meat is that?" I asked.

He didn't swallow before answering. "Venison. Aren't you hungry?"

"I've never had venison."

"What do you eat? Rabbits? You look pale. The king will not be pleased if we bring him a sick wizard."

So that's what they thought. No wonder Bedwyr thought I'd fly away.

"Eat, please." Gareth gnawed off another bite, then stopped chewing to let his eyes follow my hand as I reached for a piece of venison. My nail polish, ridiculous under the circumstances, was chipped, but Gareth seemed to find it fascinating. I raised the meat to my mouth and tasted salt. It was tough but my teeth worked off a bite. Venison proved the antidote to nausea.

"Aha! She likes it!" Gareth grinned, a piece of venison dangling from his mustache.

"It's good. Thank you."

"You are most welcome, mistress." It was a courtly response, reminding me that this rough road, this dirt, this hardship would come to an end, and we would arrive at Camelot.

My dashing young guard leaned across me to refill my cup in the stream. Accepting it, I said, "May I ask, sir? The man who drives the funeral wagon—is he your brother?"

He laughed. I thought he might even be enjoying my company. "You needn't call me 'sir.' Just Gareth. Yes, Agravain's my brother—one of my brothers. Our father is Lot of Orkney," he bragged. "Gawain's the eldest. He commands Beran Byrig. Then comes Gaheris. He's stationed at Essa to lead Arthur's troops in the southwest. Then Agravain, then me. We're all in King Arthur's service, of course. And do you know?" He leaned forward, cocked his charming chin and waited.

I shook my head. I didn't know.

"King Arthur is our uncle!"

"Oh."

"Agravain and I are as yet unproven, of course."

"But..."

"There are family privileges, yes, but our uncle is a fair man."

"Of course."

"He has fought eleven great battles. A twelfth is nigh. Agravain and I are ready."

"I'm excited to meet your uncle."

Gareth raised his dark eyebrows in surprise. "Why, you met him in the woods, mistress. He ordered Lancelot to bring you to him."

I sucked in a short breath. Was it King Arthur toward whom I had hurtled through the gap in the darkness? King Arthur, the murdering savage with the Dick Tracy jaw? "And Lancelot is...?"

"A good man. A great man! A friend. You'll come to admire him as everyone does. It can't be helped." He laughed, with a shrug of his brawny, young shoulders.

"How long before we reach Ca-Cam—?"

"Cadebir?" Three, four hours. We'd be faster without the carts. It's a good road. Roman."

Of course. I was seeing what the Romans had built, relatively soon after they'd built it. My father would have been thrilled. Briefly, I felt privileged. But Lancelot chose that moment to dampen my mood by sauntering toward us across the waving grass. Gareth rose quickly and struck a stern, guarding pose. Bedwyr snoozed against the wheel of the cart.

"I wish to speak to the lady," said Lancelot, placing a brotherly hand on Gareth's shoulder. Gareth nodded and backed away.

When we were alone, Lancelot extended his hand to help me to my feet. I had no choice but to accept. Shaking, I touched the blond hairs of his iron-hard forearm, allowing him to pluck me to my feet as though I were a blade of grass.

"Walk with me." Lancelot offered said arm and I took it. Was there a Guinevere, I wondered, to be enfolded in those arms? Was it possible Lancelot could be gentle with such weaponry for appendages?

He could. Sensitive to my wounded wrists, Lancelot patted my hand. He led me to the edge of the stream where we stood in the willow's shade. It might have been romantic if I'd bathed in the previous twenty-four hours.

Lancelot studied me. "You are not afraid of the water?"

"Should I be?"

"Perhaps not," he said, eyeing me with new curiosity.

He led me further away from the wagons, I assumed because he didn't want our conversation to be overheard. Knowing he didn't like me or at least didn't trust me, the few feet between us and where Bedwyr snoozed felt like a chasm.

"Bedwyr is in command now that we are within Arthur's borders," Lancelot whispered in his guttural, Frankish purr. "At Cadebir, the king rules. These are kind, trusting men. My friends." His glassy, blue eyes pierced. "I am kind, too, Mistress Casey. But I do not trust. I will watch you, and if you pose a threat to my king, I will kill you."

I was still wondering how the words "I will kill you" could come from such full, soft lips when he said, "It is time to go."

PETREA BURCHARD

ELEVEN

A wide, flat hill emerged in the distance. It shimmered, a dark green ocean liner on a light green sea. Black smoke rose in puffs at one end, as though from smokestacks upon the great ship's decks.

"Is that...?" I began.

"Cadebir," said Sagramore, his droopy eyes glowing. He and Lucy had taken a shine to each other. He rode alongside her behind the cart where she plodded after me, tied by a swinging rope.

We were still too far away to see turrets. "I've heard it's beautiful."

"It is the greatest fort in all of Britain," said Lancelot. His white steed swished a fly with its tail. "There is none larger, none better fortified. You see it holds a position of power. Beauty, however, is not one of its qualities."

The men laughed, gathering around, in good humor now that they were close to home.

"What's the fire for?" I asked, fearing it was for the burning of prisoners.

"Smithy." Bedwyr reined his stout brown horse alongside my wagon. "Work never stops."

"Nor does the feasting," said Gareth.

"Oh yes, the banquets," said Lancelot. "King Arthur spares no expense to entertain his allies."

"He favors his allies over his own son," said Medraut, entering the conversation like a pin enters a balloon.

"It's only politics," said Gareth. "The king's son always has a place in the hall."

"Whether deserved or no." The deep, measured voice came from the wagon behind mine. It was the first time I'd heard Agravain speak.

Medraut turned in his saddle to curl a supercilious lip at Agravain. A tense moment took too much time in passing. Then Medraut laughed. "You speak so rarely, cousin. Why must you always be right?"

The men around me laughed softly, but not freely. Conversational ease had ended. Silence returned for the most part, with the exception of the occasional cluck to one's mount or word to the rider nearest by.

I was having a little trouble following the king's family tree, but I was beginning to think that Medraut might be the Mordred of legend, King Arthur's illegitimate son. If Cadebir was Camelot, maybe the real names weren't all the same as the storybook ones. The legends had it that Mordred was the son of Arthur and his sister Morgan le Fay, who were tricked into making love by Merlin the magician. If it were true, Medraut was not only illegitimate but the product of incest. All that in a century without psychotherapy.

Closer to Cadebir hill the ocean liner began to look more like an inverted, earthen battleship, with four tiers diminishing from the largest at the bottom to the smallest at the top. No turret or flag adorned its layers. Instead, a wall of vertical logs, punctuated by stone-built guard stations, surrounded the topmost tier. It looked more like an early American cavalry fort than the medieval castle of my imagination.

I knew by the increased pounding in my left temple and the purple light at the edges of my vision that my headache was becoming a migraine. The realization brought an extra sense of dread. Surely there wasn't a prescription drug to be found at Cadebir, and being chained in a wagon in the wrong century was difficult enough without blinding pain and cognitive impairment. I hadn't been forced to endure a migraine's full progress since my doctor had prescribed a drug to stymie them. But I hadn't forgotten the steady march from purple light to nausea to weakness, all accompanied by a deep-drilling pain behind my eyes.

There was nothing for it. My migraines were caused by stress and I'd had an overdose. So when Bedwyr chained me again "for show," I took a deep, futile breath and tried to relax.

About a mile from the base of the hill, our caravan entered a small town. The one and only street, down which Lancelot and his men made an impressive procession, was lined with small buildings, made of mud packed into frames of wood and sticks. The townspeople, more finely dressed than their country counterparts (a merchant tucked his pants into his boots, a town wife shielded her skin from the sun with a hat) recognized my companions and welcomed them like celebrities. We were a parade. People stopped what they were doing and came out of their huts to see us.

"Death to the Saxons!" the people cheered, with blissful smiles and raised fists.

The soldiers shouted back, "Death to the enemies of Britain!"

Everyone loved that. Young men roared and the older folks waved and hoo-hooed. Girls cooed and blinked at Lancelot, which he accepted with a parade wave. His cousin, brawny Lyonel, even jumped off his horse and lifted a pretty, screaming lass to kiss her.

The people marveled at me, too. "It's a woman!" "Is she a prisoner?" "She's wearing trousers! Maybe she's a warrior." I might have enjoyed their attention were it not for my headache, plus my awareness of the state of my appearance. I was reminded of Roman triumphs, when the victors paraded their captives through the city. The best I could do was sit up straight and try to appear benign.

At the edge of the village, the road led out across open fields between the town and the great hill before us. To the southeast, tents spread across the land, hundreds of them, teeming with men and smoke. Arthur's armies, I guessed. To the northwest lay marshland, clouded with fog.

On we went, the mood of the soldiers climbing the heights before we even arrived at the base of the hillside. As we neared it, the hill grew steeper, and at last we came to the beginning of a path that zig-zagged up a series of switchbacks to a great, wooden gate. There, shouting guards leaned over the wall to hail us, their arms waving like stalks peeking over a garden fence and swaying in the breeze. With a groan the gate pushed open, and out poured a dozen men, shouting and rushing down the muddy zig-zag in a torrent of testosterone.

Lucy betrayed her nervousness with a loud whinny.

"Welcome back!"

"How's Gawain?"

"Did everyone survive?"

"Surely Beran Byrig has better women to offer."

I tried to ignore the jab by staring at my lap. The laughter ended when someone asked about the riderless horses tied to Agravain's cart. Questions and shouts filled the air until Bedwyr raised his hand for silence. "Get these carts up the hill," he ordered.

The brutes bent their shoulders to the work without argument. The wagon lurched, zig-zagging up and across earthen ramparts wide enough to ride two or three abreast, steep enough that an invader would be hard put to climb them, old enough that grass, weeds and even trees sprouted between their stones. Below, the town we'd passed through was laid out like a map of itself. Miles of road we'd traveled curled back across the plains, disappearing into the morning we left behind.

Anticipation built in my breast as the cart pitched and swayed, drawing near the gate. Finally we made it to the top and rolled under the high, wooden arch where the horses could pull the weight on their own. I jerked and wriggled to turn myself to see. Like the opening shot of a grand epic, my first sight of Camelot was revealed to me.

Sun bore down on a grassless camp. Men and women came and went pushing carts, trotting briskly in the dust or meandering along the wide path that led away from the gate. With the red-haired boy driving, we rode among the meanderers along a path as deep as a trough, worn to a ditch in the dark soil by centuries of rolling cartwheels and trampling feet.

Could this Cadebir be Camelot? It was a working fort, and working hard, from what I could tell. The dust couldn't settle, being constantly kicked up by activity. I had no choice but to breathe it. Even the young wore work on their hard faces. Sunburned men pushed carts loaded with produce, animal carcasses or black dirt along the path. Women carried bundles. No hand was empty. Even the animals, at least the live ones, bore burdens, pulling wagonloads of stones or wood across the hilltop. Sweat glistened on every neck, from bent laborer to plodding dray horse, dripping in dusty rivulets through fur and hair.

Our carts bumped past a row of cement barracks like the one in which I'd spent the previous night. Across a lumpy expanse, the ground rose to a promontory where a large, rectangular structure commanded the rise. Its steep, thatched roof swept up to meet a pair of beams at the crest, declaring the building to be the main hall. On the slope at its flanks several high-peaked, round huts huddled near it like campers at a fire.

We rolled to a stop at the hall's massive, wooden doors. Bedwyr dismounted and climbed aboard the wagon to unlock my chains and help me to the ground. Blood rushed into my feet and I thought they wouldn't hold me, but my ankles warmed quickly. Standing felt like a reward. I awaited instructions.

A pair of wide-eyed boys gaped over their shoulders at me as they led the riderless horses away. They took Lucy, too, my last connection to the real world. Sagramore shouted after them, "No one touches that saddle until I get there." Smoke from somewhere stung my eyes.

I hadn't heard the doors open but when I turned a tall man stood before them, waiting. Beyond him, the hall was dark. The man's beard was closely trimmed, his hands were folded at his flat belly and his steel-gray hair was twisted into a pair of neat braids. Stone-faced, he bowed slightly, like the gentleman butler of a haunted house. "Welcome home," he said.

"Caius," Bedwyr offered his hand, "All's well?"

Caius made no move. "All is well. The king wishes to see you, Bedwyr. Sagramore, too. And Lancelot. And, of course, his kinsmen." He barely glanced at me. "Bring the prisoner." He looked over our bedraggled bunch as though inspecting a delivery, then stepped down from the doorway, his perfect posture evident in every move. Then he clasped Bedwyr's hand, and suddenly they were all slapping each other on the back, hugging and laughing.

All except Lancelot. He stood at the fringes of the group, looking to the far side of the building with a gaze that would melt stone. A young woman peered back at him from her hiding place around the corner of the hall. Her long, dark hair was offset by her white tunic. She was fair, far more fair than I had ever been, even when I was twenty, even when my hair was not caked with soil and blood. No one noticed her but me before she ducked into the afternoon shadows under the eaves.

When Lancelot caught me watching, I quickly looked away.

TWELVE

In the sudden cool, the empty hall revealed itself as my eyes became accustomed to the momentary dark. Wooden poles along the length of the center aisle supported a surprisingly lofty roof. At the far end of the cavernous chamber, a long table sat on a raised platform, its wooden chairs facing out over a cold fire pit. A row of windows opened to the air high on the eastern wall, admitting individuated shafts of light. The same windows were likely responsible for the birds that roosted in the rafters and dotted the benches and trestle tables with droppings.

I wished for a mirror. I wanted to brush the hair away from my eyes. I had not butterflies, but killer bees in my stomach.

Caius led our procession along the far wall to the opposite end of the hall. Partly to show their power over me, partly to help me remain upright, Agravain and Gareth held my arms. We made our slow approach to an archway where two armed but not armored guards stood at attention. They made no move to stop us. Perhaps they already knew we were coming. Either that, or they were merely decoration. Caius stepped aside while the brothers helped me to labor up two stairsteps into a plain room that was at most twelve feet square. One small window, open to the elements, lit the tiny space.

Lancelot, Bedwyr, Medraut and Sagramore followed us into the room and positioned themselves along the walls wherever they could. When Caius was satisfied, he called through a faded, red curtain into the room beyond. "Sire, they're here."

I heard a slight rustling and the plop, tap, shuffle of small items being moved about or set down. Then nothing. At last, a chair scraped on the floor. The next sound was loud panting.

A white, wolf-like hound burst through the red curtain and bounded into the room, ecstatic to see everyone, especially me. With my arms held behind me by the brother guards, I couldn't fend him off. As the beast pressed his wet nose into my crotch, King Arthur chose to enter.

"Cavall, away," he said, in a voice at the same time harsh and quiet. I immediately recognized my square-jawed, grizzled friend. I half expected him to speak in that strange, foreign tongue he'd used in the woods. But the savage murderer had become a calm, collected bear in boots. His hair and whiskers, the color of the dark Cadebir soil sprinkled with gray, framed an expression of bemusement on a face made interesting by deep lines. He seemed to tower above the others, not because of his size, though he was tall, but because of his presence.

The dog backed off, leaving me teetering.

"Release her," the king said calmly. "Cai, send for water."

The guards let go of my arms. Gareth steadied me with a gentle touch on my elbow, making sure I could stand on my own before he moved aside.

Gareth needn't have worried. King Arthur stepped forward and took my hands in his, giving me an extra point on which to balance. Though he had gripped my hands in the bloody forest, this gentler gesture shocked me in our more civilized surroundings. Was there a convention I was expected to follow? Should I bow or curtsey? Afraid to meet his eyes I looked at my red-polished, chipped nails enfolded in his rough palms.

His grip warm and sure, the king led me to the bench near the doorway, where Caius had stationed himself, and helped me to sit. Movement aggravated my migraine. I tilted my head back, allowing the cool wood of the wall to support it. Opposite me, Lancelot leaned, languid, in the corner. I thought he was watching me but in the dimness I couldn't be sure.

Having placed me, the king turned to his men. I would have to wait to know my fate. "Bedwyr, your report."

Bedwyr stepped forward. "About a dozen escaped us, Sire."

"We'll return for the stragglers. How many did we kill?"

"Seventeen, Sire, with Lancelot's help."

"Our casualties?"

"No serious injuries among the survivors, Sire," said Bedwyr. "Three dead."

The king's forehead clamped down over his brow. "Their names," he demanded.

Bedwyr seemed to be holding his breath. "Dead are Tore, Fergus and...Dynadan, Sire."

I felt the king's weight tip the bench forward when he sat. "Failure," he said.

The dog circled, settling at his master's feet and closing his silver eyes with a sigh. The king looked around the room, visiting each man with his eyes. "There's a spy among us."

"No, Sire!" Outraged, Medraut placed his hands on his hips. His resemblance to his father showed in the smooth but still square angle of his jaw.

"It can't be!" I thought Sagramore's chin quivered.

Lancelot stopped leaning and stood up, at last interested in the proceedings.

"You were all fighting for your lives, as was I," said the king, "but they knew me, I'm sure of it, either by my dress or my face. They sent their strongest warriors and separated me from the rest of you. I killed two men but was overpowered by the third. I couldn't see how to save myself." He turned, and I felt his eyes on me. "Then help came from the sky. An angel saved my life."

Cloth shifted against skin and leather slid across wood as all turned their eyes to me. Stunned, I tried to think back: *hurtle through space, see the grizzled man, bump into a hard thing, fall.*

"How did she save you, Sire?" asked Bedwyr.

"She flew at me with fury in her eyes. With great might she forced the Saxon upon my sword." King Arthur gazed at me in wonder. "I am forever in your debt."

The fury in my eyes had been terror. The shadow I'd bumped into with my head had been a man—a man I'd killed. King Arthur was forever in my debt. He probably wasn't going to kill me.

A servant appeared with a cup of water and offered it to me.

"Thanks," I whispered. I tried to calm my breathing so I could drink.

"Tell me your name, mistress," said the king.

I swallowed. "Casey."

A soft chuckle rose up among the men. Someone said, "Oh no," and someone else said, "It's the gallows, then." The king blinked and suppressed a fatherly grin.

Caius bent down from his considerable height to whisper, "You will address the king as 'your majesty.'"

"Oh. I'm sorry. It's Casey, your majesty." My voice sounded timid, not like a furious, avenging angel.

"Kay-see," the king tried it out on his lips. "An unusual name. You are most welcome here, Casey. Have my men ill-treated you?"

They just wanted to go home and get some sleep. It was in the look

Bedwyr exchanged with Sagramore and in Agravain's yawn, and the way they all slouched against the wall. By then not one of them was holding himself up with his own power.

"No, your majesty, they've been nice."

He shook his head. "I'll forgive you that lie because you don't know me yet. I can see they've been rough. You will be honest with me henceforth. I do not accept lies." He turned on the bench to face me squarely. "I owe you my life. I wish you no harm. I only wish to keep you. With your powers, you can be of great help to me."

Lancelot cleared his throat.

"What is it, Lance?"

"The stream did not frighten her, Sire."

"That is inconclusive."

Bedwyr spoke up. "Sire, if I may."

"Bedwyr."

"The lady has given her word to stay and has abided by it so far. She accompanied us the latter part of the day without chains."

I wanted to say, "Where else would I go?" but I sensed I shouldn't speak until spoken to, regardless of my magic powers.

The king folded his arms across his chest. To me he said, "Will you allow my wizard to nurse you?"

I nodded, then remembered, "Yes, your majesty." I thought I might pass out again if I didn't get something to eat or at least a place to lie down and let the migraine finish its evil work.

"Good. Cai will see to it that you get to the dell. Order the cart to the kitchen door, Cai."

Caius disappeared through the archway. The dell, whatever it was, had better be nearby.

"Can you walk?"

"I think so, your majesty."

Careful of my chafed wrists, the king helped me to my feet, holding my elbows with his big, bear hands. He put a protective arm around my shoulder and we moved with halting steps through the archway, down the stairs and into the hall, leaving the others behind. I held myself up, wanting to give over my strength to him yet not sure I should.

"I've never seen a hauberk like yours," the king whispered as we made our measured steps to the back door. "Is it magic armour? Can you make more of it?"

"I...I'm afraid I can't, your majesty," I said, glad he'd at least mentioned my armor so I had a general idea of what "hauberk" meant.

"Who made it? Perhaps I can persuade him to make more for my men. The hood is especially fine."

"I don't think so," I said, forgetting myself in migraine and exhaustion. "I got it at the Gap."

He stopped, turning me to face him, gripping my upper arms too hard. His gray eyes held mine, eyes that made me hope Guinevere, if indeed she existed, was not his wife. I'd never seen gray eyes before, at least not up close. Within them, relics lay buried. Chasms ran deep with hope, loss, and too much knowledge.

"I mean, I got it at the Gap, *your majesty.*" Stupid, stupid, I thought. Remember where you are. He doesn't know about retail.

But his eyes brightened with revelation. "I see!" He looked over his shoulder toward the men, then back at me, lowering his voice to a whisper. "We'll speak of it when you're well. Now go to the dell. Myrddin will know what to do with you."

THIRTEEN

Sick of rolling, sick of wheels, sick of feeling sick, I lay in the bed of another cart, this time unchained. On the downhill lurch I slid against the wagon side, bumping my pounding head. The cart rattled under branches of forest canopy while twilight crept over me like an animal padding over a bed of fallen leaves. I wanted to pull myself up to look around but could only wonder at the great height of the trees while details of their leaves diminished into darkness.

After time, long or short, someone lifted, moved, floated me to a surface where at last movement stopped. I lay listening to the whooshing in my temples, until a tiny light invaded the space. Soft footsteps padded toward me.

"Help me, Drostan." A rumbling, confident voice.

Strong arms propped me up to sit.

"Drink this."

A veined hand offered a steaming cup containing hot water and what looked like a bit of tree bark. The concoction burned my tongue and tasted bitter. It would cure me or kill me. Either would be a relief.

"Drink more."

"Whzzt?"

"Bark of the white willow. Good for aches, especially of the head. Drink every drop."

I did. The helper laid me down.

They moved away. When I opened my mouth to say "thank you," my stomach retched and my body curled in convulsion.

His robe swishing, the deep-voiced one returned to my side. "Some don't take well to willow bark," he soothed. "Pail to your left."

If I dreamt, I didn't remember. I woke, wildly hungry, on a comfortable cot in a clean hut. Sun and birdsong beamed through a window, opened to them with no glass to keep them out. Most of me was still filthy but my wrists and ankles had been cleaned and salved.

I rose slowly, allowing my joints to release their stiffness like paper once scrolled and reluctant to unroll. My feet, now bare, felt like they'd spent the last few days in vice-grips instead of expensive boots. With tentative steps I crossed the room and opened the door to peek out, jumping back when I nearly broadsided a small woman who rushed by. She wore an off-white tunic and carried an armload of clean rags.

"Good morning," I said. She ignored me and trotted past, disappearing down a path that was shaded by a pergola overgrown with woody vines. I followed her, meandering between huts and enjoying the morning's soft air until the path opened onto a sunny garden. The woman had disappeared. Across rows of vegetables and greens, an old man in an off-white robe watched me from the doorway of a large hut. When our eyes met he waved me to him. I cut between rows of lavender, rosemary and poppies, inhaling the mixture of their scents as I crossed the garden, my feet warm on the earth. The old man watched my approach, his pate reddening in the sun, his thin lips framed by a white beard.

"You're better this morning," he said in his rumbling voice. "You must be hungry."

I followed him into the shade of what I at first thought was a kitchen. Herbs hung in bunches from the ceiling to dry, giving the place a wild, fresh smell. Every surface was cluttered with bowls of seeds, vials of powder, and organized arrays of bones. I turned away from what looked like an odd biology experiment but turned out to be the dissection of a hapless squirrel. Not a kitchen. A laboratory.

The old man gestured a skinny arm to a table laden with food. "Sit and eat." He padded in bare feet to the corner, his dingy robe dragging on the packed dirt floor. He picked up a couple of stones, smacked them together, and blew gently on the sparks they created in the fire pit. It seemed like magic.

He looked up. "Eat," he said. "I've eaten already. I hope you don't mind."

I took a seat at the table. He dipped a cauldron into a barrel of water and hung it over the small flame.

"Are you...?" I had so many questions.

"Am I what?"

"Is your name...?"

"Myrddin," he said. It sounded like *Merthin,* just as King Arthur had pronounced it. Almost, but not quite, *Merlin.* Without looking, he took pinches of herbs from a bunch hanging above his shoulder and tossed them into a pair of mugs. "This time it's only tea."

Laid out before me was enough food for four people: small pies, baked buns, sliced apples, nuts and berries. No silverware. No matter. He was right, I was starving. I plucked up a warm roll with dirty fingers and inhaled the aroma of freshly baked grains.

"Are you a wizard?"

"You first." He brought my tea to me and took his to a desk in the corner, behind which leaned precarious shelves overloaded with bottles, scrolls, and rusted tools. There he sat and regarded me.

I chewed, hungry but self-conscious, not sure what to say, wondering what the king had told him about me.

"Did you come from a star?" asked Myrddin. "We have legends of people from the stars. Did you really appear out of nothing? Arthur mentioned a gap. You received your garment there?"

"Uh, yes."

"Is it a gap in the sky?"

I picked up a piece of pie. "No. I think it's a gap in time." Egg pie, it looked like. With cheese.

Myrddin brought his fingers to his lips. "I like that. Explain." He rested his chin on bony hands and waited.

My instinct was to trust him. I hadn't felt that instinct in years. Though Myrddin was old and cheerful unlike my young, sad father, my dad was the one who had listened, like that, with his chin resting on his hands.

"All I know is I was riding Lucy in the rain and a car came along. Lucy panicked, the car slammed on its brakes and I flew. When I landed it wasn't the twenty-first century anymore."

"Carrrr," Myrddin muttered, taking up a quill and scratching it on a flat piece of leather. "Brakes. Twenty-one." He stopped. "Lucy. A horse?"

I nodded.

He glanced back at his notes and frowned. "You came from the twenty-first century?"

"Yes."

"By what reckoning?"

"Well...have you ever heard of Jesus?"

"Why?" He eyed me with suspicion.

"Years since Jesus lived. That's kind of how we count it."

"That bodes ill." Myrddin sighed. "Poor, fatherless boy. Tragically misunderstood. He's all the rage with the young people these days."

"What year is it now?"

"By the same reckoning?" He bent over his scratchings. "Alas, from his death I calculate...oh, five hundred years. Or so. Perhaps fewer. Certainly not more."

I put down the meat pastry I'd been munching. Myrddin laid his quill on the desk. We gazed at each other. I wondered if he'd almost stopped breathing, like I had, at the thought of it.

I'd lost fifteen hundred years. My nose tingled.

Myrddin's black eyes glowed. "Your people must be looking for you."

"I don't think so." Mike had his wife and baby. Hollywood and *Gone!* were finished with me. My mother wouldn't notice I was missing until she didn't get her Christmas e-card. I didn't matter to anyone in the world. My eyes misted. Among the apples, pastries and nuts on the table was not one, single napkin.

"You didn't choose to come here?"

"No. I don't know how I got here, or how to get back. I could die here." My stomach churned and sank like a dying motor. I was a negative. I had to get back, even though I had left nothing of importance behind. "Myrddin, have you ever heard of Camelot?"

"No. What is it?"

"It's the greatest legend of all England."

"Angland?" He stiffened. "Don't tell me the Angles are going to win?"

"Oh—uh, I'm not a historian."

Myrddin glared.

"Well. They don't exactly lose." He continued glaring and I hurried to mollify him. "The trouble is, not a lot of detail is known about how it happens. King Arthur and you, you're legends in my time. But there's no proof of your real lives."

"That is not to be tolerated." He stood, surprisingly agile, and began to pace. "You shall take proof back with you. You certainly brought things—your horse, your pack, your clothes."

"But I don't know how to go back."

"Well, you can't stay here." He stopped pacing, towering above me, eyes gleaming. He must have been fearsome in his youth. Even then I cringed at the foot of his power. He calmed, speaking almost apologetically. "You and I are intelligent people. We know how to solve problems. We shall study this one together to determine exactly how you got here. When we know that, we'll know how to return you to your time."

It seemed impossible. But my presence there was impossible, too.

He returned to his desk and plucked up my passport. "Let us begin with this. Do you know what these markings are?"

"It's writing—words."

"Can you read these words?"

"Yes."

"What do they say?"

"'Passport, United States of America.' That's where I come from."

"I've never heard of it."

"It's a new country."

"A new country. Oh!" He closed his eyes and allowed a thrill to shudder through his body. Recovering, he waved the piece of leather he'd been writing on. "And this? Can you read the words on the vellum?"

Lines and scratches. "Is it Latin?"

His eyes widened in surprise. "Yes, it is."

"I can't read it."

"But you recognize it."

"Where I come from, lots of people would recognize it. But you're not speaking Latin."

"Our language isn't written. To create a dispatch or a record, I must use Latin. But few people know it—the educated few. And none of them are women." He tossed the vellum to the desk, still watching me. In a single, swift movement he was sitting across from me. "Your society—mostly educated, eh?"

"A lot, yeah."

"Hmm." He flipped through the passport and opened it to my picture, which showed me grimacing as if I'd just eaten a dissected squirrel. "This likeness—it's uncanny. Tell me how it was made."

I'd be lost if I had to explain photography or any other modern innovations, from computers to can openers. "I'm not good with technical stuff like photography, or cars, or air travel—"

"Air travel! Oh yes yes yes!" He clapped his hands like a six-year-old at Christmas. "Tell me all about flying. I must know how you did it! If you are from the future, I'm thrilled to learn what I can from you. If not, your lies are grand." He then quickly composed himself. "In either case, your presence is perhaps not best for our cause, despite Arthur's delight in you."

"I'm glad he's delighted."

"Oh, he believes you've come expressly to protect him. That's why he wants to keep you."

Ah yes. I was King Arthur's property.

"Of your true purpose, however, I'm not certain. We're at war,"

Myrddin went on, popping a handful of nuts into his mouth. "A king has many enemies."

"Sounds like he's insecure."

"Watch what you say, my lady. Besides, every king is insecure, as well he should be. An attempt was being made on his life even as you appeared. It happens all the time."

"That's no way to live."

"It is his calling. He has no choice."

That, I knew from the stories. I had thought of it as grand and heroic, as opposed to burdensome.

I sipped my tea. "What if he didn't want to keep me?"

"That would depend upon you." Myrddin selected a meat pastry. "If you committed an offense, perhaps, like treason—if you lied, for example—he'd have to kill you." He took a bite and continued. "If he tired of you or you became useless, he'd simply turn you out."

"I won't commit treason. I'll be useful."

"That doesn't mean you belong here."

I wondered how I was going to make myself useful. I couldn't imagine fending for myself on the open plains, but what did I have to offer a king? I didn't even have the skills to survive Hollywood.

"The king called you his wizard," I said. "Can you teach me?"

"I'm afraid he used the term broadly. I'm a natural philosopher, a physician. And I'm blessed with a plethora of assistants." Finished eating, he wiped his hands on his robe. "Arthur knows *my* limitations." He looked deep into my eyes. "He tells me you have magic."

"I have...*some* powers," I said, unable to hold his gaze. "But I wouldn't mind picking up some other skills." I had to buy time until I came up with a way to make myself indispensable.

"I'm pleased and amazed that magic exists in the future," said Myrddin. "Here, it has almost disappeared. Arthur still believes, but he's old-fashioned." He stood. "Well! Soon enough, you and I shall begin seeking a way to send you home. Just...let's not mention it to Arthur, shall we?" He wiped his mouth with his sleeve, towering over me once again. "Today, you rest. Tomorrow you have an audience with the king."

FOURTEEN

I had to jog to keep up with Myrddin's confident stride. My painfully stylish boots pinched my toes with every step. We retraced the path I'd taken from among the infirmary huts the day before, following it past my hut, deep into the green, buzzing forest until we stood at the bottom of a seemingly insurmountable stone stairway dappled in sunlight. Each of its risers was so steep and uneven I thought the old man wouldn't make it to the top. But he skipped up it, his long, slender legs sticking out under his flowing robe. I scrambled up behind him as best I could, grabbing branches to balance myself and stopping to gasp for breath.

At the top of the stairs, a boy waited with two horses. His off-white tunic marked him as a member of Myrddin's staff. Without a word, he blew a puff of air upwards to push brown bangs from his eyes, then formed a lift with his hands to give me a leg up onto the back of a brown mare. The "leg up" business was clumsy (stirrups made so much more sense), and while I was at it Myrddin had already leapt aboard his fine, black steed and ridden away into the forest. Seated at last, I clucked to my mount, who was willing to trot. Further effort to catch up was outside her circle of interests, but when Myrddin's horse slowed to a walk we were able to overtake him.

At first the wide, clear path was lined with rocks. Soon we came upon a pair of giant stones posed like sentries at either side of the way. Myrddin reined his horse to a stop and leaned so far to the side I thought he'd lose his leather cap in the underbrush. "These stone columns mark the entrance to my compound. But it wasn't always mine. Look." He pointed to deep curlicues carved into the giant stone. "A message from our ancestors. There have always been people here. There always will be." He sighed. "I wish I knew what they meant to say. But do you see? It's entirely possible to send messages to the future. It makes me hopeful we can send people as well."

My mount swished a fly with her tail. I leaned across her neck to trace my finger along the intricate patterns in the cool, white stone. How deep in time had the inscription been made if even Myrddin couldn't read it? Maybe we could send messages ahead, but the only people I knew of who went to the future were found there in the form of mummies and bones.

Beyond the stones the woods grew wilder. I was forced to ride behind Myrddin much of the time because abundant flora crawled its way over the edges of the path so profusely we couldn't ride two abreast. The trees were close enough to touch, and I sat astride my gentle mare paying little attention to what lay before me while reaching up, looking sideways, turning to follow a sound in the underbrush. Sometimes I was forced to duck to avoid being knocked off by low branches. Eventually our way grew so thick with growth it seemed not to be a path at all. At times I thought we were lost. Yet in less than an hour the forest thinned. Dark green paled to yellow at the edge of the woods, and we emerged from the trees into bright morning.

Our path met a road that led up the shaded west side of Cadebir hill, a road so wide it didn't require switchbacks. At its summit stood a stone gatehouse about twice as large as the one atop the zig-zag path on the other side. This more impressive entry was well-provisioned, with armed men and a store of weapons.

A dozen guards greeted Myrddin with a respectful "Good morning, sir." They bowed slightly to me, as though I gained respect by virtue of being with the old physician regardless of my blood-caked sweater and muddy cargo pants. I'd lost track of the number of days I'd been wearing those pants. I'd been wearing the underpants even longer.

"Good morning, good morning," Myrddin doffed his leather cap again and again, bowing like a showman. All attention was ours as we rode through the gate, like a famous client arriving at her trial with her celebrity lawyer.

The path from the entrance rose directly to the promontory where the hall sat with its cluster of huts. There, Myrddin dismounted and gave his reins to a groom. I followed his example, landing with a wobble. The groom bowed to Myrddin, watching me out of the corner of his eye.

Trotting to keep up, I followed Myrddin along the back side of the hall, where the fort's wall came within yards of the main buildings. A few cows stood stamping and blinking in a sunny pen near the wall. In the shade of the eaves of the hall, dozens of wild-looking fowl clucked in their pens. Outside a low building annexed to the larger one, a pack of shaggy dogs barked at us, standing their ground.

Two young women waited there beneath a wooden awning. The brunette stared at her hands, which were folded across her very pregnant belly. The redhead shooed the dogs away and gave Myrddin a coquettish smile. "The gentleman is required to wait outside," she said.

"Of course." Myrddin made no move to leave. "Casey. Lynet and Elaine will provide you with a bath in advance of your audience with the king."

"Oh! Thank you." I desperately needed a bath.

"This way," said the redhead, leading into the annex with the light step of a dancer. We followed her into cool dimness where I collided with an animal carcass that hung from the ceiling. Bits of the unfortunate creature's skin stuck to my sweater between the clumps of mud and dried blood already there.

"Sorry, I should have warned you," said the redhead. "Careful. The floor's slippery, too."

We picked our way through a busy kitchen. The fragrance of spices mixed with the wet-raw smell of fresh meat. A woman stirred an iron cauldron, laughing with the men who stacked ceramic jugs atop lidded barrels. Fresh vegetables, the dirt still on them, lay heaped on wooden countertops by the windows.

Myrddin stopped to talk to a big-boned woman with red cheeks. "What's to eat?" he asked her.

With a formidable cleaver, she whacked the head off a small, skinless creature. The *whump* of the knife hitting flesh and wood cut off her answer.

I followed my leaders through an archway to a workroom beyond the kitchen where the temperature was several degrees warmer, thanks to a fire burning in a pit in the far corner. The brunette scurried to the pit, skittering around piles of clothing on the floor. She stared at me from beneath lowered lids until I caught her eye. She blushed, looking away.

"Elaine thinks you're going to cast spells on us," said the redhead. She, then, would be Lynet. She looked all of seventeen and Elaine wasn't much older. Lynet pulled a curly lock behind a pink ear, jangling the brass bangles on her arm. "Protection spells are fine but if you've any others, please save them for after the bath." Her mischievous smile warmed me to her. "I'll take your...er...garments." She extended her dainty pinkies for me to hang my clothes on, thus allowing as little as possible of her surface area to come into contact with my odious apparel.

The women's eyes grew wide as I unzipped my boots, but neither commented, and I set the boots aside. The rear pockets of my cargo pants dangled by threads. I peeled them off and hung them on Lynet's pinkie by a belt loop. My tee shirt couldn't be saved, but I gave that over, too. The chain mail sweater I'd thought so apropos was stiff with mud and bloody remnants of the horrors it had seen, not to mention what some poor deer had seen. Lynet bundled them all at her feet.

The ragged chafing on my wrists and ankles had hardened to scabs. "I've never seen wounds like yours," said Lynet. "Have you, Elaine?"

"Not on a woman I haven't." Elaine lumbered to the iron bath tub near the window, carrying a heavy pot from the fire. I didn't think she should lift such things in her condition. She looked like she'd deliver in a matter of days. She poured the hot water into the tub, set down the pot and stared, dumbfounded, at my chest. "What's that?"

My bra had suffered from the ordeal, but it was recognizable.

"It's a bra. For...you know, managing my...breasts."

"Ouch," said Lynet.

"But your breasts don't require management," said Elaine.

Lynet laughed. "We bind with cloth, for comfort." She gestured to the tub. "We'll show you after the bath."

Yes. The bath. Inhaling steam, I gripped the edges of the tub and raised my leg to swing it over and dunk a grimy toe. The water was just as I like it, on the edge of too hot.

"Wait." Lynet drew in a little gasp. "Your wounds. The water will smart. Give me your foot."

"Okay." I balanced on one foot while Lynet folded her palms around my other ankle. She submerged it slowly, cushioning my raw skin from the sting.

"That's got it?"

"Yes. Thanks." Once both legs were submerged I lowered myself to sit, marveling at Lynet's thoughtfulness, and, at the same time, the water's blessed sting.

Elaine followed Lynet's example and helped me submerge my wrists. "Brutes." She shook her head. But the sting was past. "Do all Saxon ladies wear toenail paint?" she asked.

"Oh. Uh, some," I said, going along with her assumption. Perhaps rumor had it that I was a Saxon lady.

I hadn't been washed by anyone besides myself since I was a baby. My dad had relished the opportunity to teach me about soap, bubbles or whatever was available. My mother must have washed me at some point, but I found it difficult to picture her involved in such a maternal task. She wouldn't have let me drown, she'd just have forgotten to rinse my hair.

Elaine and Lynet were careful, their touch a comfort, a mothering. The rough soap they scrubbed me with smelled vaguely meaty. But the suds it made broke up the grime that had become caked on my surfaces. I closed my eyes and rested my head against the side of the tub, allowing myself to relax while the women scrubbed and chatted.

"Your husband will be here for the birth, then?" Lynet washed between my toes, which felt divine if she didn't squeeze.

"Yes," said Elaine, careful to pat softly around the bruise on my forehead while she lathered my hair. "Beatha says I've got a girl."

"Lance must be disappointed."

"He's been sullen since his return from Poste Perdu. I don't know why." Elaine scratched the sides of my head a little too hard. "But Lancelot will do his duty by me."

That couldn't be right. Lancelot was glamorous. Elaine was artless and simple.

She changed the subject. "Have you seen Gareth yet?"

"Oh yes."

I opened my eyes. Lynet blushed and flashed a bright smile. "Gareth and I are hand-fasted," she told me.

"What's that?"

Elaine stopped rubbing. "Don't Saxons hand-fast?"

Maybe they did. "Um...no."

"It's a marriage vow for a year and a day," said Lynet. "It's taken at the festival of Calan Awst." She skipped to the fire to retrieve another pot of water, holding the hot handle with a cloth. "If it doesn't suit, you may undo the marriage the day after next Calan Awst."

"Unless a child is conceived, then it stands," said Elaine. There was my clue.

"And if you don't undo the hand-fasting, you're wed." Lynet leaned against the tub. "Gareth and I will not be undoing. He says he's destined to be tormented by me forever." She tested the water's temperature with her finger. "Ready to rinse?"

I nodded and closed my eyes. Warm water splashed the top of my head and flowed over me.

"Maybe you'll meet someone here, Casey," said Lynet. "It's less than a month 'til the festival. Or perhaps you've a love at home?"

"I'm not seeing anyone."

"That's a funny way to put it," said Elaine, handing me a cloth.

I stood to dry off. "It seems there aren't many women here."

"Mostly serving women," said Elaine. "We're not serving women."

"Of course."

Lynet offered a carved, bone comb from the pouch at her belt. "But everyone must work. I sew. Elaine oversees the washing. We have servants to help us." Presenting moisturizer in the form of rosy-smelling oil she said, "Imported from Italy."

"Such luxury."

"Oh, not nearly. At the castle we have all the finest things." She sighed. "I miss the coast. Elaine returns there soon."

"Really? Why?"

Elaine handed me a splinter and a handful of leaves. "A war camp is not a place for babies." She frowned, making her small nose wrinkle.

"Oh."

Elaine pointed to the items I held. "That's for cleaning your mouth."

"Oh!" Splinter and leaves; a toothpick and fresh mint. Gratitude made my nose tingle.

I found binding to be more comfortable than a bra, though the ladies tied the fabric tight to keep it from slipping. Next came a linen underdress with a round neckline and long sleeves. It shielded my skin from the itchy wool tunic that went over it. Soft, leather shoes, a cross between moccasins and ballet slippers, replaced my painful boots. The straps were supposed to tie around my ankles but for the time being, I laced them up my legs to allow my wounds to heal.

Someone, presumably Lynet, had repaired my fanny pack with strong stitches where Bedwyr had slashed it, making it a usable, if not beautiful belt. My money and credit cards, worthless at Cadebir, were still inside.

"You need something else." Elaine untied a ribbon from her hair and with it, pulled together a lock of mine. "Keep that," she said. "You'll want to use it again."

Lynet gave me one of her bracelets. "I have plenty." She stood back to admire me. "King Arthur will be pleased, don't you think, Elaine?"

"I do."

I smiled, letting gratitude fill me. "Is there a mirror?"

Lynet laughed. "The queen has a looking-glass, but I don't suppose you ought to go into her chamber."

So there was a queen.

"We use the well to see our reflections if we must, but there isn't time now. You look quite presentable," said Lynet. "Myrddin's orders."

"Thank you. I...I love baths."

"You look pretty," said Elaine.

I released a breath. Though I feared "pretty" would not be enough, I wanted very much to look pretty for the king.

FIFTEEN

"Wart!"

Myrddin and I stood in the small audience room where I'd met the king the day before. Or two days before. In losing time, I had lost track of it. I shifted from one foot to the other, picking at the edges of my muslin sleeve.

Myrrdin called at the faded red curtain. "The lady wizard is with me."

"Enter."

The old man pulled the curtain aside. Touching my shoulder, he guided me through the archway into a low-ceilinged chamber. Daylight found its way through tall windows at the far end, where a ladder led up to some kind of loft. At the room's center, King Arthur sat behind a crudely-made wooden desk, studying a vellum document. Behind him, hanging from an iron hook that pierced its eye, leered the sideburn helmet of the Saxon I'd watched him kill.

The king did not glance up. "Please refrain from addressing me as 'Wart' in the presence of our guest."

"Sorry, Arthur."

Myrddin chose a chair facing the desk and relaxed into it, crossing his legs. I awaited instructions.

With his arms supporting his head like columns support a roof, King Arthur rubbed his temples and sighed. His salt and pepper hair was tied into a ponytail with a leather thong. The sleeves of his linen shirt were rolled up to the elbows, revealing a cloth bandage where his forearm had been sliced in the fight with the big Saxon in the woods. The document he perused was a map, which didn't surprise me. What I didn't expect were the stacks and stacks of vellum sheets, bolted between slabs of wood, piled on the desk and floor. Books. Everywhere. Quills, too, with little ink pots like Myrddin's. Maybe Myrddin wasn't the only well-read man at Cadebir. But with shoulders hunched and shirt draping open, King Arthur wore the look not of a scholar but of an aging prize-fighter, stony with muscle and etched with scars.

Tapping a thick finger on the parchment before him he said, "Come around this side, mistress. I'll show you."

I didn't expect to find the wolf-dog behind the desk. Cavall growled. Startled, I tripped over the king's sword, which was propped against the desk in its scabbard.

"Hush, Cavall. Go away."

Cavall cocked his big head, looking innocent.

"Go."

The dog obeyed, slinking off to curl himself onto a pillow by the cold fire pit.

"Sorry, your majesty," I said. Nervous, I righted the sword. It wasn't a broadsword but shorter, and a good deal heavier than it looked. When I finally stood beside the king I saw my passport lying atop a stack of vellum on the desk, weighted by a smooth stone. I was also in a position to see the queen's mirror, the looking glass Lynet had mentioned, hanging on the far wall near the ladder. A ray of sun glinted off its edge with a golden spark. It was too far away for me to get a glimpse of myself.

King Arthur reached a burly arm across me, brushing against my sleeve and recalling my attention. Standing so close to his shoulder, I could see the weave of the rough fabric of his tunic. He pointed to a spot on a crude map of southern England.

"You know Londinium."

"Yes, your majesty."

He moved his finger a couple of inches west and slightly south. "Here's the Giant's Ring. And there," he pointed a bit southeast of that, "is Poste Perdu." Indicating a mark further west he said, "This is Cadebir."

Mesmerized by his cracked nails and weathered skin, I followed his hand along the uneven triangle he traced between the Giant's Ring, Poste Perdu and Cadebir. On his middle finger he wore a silver ring with concentric circles etched on its round, flat face. Inside the smallest circle was a horseshoe shape and inside the horseshoe a little mark, like a hyphen. It was fine, meticulous work.

He was watching me. "You admire my ring?"

"Yes, your majesty."

"It's fashioned after the great stones of the Giant's Ring." He lifted his hand for me to get a closer look.

I bent to examine the Stonehenge pattern, inhaling his scent of herbs and something like oatmeal. "It's beautiful, your majesty." Unnerved at being so close to the man, I tried returning my attention to the map. Pointing to a spot slightly north of the Giant's Ring, I changed the subject. "Is this about where you found me, your majesty?"

"Where *you* found *me*, yes. Nothing there but deep forest and wolves. Except the road. Tell me, how did you come to be there?"

His gray eyes challenged, his direct gaze flustered me. He could easily ruin me, as if I were a dry dandelion bloom and he a breath of wind. I remembered what Myrddin had said about lying to the king. "I don't know."

"Who sent you?"

"No one. I came on my own."

"But you came to save me."

"I guess..."

He turned away, releasing me from his eyes. "You may sit."

Relieved, I stepped back around the desk, avoiding the sword, and took the chair next to Myrddin's.

"The Saxons knew we'd be at that spot at that time."

I sat erect. "I'm not a Saxon, your majesty."

Myrddin picked through a jar of quills, looking for something with which to entertain himself. "Wart—Arthur—"

"I want to hear from the lady." King Arthur sat back and waited.

I hesitated. Behind me at the fire pit, Cavall gnawed a bone, his teeth grinding against its surface. Mindful of the penalty for lying, I decided it was best to go ahead with the full truth. "Your majesty, I'm...from the future." That was true.

"I see." He didn't believe me. "Has this to do with the Gap?"

"Yes, your majesty." That seemed reasonable, in an unreasonable way.

"She arrived here through a gap in time," Myrddin said, as though it were obvious.

"Do you have proof?"

I was reminded of the perilous position I held somewhere between dead prisoner and live avenger. I didn't know the truth.

"I'm not sure how to prove it to you, your majesty. But I've known about you all my life. You're a legend in my time. Books are still being written about you, fifteen hundred years from now. Stories are still being told."

"What sort of stories?"

"I don't know if they're true."

"Tell one."

"Well. Um. Okay." I thought of my storybook, tucked in a drawer in a place called a condo, where there was electricity. "One says your sword is called Excalibur."

"I've named my sword?" He suppressed a smirk.

"Yes, your majesty. It shines in battle and it has magical powers."

He laughed softly. "Would that it were magic."

"You do keep it shiny," said Myrddin. With a glass ink bottle, he absentmindedly made sunlight prisms on the floor.

The king leaned back, tipping his chair against the wall. "Go on, my lady. I'm entertained."

"Okay. Uh...as a boy, you pulled your sword from a stone."

"Perhaps Lancelot could do such a thing."

"It's how everyone knew you were destined to be king."

"Not because the people needed me to lead them?"

I rushed to say, "I'm sure they did, your majesty."

"Continue." He let the chair land on all fours again.

"Have you sent Sir Galahad and the knights on a quest for the holy grail?"

"I haven't. I've never heard of this Galahad."

"Oh. Supposedly he's the strongest knight. But maybe that story doesn't happen. Or maybe it's later. Or the other knights went."

"These nights—?"

"Your men. It's a title. But knighthood, uh, maybe that was a later invention? Jousting too, probably."

"Probably. What is it?"

I scooted my chair closer to the desk, enjoying his interest. "It's a competition. The knights knock each other off their horses with a lance."

"They kill each other for pleasure?" asked Myrddin.

"They don't kill each other, mostly. I think the lance tip is blunt. It does sound ridiculous, though, now that I think about it."

"Highly impractical," said Myrddin, "at least during war time."

"Yes," said King Arthur. "I can't imagine why, with such silliness, I'd be the legend you say I am. Though I admit it's amusing." He laughed. Myrddin and I laughed with him.

"So you're not going to seek the Holy Grail?" I asked.

"I've a war to fight, my lady." He patted the desk. "But come, are there more stories?" His smile encouraged me to speak freely.

"Yes, many. Myrddin taught you things by turning you into animals. That's one of my favorites."

They looked to each other with raised eyebrows. "That's true, in a way," said the king. "Myrddin has his tricks. But tell me, will I not lead my army to battle, defend my people? Are there no stories of my might?"

"Oh tons," I blundered on, emboldened. "There are at least a dozen battles. And castles, and fair maidens, knights in shining armor—oh, but you don't call them knights, so I don't know how much of it is true. I wish I knew all the stories, there are so many. The most famous one's about Lancelot and Guinev—" I stopped.

"What happens in that story?" King Arthur was no longer smiling.

"It's probably not true," I said.

"Tell it." He ignored the strand of hair that had come loose from his ponytail to hang across his cheek.

My mind sought a quick lie but came up empty. "Legend says there was a...love affair."

A loud clatter startled me.

"Sorry." Myrddin climbed down from his chair to retrieve an ink bottle from the floor. "Tiny spill."

"Continue." The king hadn't moved.

A vinegar smell rose from the ink spill. Wishing for a tissue, I wiped my nose on my sleeve and looked at my lap. "I'm sure it's not true, your majesty. In the story, the affair is revealed by your illegitimate son, Mordred."

"His name is Medraut." His voice was flat.

"The legends got a few things wrong."

"Not as many as one might hope."

Myrddin returned to his chair. The two men eyed each other.

So, the queen was indeed Guinevere.

"Splendid," said the king. "I've gone down in history as a cuckold."

"Oh no, your majesty," I said, reminded of death sentences. "You're known as righteous and wise, fair, judicious, and...and...kind..."

"We shall see." Like lifting a heavy burden, King Arthur hoisted himself from his chair. He took up the stone from atop my passport, absentmindedly tossed the rock in his hand and ambled to the windows to gaze out over the camp. A breeze wandered in and tousled the muslin curtains, bringing work sounds with it: pounding hammers, men calling to each other, horse hooves trotting, a cart rolling by. King Arthur caressed the stone in his hand, thinking.

Myrddin caught my eye and shook his head ever so slightly. I didn't know if he meant "Don't worry," "Don't say anything," or "It's all over for you."

Cavall stretched and yawned, then sauntered to his master's side. The king pulled the shutter closed and scratched the dog's big, white head before turning to me. "I believe you," he said. "You are from the future. And for saving my life, I'm grateful."

Relief made my nose tingle. I bowed my head, fighting tears.

"If you're to stay you must abide by my terms. You are not to practice sorcery, not the tiniest trick, without my express orders."

That was a relief.

"As far as the others know, you are not from the future. You are a Saxon wizard who has defected to our side. You will not speak of the future, of the legends or of the affair, on pain of death."

"Yes, your majesty."

"There is no proof of this affair, of course."

"Of course, your majesty."

King Arthur strode back across the room to loom over the desk, supporting his weight on arms as strong as girders. "I'm sorry if I seem ungrateful, my lady. I am in your debt. But I must be clear for the sake of our cause."

I nodded.

"We are at war. Everyone works for his keep. Your job shall be Protector of the King. For now there's little for you to do, but I will call upon you. You may recuperate here on the hill or visit Myrddin when he wills it. But I must ask you not to leave Cadebir without my permission."

Because not everything the king said was a direct order, I was beginning to think he didn't know the extent of my powers. "Yes, your majesty."

He lifted my passport and handed it to me. I zipped it into my pack.

The king studied me, scratching his stubbled cheek. "You haven't answered one of my questions."

I didn't remember which one.

"Why did you come here to save my life?"

Why had I flown down through the ages to this time of all times? Why had the universe opened up and swallowed me? The question weighted my chest with the wonder at where I was and who he was. Why him? Why me?

He watched me, intent on Casey the wizard. Casey the actor had once wanted to command such attention but Casey the person had failed. I'd spent my life thus far desiring greatness and becoming nobody. In that rickety chair I sat facing someone truly great, history's idol, the world's, my father's, mine.

"Because your life had to be saved, your majesty. Because Britain needs you."

A lie, though I meant it with all my heart. I didn't know the truth.

He considered it. Then he released the desk and stood, no longer needing to hold himself up. "I *will* save Britain."

I didn't correct him. The legends did not say King Arthur would save

Britain. They said he would return one day when Britain needed him again. While the king and I gazed at each other the Saxons, Jutes and Angles who gnawed at Britain's shores were in the process of defeating him. It would take years, but Britain was already becoming Angle-land. England.

It was a lie of omission, but a lie nonetheless.

It was also my first act of treason.

SIXTEEN

"How did I do?" I trotted in the dust at Myrddin's heels. "Am I safe from burning for now?"

I slammed into him when he stopped and turned on me, his black eyes hot. "I suggest you lower your voice when referring to the subject of flames." He sounded stern but he was more interested in what he saw beyond my shoulder.

I turned to look. Two men sauntered by, carrying a deer carcass strung on a pole between them. When I looked back, Myrddin was licking his lips. He glanced sideways, then pulled me off the path.

"Try to see it through Arthur's eyes," he whispered. "The Saxons are maddeningly close. Marauders disrupt our trade on the seas. What's left of the British tribes is in disarray and has been so since the Romans left years ago. Arthur must coordinate these mobs into an army, and quickly. If we don't defeat the enemy we'll no longer exist. It's that simple."

"That's a lot of pressure for one man. Not to mention his wife is sleeping with his—"

Myrddin slapped his hand over my mouth. "Don't speak of it!" He quickly removed his hand and held both behind his back. "I beg your pardon. But perhaps you don't understand. The queen's indiscretion is treason, punishable by death at the stake."

"Wow." Myrddin's glare was unnerving. "Sorry. I won't mention it again."

He continued to glare.

"Um...you have my word?"

"Good." With an exaggerated sigh he offered his arm and we began to stroll. "There's also the strategic alliance to be considered," he whispered. "Arthur's friendship with Lancelot is crucial. Poste Perdu is a mere three hours away at a gallop. Lancelot brings with him the allegiance of the Belgae."

"I hadn't thought of it that way."

"Do. Now. I'll be with you tonight at supper, but I recommend you keep your mouth closed at table, except to put food in it."

"I'll be careful. What are these buildings for?" We were strolling among the huts clustered near the hall.

"People live in them, those in Arthur's circle. Lancelot and Elaine, for example. Caius and Andrivette live in the large hut just there. I'm not sure about the one across from it. Empty, I believe. Caius is the king's foster brother, did you know?"

"Oh. Cai. Sir Kay."

"From one of your stories, perhaps. Arthur also uses spare huts for allied chieftains, though some prefer to camp with their armies."

"The tents below the hill?"

"Mmmhm. All in preparation for what's to come."

The war. A tingle heated the back of my neck, softly, like a beam of late afternoon sun. Cadebir fort may have been the most imposing in the land, but it was no larger than a Hollywood backlot: big enough to house the pretense of a full-out war, but not the real thing. Myrddin and I traversed it diagonally on the path that connected the southwest and northeast gates, passing hunters with the day's catch and servant women with their baskets. We'd all smile or nod, then, when they got past us, I'd hear excited whispers.

"Tell me," said Myrddin, feigning disinterest, "do the legends say anything else about me?"

"Yeah. At least I think it's you."

He laughed. "Did they mistake my name as well? What did you call Medraut? Morbid?"

"Mordred. They call you Merlin, but I'm pretty sure it's you."

"Close enough. So?"

"Sorcerer, poet. Some say you live backwards, getting younger. There's one that says a sorceress imprisons you inside a tree."

"Is she pretty?" He wriggled his eyebrows, making me laugh.

"I don't think she'd manage it if she weren't. You'd better look out for her."

"I will, most certainly."

"You should already know who she is. The legends say you can see the future."

"Hah! Now that you're here, that's true."

"Would these be the barracks?" We were passing the buildings along the sunken path near the gate.

"Avoid them," said Myrddin, "unless you take delight in drinking and fighting."

"Where do the king and queen live?"

"Their private quarters are above Arthur's office."

I'd seen the ladder. It couldn't be much of a place up there. Considering the size of the office, the royal bedroom was merely an attic. "Do they—Guinevere and Lancelot—do they know their crime is punishable by death?"

"Shh! Of course they do."

Arm in arm, we strolled out of the northeast gate, the one through which I'd entered as a prisoner my first day. The guards were not the least bit surreptitious about observing our progress to the top of the zig-zag path. Several yards below us on the hillside, servants filled jugs at a wellspring, their voices wafting our way.

If there was such a thing as safety in that land, perhaps it could be had at Cadebir. King Arthur's stronghold stood at the highest point for miles. One couldn't approach it without being spotted. Two riders on the road far below were easy to see, dark against white stone. Any ruler would have chosen the hill, being able to tame the countryside by virtue of living above it. The city of a thousand tents smoked and seethed in the southeast, an adjunct to Cadebir Town with its huts and merchants. In the northwest, across the shimmering marshes, one prominent hill rose above smaller ones like the back of an enormous, sleeping beast.

"What's that?" I asked.

"That is Ynys Witrin," said Myrddin, "the Tor. A settlement of priestesses lives there. Women of the old ways."

"Druids?"

"Not that old."

The last sliver of sun gleamed metallic on the marshes. I shivered.

"It's almost time to dine," said Myrddin.

I hadn't eaten since breakfast. There had been no mention of lunch. We turned to re-enter the gate.

Far to our left, in the shade of the wall, a couple tiptoed in the grass on the topmost rampart, their arms around each other. I could barely make them out in the fading light.

"Isn't that—?" I stopped myself when I recognized Lancelot. With him was the dark-haired beauty I'd watched him undress with his eyes outside the hall a couple of days before. The pair disappeared into a thick copse of trees.

Myrddin tugged my arm. "You don't see a thing," he said.

SEVENTEEN

Two rows of fiery torches lit the pathway to the hall. Myrddin and I stood beyond the light, watching the crowd file in. My stomach burned with nervous dread, as though I were about to enter a Hollywood party where I didn't know anyone, and knowing who was who meant everything. But all parties were like that. I had long been in the habit of keeping to myself. To have friends one had to reveal bits of one's self and my bits were best not revealed.

"I have a gift for you."

Myrddin drew from his sleeve a small, golden scabbard about eight inches long, etched with intertwined symbols I couldn't read. He offered it on his extended palm. The bone-handled knife I drew from it had a shiny, black blade—uneven, imperfect. Not like something you'd buy in the housewares department. Not a knife like a thousand other knives.

It stopped my breath for a moment. "It's beautiful. Thank you." I hooked the scabbard to my belt.

"You're welcome. It was made right here at Cadebir," Myrddin bragged, "although the gold was imported from Dolaucothi. Keep it with you. At dinner, watch what I do with mine. Actually, eh, watch somebody else. Watch a lady. Watch the queen. Ready?"

"No."

His black eyes shone. "You will appear to be ready, even so."

I thought about how a defecting sorcerer would act in the hall of Britain's king. Grateful for amnesty but confident, sure of her power. I threw back my shoulders, lifted my chin and hoped I was up to it. Saxon

89

wizard was a more challenging role than Mrs. Gone had ever been.

Most of the crowd had already gone inside. I wiped sweat from my forehead with my sleeve. Myrddin frowned, giving me a final appraisal. "Posture's good," he said, speaking over the noise that wafted to us from inside. "Chin down. No need to frown. That's better." He offered his arm.

My heart thudded.

"Please don't grip so hard."

"Sorry."

Up the aisle of torches we walked at a regal pace, agonizingly slow. Three or four yards felt like a mile. Finally, we stepped into the hall.

Torches blazed in sconces along the walls. A fire glowed in the pit. It illuminated the crowded cavern with jagged edges and blackened the shadows by contrast. The smoke that stung my eyes smelled of burning oil and cooked meat. For a second, the dinner conversation of a hundred and fifty tribal voices assaulted my ears. Then all eyes turned to us and the noise stopped.

Myrddin patted my hand, which reminded me to stand up straight, and we stepped down two stairs into the shadows. Except for the occasional burp from the benches, the swish of our clothing was the only sound.

Soldiers, chieftains and the intermittent lady stared, having stopped mid-sentence or -sip, making no attempt to hide what felt to me like rudeness. Here and there a glint of earring or bracelet flickered in firelight as men and women turned to gape at me, unmindful of the dribbles on their chins. Only the skinny dogs continued their arguments over bones in the corners of the hall.

How did movie stars stand such scrutiny? It made me squirm. But Myrddin was determined not to rush. I focused on the head table on its raised platform opposite the door, and we proceeded down the center aisle. Four men I didn't recognize sat at one end of the table, their expressions arrested between smiles and frowns. The two empty seats at the middle were presumably reserved for the king and queen. At the other side of the royal chairs sat Lancelot and Elaine, Lancelot smiling politely at me and Elaine looking back and forth between us, blinking. Two more empty chairs waited at Elaine's side.

Myrddin and I headed for those. We skirted the fire pit and stepped onto the platform, passing a wide-eyed boy who stood in the corner, clutching a zither-like instrument to his chest. Myrddin pulled out a splintery chair for me to sit beside Elaine, who granted me a shy smile. Then, to my delight, Myrddin glared at the crowd and made a sudden shooing gesture, startling the gawkers. Like flighty pigeons, they turned quickly away, and conversation began to buzz.

"Play your instrument, young man," Myrddin said to the boy. The terrified lad strummed with all his might. Myrddin took his seat at my side.

Almost immediately a chair scooted, then others. Myrddin stood again. Everyone did, so I did, too.

King Arthur entered from his quarters with Guinevere, his petite, dark-haired queen. It was indeed she who had peeked at Lancelot from around the side of the hall. It was she I'd seen with him on the rampart. Now she aimed her adoring gaze at the king. She was dressed all in white, the better to set off her coffee-colored hair, pink cheeks and pale skin. She was barely eighteen, but it was more than age that made her King Arthur's opposite. She was a rose, he was a bludgeon. Yet he held her hand as though holding the sweetest bud, and the pang of jealousy that heated my throat came to me as a surprise.

Because Guinevere was seated on the king's far side where I caught only the occasional glimpse of her, I used Elaine as my exemplar of table manners. She ate methodically, spearing each morsel of stew with her delicate knife, then lifting it to her pouty lips. She and Lancelot stared over the assembly and conversed in rare, quiet snippets.

I watched Lynet's example as well. Seated between Gareth and Agravain at the table just below ours, she drank mead and joked with the men, obviously comfortable being the lone female in her group. Gareth flirted with her, though their playfulness only seemed to make Agravain quieter. Medraut and Pawly huddled at the same table, Pawly relishing Medraut's every word. Everyone was arms to elbows, thighs to knees, packed in on the benches and shouting in close conversation.

When Lancelot leaned back or King Arthur stood to greet someone I caught an occasional glimpse of Guinevere. It was obvious why both men found her captivating. Chatting with her husband's guests, her white tunic bright in the firelight, she was an oasis of poise in the chaos of the hall. Her expression was open, as though she absorbed everything without judging. When her companions spoke she listened, rather than pretending to appear to listen. When servants came to replenish platters she looked them in the eye and thanked them. They responded with familiarity, comfortable with her.

My plate, which Myrddin called a trencher, was a square piece of wood with a little trough carved around the edges to capture drippings. Myrddin and I got into a brief discussion about the qualities of wood. I thought to tell him it was the wrong material for dinnerware because the wood's porous quality made it a good place for germs to proliferate, but I was in over my head. Germs were just one more subject I couldn't fully explain. If I started talking about them Myrddin would ask questions I couldn't answer, and if I allowed myself to think about them I'd never get enough to eat.

I ate slowly, awkward with the knife. The leeks and root vegetables were over-spiced but the meat, whatever it was, was delicious and full-flavored. I was pleasantly surprised by the wine, which was stronger than wines I was accustomed to. As I emptied my goblet a servant appeared and filled it again. When I followed the queen's example and thanked him, I caught Guinevere watching me with that open expression of hers. She stood, plucked up her goblet and glided across the platform to stand beside me. Elaine and Myrddin rose to their feet as she arrived, so I did, too.

"Oh not so formal. Please sit. Good evening, Myrddin. Hello Elaine, sweet. Mistress Casey, at last I've an opportunity to welcome you. We're so grateful you've chosen to be with us."

She held out her graceful hand. I wasn't sure what to do with it but I hadn't seen anyone kiss it, so I took it and bowed my head a little. The ring she wore was a smaller version of the king's, with the etching of Stonehenge on its face.

"I'm grateful to be here, your majesty."

"I trust everything is to your liking?" she swept her arm sideways, presenting the table with goblet in hand.

"It's all delicious, thanks." I raised my glass. "Good wine."

She lowered her alto voice. "Arthur gave orders to the kitchen to show off. For the other guests, too, but mostly for you." Louder, she said, "Sorry we don't have our usual bard, but war makes everything difficult."

"Well, I am impres—"

"I've never met a lady wizard before," said Guinevere. "It's exciting. don't you think so, Elaine?"

"Mmmhmm."

Guinevere rested her hand on Elaine's shoulder. "The midwife has spells, but it's not the same, is it?"

I didn't know if it was or not. I glanced Myrddin's way for help, but his attention was on his food. "There may be some crossover."

"Perhaps you'll be of assistance when Elaine has her baby."

"I don't think—"

"Will you be casting protection spells over the fort?"

"Uh, no."

"Good." She smiled, revealing straight teeth, another thing that made her stand out. "I wouldn't want to be fenced in. I like to go to

Cadebir Town from time to time."

"Or to stroll on the ramparts, my lady, as you did this afternoon?" The voice came from the table below us.

Guinevere spilled her wine.

Medraut continued, fending off Pawly's elbow from his skinny ribs. "Pawly and I observed you and your *friend* as we rode in from town." Lancelot began to rise from his chair but changed his mind. Medraut ignored him and gazed sweetly up at the queen.

Shouts arose from the opposite corner of the hall, where two Belgic soldiers began to argue about something unintelligible. Their drunken friends egged them on to fight. People backed away to make space. Like water, everything in the room shifted, pressing on everything else.

Pawly wriggled on the bench beside Medraut. Across from him, Agravain watched Lancelot, waiting. Most of the others at their table were concentrating on the fight but Lynet and Gareth, glancing side to side, only pretended not to listen to what was happening at our table. I wondered if others might be doing the same. The chieftains on the king's opposite side gossiped among themselves, peering occasionally at the queen.

The king had heard. "Take care, Medraut," he warned over the noise. While the fight began to rage in the corner, the king and his son glared at each other. The queen's face could not have been more pink. Tension froze the high table into silence.

"Strolling is healthy for women," I said. The authority in my voice surprised me.

Arthur and Medraut unlocked their gaze to look at me. Even Lancelot turned his blue eyes my way.

"Is that true, Mistress Casey?" asked the king.

"Absolutely, your majesty." I sounded sure of myself.

Guinevere returned to her husband's side. He encircled her waist with a single arm, a gesture designed to be witnessed. He waved for me to continue.

I spoke louder, to be heard over the upending furniture at the back, none of which seemed to concern the royal party. "Regular exercise is essential for the body and mind. Your men get it from riding and fighting. Women need it, too. Obviously the queen knows this."

Elaine stared demurely at her plate. Lancelot put his arm around her, stealing an unreadable glance at me.

"You've given me an idea, Mistress Casey," the king shouted over the melee. "You will lead the queen and her friends on a daily walk. Inside the walls, of course."

"I'd be honored, your majesty," I shouted back.

"You may call me 'Your Grace.'" He raised his glass. "To Mistress Casey! Welcome to Cadebir fort!"

A drinking song broke out at the back, signaling the end of the fight. While the king and his guests toasted me, warriors righted the tables and benches, laughing and slapping each others' backs and buttocks as though they'd just performed a comedy routine and were not bleeding from their lips and noses.

With the subject changed, the king returned his attention to the guests at his end of the table. His expression betrayed no relief or gratitude. Nor should it have, I thought. I had pleased him and that pleased me.

I looked to Myrddin to seek his approval, but he had snored through it all.

"You'll stay here, next door to Cai." Bedwyr's torch came precariously close to fingering the thatch above a red-painted wooden lintel. A single spark and the hut would disintegrate in flames. No streetlights lit the pathways. The waning moon was enough to light the promontory. A few drunken soldiers stumbled past, laughing and shouting on their way to the barracks. A couple walked by on the path and said, "Good night." I felt a chill.

"You'll need this, mistress." Sagramore's dinner had complicated his aroma. He unpinned his heavy, brown cloak and draped it over my shoulders, careful not to touch me. I could almost hear him blush in the dark.

"And this, to keep it on," said Bedwyr, not to be outdone. He removed the brass pin from his cloak and placed it in my palm, aiming the spike away from my skin.

I traced the pin's golden inlaid curlicues with my fingers. Was a powerful wizard to expect such tributes? Did Sagramore have another cloak, Bedwyr another pin? According to Lynet they'd all left the fancy stuff at their castle on the coast. These must be special things.

"Chivalry," I said, before I knew I was speaking. From the confusion on their faces the word was new to my escorts. I clarified. "Thank you for these kindnesses."

Bedwyr grumbled."Let's light the lamp, then." He handed the torch to Sagramore and entered the pitch-dark hut, returning with a lidded metal bowl. It had a wick at one end and a handle at the other. He held the wick to the torch then gave me the lamp, handle first. "You'll sleep well, mistress." To Sagramore he said, "They had wine at the king's table." For my benefit, he added, "*We* get mead from the village."

"Not very good mead," said Sagramore.

"Better than no mead," said Bedwyr.

"Blast the embargo," said Sagramore.

They ambled off toward the barracks, grumbling quietly. I watched them go until their torch disappeared beyond the huts. Then, holding the lamp before me, I stepped inside. The lamplight softened the darkness and showed a room large enough only for a small, lopsided table, a bench and a cot. The walls were made of a combination of mud and straw and something else; the hut smelled vaguely of livestock. There might once have been shutters on the open window above the bench, but as it was, I would have to find something to cover it. For the moment, the night air freshened the room.

The table was sturdy despite being crooked. I set the lamp there and emptied my fanny pack of loose change, credit cards and English paper money. At Cadebir it was a useless pile.

Someone thoughtful—Elaine? Lynet?—had left a stack of clothing on the bench for me. Two wool tunics, a couple of linen underdresses, a pair of leggings and a loose muslin sleeping gown were neatly piled there.

A burst of drunken laughter erupted on the pathway outside, startling me. I jumped away from the bench to a spot near the door, where I couldn't be seen through the window. The drunks stumbled by, probably on their way to the barracks. The room had aired enough. I tucked one of the underdresses around the corners of the window to cover it.

I disrobed and donned the muslin gown, shivering. It would be nice to have a mirror, but the only one who owned such a treasure was the queen. What must be going on in her quarters now? Did the king and queen discuss what had happened at dinner? Did they talk of the affair? Fight? Make love? Perhaps they lay awake, their backs to each other, silent.

Noticing something under the bench, I moved the lamp closer and discovered another neatly folded pile: my twenty-first century clothes. They'd been washed. The T-shirt was almost white. The chain mail sweater had been cleaned so thoroughly it was soft again, like new. Someone had sewn the pockets back onto my cargo pants and scraped my boots clean. I would need those clothes for my impossible return to the twenty-first century.

I sat on the bench and pulled a corner of the cloth away from the window, just enough to peek out. I had to get back to my time, my place, my element. I wanted to wash my face and brush my teeth. I couldn't even lock the door. How long could I keep up a pretense of wizardry and remain on the king's good side? How long could I stay alive at Cadebir? Long enough to figure it out, I hoped.

I moved the cloth further aside and leaned on the splintered windowsill, taking in the sharp, cool air. Laughter and the shouts of inebriated soldiers drifted from the barracks on a breeze. Cai's hut blocked my view of the hilltop, but not of the black sky and countless stars above. Near the kitchen a dog barked, lacking enthusiasm. Closer to my hut a cat meowed, then a smaller animal, a mouse or a rat, screamed its last scream.

Maybe I was dreaming. Maybe I was dead and Cadebir was the afterlife. But I knew I was alive. They could have killed me a thousand horrible ways. Instead they'd given me gifts. The king had raised me to a high position. It was life, it just wasn't *my* life.

Close by on the path, footfalls came. I closed my makeshift curtain and plastered myself against the wall like I'd seen people do on TV.

Men, more than one, conversing in low tones. They cut between the huts and went on. I dared one more peek.

It was only Medraut and Pawly on their way to the barracks. Whatever I was afraid of, it wasn't them.

EIGHTEEN

Squatting above the brass chamber pot, I was momentarily grateful to have been designated a wizard instead of the servant whose job it was to empty it. But I missed toilet paper almost as much as I missed toothpaste.

"Should we wake her?"

The treble notes of women's voices floated to me from beyond the door.

"Wizards need more sleep than we do. You know Myrddin and his naps..."

Giggles.

After an awkward finish with a rag, taken from a pile which I presumed and hoped had been left beside the pot for the purpose, I threw on the green tunic and hooked my fanny pack around my waist while the conversation continued outside.

"If she snores like Myrddin it's no wonder..."

When I opened the door Guinevere was making a loud snoring noise, squinching her cute little nose. Lynet and Elaine thought it hilarious until they saw me. I thought it was funny, too, but I didn't say so.

The queen recovered first, giving me a smile that showed off her teeth. "Good morning, Mistress Casey. We're ready for our stroll." She wore her usual white tunic. A diaphanous, white scarf protected her face from the sun.

"I don't suppose there's any coffee," I mumbled, covering my mouth. My breath could've set torches aflame.

"I've brought breakfast." Lynet offered a bundle of cloth. "It's not nearly sufficient."

To avoid breathing on her I accepted the package with a closed-lip smile. "Thanks. You're a lifesaver." The bundle contained a small, reddish-green apple and a couple of muffin-sized loaves. I didn't see any mint, but a bite of apple would refresh.

"Perhaps you need more time for your toilette?" the queen said, looking me up and down.

I ran my fingers through my hair. "I wouldn't like to keep your majesty waiting."

"If you care to rise early tomorrow," said Guinevere, "you may join us in the hall for breakfast. The meal is finer."

Elaine tied on her scarf. "Will the stroll take long? I've so much work."

"It might," said Guinevere. "My husband says Mistress Casey is to lead us around the entire circumference of the fort."

"You can hardly call that a stroll," said Lynet.

"A march, then." Guinevere stepped out from under the eaves into the sun. I followed.

Elaine remained by the door. "I don't think I should go."

I'd heard that walking was healthy for pregnant women, though I couldn't cite my source. From the size of her belly I guessed Elaine would deliver soon. "It'll be good for you and the baby," I said, stuffing down a bite of muffin.

"If you say so." Elaine hung her head and slogged after us. I wondered if I'd made a *faux pas*. Maybe she just didn't want to go. With all the hush about Guinevere and Lancelot cheating on the king, it was easy to forget Elaine was being cheated on, too.

At the promontory's edge the land sloped downward toward the wall. Dampening our shoes and the hems of our underdresses in the dew, we walked, sometimes skidded, down to where dirt met wooden posts and the grass grew as high as our knees. I tripped.

"Oops."

"Did you hurt yourself, Mistress Casey?" Guinevere was overly solicitous.

"I'm okay. Hey." The grass had overtaken the edges of a large, iron disk on the ground.

Lynet bent to examine it with me. "What have you found?"

"A manhole cover?"

"The oubliette! I'd forgotten." Guinevere laughed at her joke and started up a nearby ladder. "Everyone's behaved so well we haven't had to use it this summer."

I remembered my high school French (my "Gallic") well enough. Being thrown into a hole to be forgotten forever was a nightmare as horrible as burning. I pulled the grass aside to get a good look. An iron handle on the disk allowed for a jailer to open it. But it must have been locked; I couldn't move it. A rat-sized opening beneath the handle would let in a little air. It would take ages to die in there in the dark, starving, thirsting, and unable to move or see anything but the little circle of light admitted through the hole. One would hear whatever life passed by. I peered into the opening and saw nothing.

"Mistress Casey!"

My charges waited for me atop the wall. I had a duty to perform. Leaving the oubliette, I started up the ladderway.

Heavier than ladders yet more portable than a permanent stairway, the ladderways improved upon both with a simple design: they consisted of two aligned poles with planks secured between them like stair-steps. A sure-footed soldier could run up and down with his hands free to wield his weapon. These ladderways leaned against the interior of the wall at intervals.

The ladderway looked innocent from the ground, but I got nervous halfway up. Without the customary railing, the climb felt precarious. I knelt to crawl, like a toddler going up the slide the wrong way. Elaine was still panting when I reached the top. She had struggled up the steps as well, though her excuse was better than mine.

The sight of Ynys Witrin, glowing green across the northern marshes, was our reward. A mist of fluffy clouds rolled around it, revealing the hill then hiding it, then revealing it again. I saw then that it was an island, surrounded by a glassy, black lake. I could have stood there for an hour watching the island change, but the walk was my first shot at being useful to the king and I wished to avoid such things as oubliettes.

We settled to walking in pairs, Guinevere marching beside me in the lead, Elaine and Lynet arm in arm behind us. The soldiers who patrolled the wall made way, nodding their respect to the queen.

Elaine halted at the fort's west end. Myrddin's woods lay below us. It had seemed vast when I was under its cover, but from atop the wall I could see its borders.

"I'm already tired," said Elaine, propping herself against the wall. "I don't understand why we have to do this. I should be at the well. We'll never finish the washing."

"The women know what to do," said Guinevere. "They can manage without you for a time."

"I don't mind a break from work," said Lynet.

"Truly," said Guinevere. "Since we must endure this 'exercise,' let's enjoy it." She walked on. We had little choice but to follow. I thought her pace too fast for Elaine, especially because the sun was high and a wool tunic wouldn't have been my first choice for such an outing. But the southwest gate wasn't far, and the young soldiers there were as glad as puppies to see us.

"Here they come."

"Careful, Jonek, these ladies are in fighting shape."

"Think so?" Jonek tossed his ponytail over his shoulder. "Will they take us on then?"

"You'd like that, wouldn't you?" said Guinevere, perhaps a bit more flirtatious than a queen ought to be.

"I'd look forward to it, your majesty," said a dark-haired soldier with a crooked but charming smile.

"Beware, Hew," said Lynet to the swaggering guard, "we'll soon be as strong as soldiers."

"I doubt it not," Hew answered. "Both you and her majesty already have the muscle to lick me."

Then came a good deal of laughter of the har-de-har sort. I thought the young men wouldn't have been so brazen if Gareth or King Arthur had been present, but the women didn't seem to mind. All these men out in the middle of nowhere, with so few women around, had to be feeling a powerful hunger to say the least.

Flirtation was as good an excuse as any to stop in the shade of the guard house. On a stone bench inside, under which lay a cache of axes, Elaine took the opportunity to rest her feet.

Not Guinevere. "You'd best not tangle with Mistress Casey," she told Hew on her way through. "She knows well enough to be on our side."

"I wouldn't dare, your majesty," he said, bowing his tall, brown head to her, then to me.

I liked that. I gave him my best smile.

"Good morning, Mistress Casey." I recognized the red-haired, peach-fuzzed boy who'd driven my wagon on my first day in the Dark Ages. Apparently guard duty was reserved for the young.

"G'morning," I said, waving as I trotted past. "Nice to see you again." I was hoping to be introduced, but Guinevere had already moved on. The king had asked me to lead the walk, but his wife was taking over. I had no desire to thwart her authority. Lynet stayed behind while Hew and the other soldier helped Elaine to her feet. Maybe we wouldn't make her come with us again.

I caught up with Guinevere along the southern wall, where she had stopped to wait for me. Cattle waded in the stream far below, sinking their maws for a drink of clear water. Watching them made me thirsty. On the opposite bank, a herder grazed his sheep on a gentle slope.

Guinevere's soft cheek lay on her hand and she gazed to the southwest, where a single road curled away, a silver trail blending into the green.

"Where does that road go, your majesty?" I asked.

She sized me up for a second, then returned her gaze to the road. "You may address me as Guinevere."

"Thank you, Guinevere." I tried a curtsey.

"The road leads home. I haven't been there in a long time."

"The castle on the coast?"

"No. *My* home." She watched the road a moment longer, as if hoping to see a friend approach. When she turned to me, her voice was as direct as her gaze. "Everything you see is Arthur's. All of it."

"So it's yours, too, I guess."

Her laugh was short, but not bitter. "I'm not his ally, Mistress Casey. I'm his property. Like the land."

"I see." We began to walk again. "If I'm to call you Guinevere, shouldn't you call me Casey?"

"Yes, of course I will. Hello, Berrell."

A sentry stood at attention against the wall, allowing us to pass. I nodded to the sentry and kept up with the queen's pace. "I'm sorry."

"What for?"

"I don't think I would like being owned by someone."

"There's no greater position for a woman than mine. I'm fortunate that my father made this alliance. Besides, what makes you think you're not owned?"

Owned by the king. If I was to survive I had to think of myself that way. I stole a glance at the queen. If she felt anything other than serenity it didn't show on her face. "I have a lot to learn, your majesty."

"Guinevere."

"Right. Guinevere."

"But it's my understanding that you know and see all," she said, still gazing calmly forward.

I was tempted to let her believe in my prowess, but I knew I'd be found out. "No. That's beyond my powers."

She puffed a out sharp breath of relief. "Oh."

We came to a stop where the wall ended, crumbling almost beneath our feet and leaving the hilltop vulnerable. Inside the fort, to our left, the way was lined with storage sheds. Outside, the steep ramparts tiered from high to low. I imagined an army crawling up them, like black bugs on the green. Below us, at the foot of a ladderway, a sun-wizened foreman oversaw a tattered crew.

"Rufus," the queen called down to him, "how goes the work?"

"We're getting nowhere, your majesty." Rufus spat. "These Saxon slaves. Too belligerent to be good workers."

"Respect, Rufus." Guinevere began walking down the ladderway. "You've not met our new wizard, Mistress Casey."

From the way he paled when he saluted I guessed he'd heard of me. "I mean no offense, mistress," he said, shifting his weight and bowing a little too deeply.

I nodded sagely and gifted him with my most benevolent glance. I followed Guinevere down the ladderway toddler-style, feet first and holding the sides. Below the wall, slaves handed rocks from one man to the next, the boulder version of a bucket brigade. Here and there a bleeding hand stained the stones. Their ankles were chained as mine had been, but their scars represented months of endurance, not days. They worked methodically, rock to hands, rock to hands, manacles clinking, eyes downcast, anything but belligerent. To be owned by King Arthur could mean many things.

"Give the slaves a rest and some food," the queen said to Rufus. "The wall can wait."

"Yes, ma'am."

To me, she said under her breath, "No matter how he works the slaves, there isn't time to finish the wall before we fight. There is always fighting."

My stomach clenched. The gap in the wall was only twenty-five feet at its widest, and the workers seemed to make progress even as we watched them.

"You're a fast walker, Guin," Lynet called from atop the wall. "It's as though you're late for an assignation!"

"I'm only enjoying my exercise."

"Let's not climb back up," said Lynet, starting down the ladderway. "It's too hard on Elaine." Elaine followed Lynet, lugging herself down the ladder, huffing and puffing, while Lynet watched her from below. By the time they reached the bottom Elaine's cheeks were as red as the last flecks on my fingernails. Lynet blushed a rosy pink.

"We'll go through the pasture," said Guinevere, kissing Elaine's forehead like a mother kisses her child. "Would you like that?" She led us past the slaves at a slower pace, scuffling through the grass to the gate and lifting the wooden latch. "It doesn't matter what we do," she said. "Arthur wants me out of his way, that's all. We might as well enjoy ourselves."

"I think I'd enjoy sitting down," said Elaine. She giggled, which was a relief to me. I was afraid we'd overtaxed her. She was cute when she smiled. I saw what Lancelot must have seen in her before she gained her pregnancy weight and still had her hopes.

The pasture was less trafficked than the paths. Grass grew thick there. Tiny, blue and yellow wildflowers filled the corner where the fence met the wall.

"Come," said Lynet, "you shall rest in the barn." She took Elaine's arm and they moved off, Elaine dragging her feet, Lynet pirouetting, a thousand years too soon for the ballet to have been invented for her.

"Is that your mare with Arthur's horse?" Guinevere pointed to several horses grazing together among the wildflowers near the barn. Lucy stood in their midst, watching us and chewing. The brown stallion beside her was the only other horse that came close to her in stature.

"That's Lucy." I felt pride of ownership even though the big gray wasn't mine. Her coat shone, a benefit of the break in her rental routine. She seemed to make a decision and begin to stride toward us. Perhaps it was because she was more accustomed to people than to horses, but I allowed myself to hope it was because she was happy to see me. She walked directly to me. Cooing to her and petting her soft muzzle felt familiar, although I had never done so before. I wondered if horses had memories, if she knew we shared a different time than the one in which we found ourselves. When she slobbered green foam on my fingers, eating the wildflowers I picked for her, I wondered if she felt the bond I felt, my friend from another time.

The barn door clattered open. Lucy shied and trotted away.

"*Bonjour,* your majesty. *Bonjour,* Mistress Casey," Lyonel surged through the door, not bothering to sidestep a well-placed pile of manure. He held the door for us, bowing to the queen and watching me from the corner of his eye.

I had liked it when Mike looked at me that way, the way that meant he wanted me. In private moments, he'd bite his lower lip, allow his eyelids to droop, and give me a secret smile. I didn't want Lyonel to look at me like that. He upset my balance and I was already unsettled.

"Good morning, Lyonel." Guinevere was all business. "You've been seeing to Lancelot's horses?" I could see by the way she turned up her chin that she didn't much care for the man, either.

"I have, your majesty," he said in his oily voice, giving her his attention. "Everything is satisfactory." For a moment I detected that heavy-lidded look directed at the Queen. "Lancelot will be sweetly satisfied." He licked his thick lips.

If the queen took implicit meaning from Lyonel's words, she ignored it. "Very well." She flounced past him into the barn, skirting the pile of manure. I followed, leaving him outside with his insidious smile.

Stepping from sunlight to shade I blinked, shaking off Lyonel's taint of imagined sins. Instead of the expected alfalfa and manure, my nose smarted at the scents of hot metal, leather and oil. Under the low ceiling, about thirty men worked in a central room. Some sharpened blades and repaired weapons. Most of them, though, were making copies of Lucy's saddle.

The saddle was perched prominently on a wooden stand in the middle of the main space. Light spilled in from the back door, showing the saddle to its best advantage. I heard not one neigh or moo; instead, men's voices discussed the work: "It needs to be thicker there. Use more padding." "Sagramore says that's good." "Here now, give a quick cut, will you?" Mostly the *pound! pound! pound!* of hammer on nail and the *whap!* of leather slapping against leather.

I allowed my palm to feel along the seat of one of the copies. The hide they'd used to make it was soft, undyed brown, with short tufts of hair still on it. Brass rivets, their small, round heads etched with intricate designs, attached the wooden stirrups. I tugged on the stirrup leather. Solid.

"I think Elaine's going to faint." Guinevere sat on a stool near the open back door, where Elaine had plopped herself onto a bench. Lynet was fanning Elaine with her scarf and dabbing sweat from her friend's forehead.

Sunlight from the door shone directly into Elaine's eyes. "I'm not going to faint."

Sagramore crunched across straw and scraps to block the offending light with his bulk. "Are you ill, my lady?"

"We've been having our exercise," said Lynet.

"Arthur's orders," said Guinevere.

"I'm fine," said Elaine.

"I have water, fresh from the well." Sagramore darted out the door. I had not thought Sagramore could dart.

"One day I'll get the nerve to suggest he try some mint," said Lynet.

"He's sweet." Elaine squinted and pushed herself to sit up. "I'm sorry. I'm not much good at exercise."

"We shouldn't have made you come," I said, leaning on Lucy's saddle. "It was too much for you."

"Here." Sagramore arrived and knelt at Elaine's feet to present a cup of water.

"Thank you." When Elaine smiled, the big man blushed and cast his bashful eyes at the floor. "I...we...we're..."

"You're very kind." Elaine drank.

"You've been making copies of Casey's saddle," said Guinevere. "They're quite fine. Arthur will be pleased."

"Thank you, my lady."

"What do you think of it, Casey?" asked the queen, sitting erect on her stool and appearing to be interested.

"Yes, what do you think, mistress?" Sagramore's droopy eyes looked up with hope.

"It's remarkable," I said. "Almost perfect."

"But something's missing." This Sagramore said with the conviction of the old "death and taxes" joke, as though something were always missing for him and that was the way of the world.

My instinct was to be more positive, especially in front of women I thought he might want to impress. "Only one thing. It's important, but I'm sure it's easy to fix. Look." I demonstrated with Lucy's stirrup leather. "See? The stirrups are adjustable. That way the saddle can be fitted to the man."

A light went on in his somber, brown eyes. "Ah, for leverage. Ingenious." He almost smiled.

"It is," said Guinevere. "Do you think that will be simple to fix in the time we have, Sagramore?"

"Simple enough, I suppose."

"Wonderful." The queen stood. "My friends, reward yourselves. Go on to the well and soak your feet." She looked away from me, from Elaine, and especially from Lynet to fix her gaze on Lucy's saddle. "I'll stay here and...inspect the work. To report back to Arthur."

Lynet straightened. "Surely Sagramore can report his own progress to the king."

In the silent second that followed, Sagramore focused on Lucy's stirrup. Elaine sipped her water. I wasn't sure what had happened.

"I will see for myself," said Guinevere, refusing to look at us.

She was the queen. It was her final word.

Unaccustomed to life without a mirror, I hoped for a glimpse of myself in the waters of the wellspring. I hadn't seen my hair in days. I wondered if the clothes I wore flattered my figure. Did the color of the cloth enhance my skin tone? Did I resemble a fair, Arthurian maiden or was I just Casey in a green tunic?

It wasn't my day to find out. When we arrived, half a dozen women were already dunking shirts and tunics and strangely familiar rags in the well and slapping them against the stone. They ceased their work only long enough to make way for us to sit.

Elaine, finally at ease, chattered with her workers and moved among them, inspecting their morning's efforts. Lynet sat and removed her shoes to kick her feet in the same well from which Sagramore had given Elaine a cup to drink. I untied my shoes but decided not to soak my feet, not in that well, not ever, no matter how tired they got.

"I forgot about that, sorry," said Lynet.

"About what?"

"Wizards and water. Shall we sit somewhere else?"

"No, thanks, I'm fine." I rested my head against the stones that lined the spring. Sending up a prayer to the gods of dysentery, I thanked them for not visiting me.

Lynet splashed unenthusiastically. For a minute we watched the plain far below the hill, where men as small as bugs crawled amid the tents of the camp. Then Lynet leaned close to whisper to me, changing the subject of my thoughts. "Guin says Arthur wants her out of his way. I think he merely wants to keep her occupied. That's what the walks are for. Do you see?" She sat back and eyed me sharply, trying to tell me something without telling me.

Did Lynet know of the affair? "You mean it's my job to occupy her?"

"Not exactly. No. I don't presume to know the king's wishes. I can only guess. But you have his power behind you."

Our eyes locked. I considered my response. I wanted to trust Lynet. I thought she wanted to trust me.

"I can't tell the queen what to do. Can I?"

She shrugged. "Perhaps not directly. But you *are* the king's wizard. Like Myrddin, right here on the hill."

NINETEEN

"I've put many hours of thought into the circumstances surrounding your arrival."

Myrddin set steaming mugs on the table in his laboratory, where I sat hoping for an easy answer. "To send you back we must recreate those circumstances exactly."

I hung my head. Impossible.

"You arrived with the full moon. That may be important. Then there's the car. Tell me about this car." He pronounced the word carefully, setting it between vocal quotation marks.

"It's a motor vehicle. You drive—"

"—Moe-tor?"

I sighed. I had to explain everything and most of it confused even me. I gazed out the open doorway to where Drostan the gardener squatted among the herbs, weeding and humming. "A motor is...it doesn't matter."

Myrddin tilted his eyebrows and waited.

"Okay. It's a...a thing. It moves other things. It's powered with fuel so it moves on its own once you start it."

"What sort of fuel?"

"Gasoline."

Up went the eyebrows again.

"Liquid gas. Pumped from the ground. They do something to it. Refine it. Same as airplanes, except a car runs on land."

"Go on."

"The motor powers the car. The car's got wheels and you sit in it to drive it. It's a lot like a cart but you don't need horses. You steer it, and you control the speed with pedals. With your feet." From my seat on the stool, I demonstrated. "In my city, everybody has one."

"Why?" Fascinated, Myrddin pulled up a stool to sit. "Is your Lucy a rarity? Have horses gone the way of bears?"

"What way have bears gone?"

"They once roamed the forests, but we've hunted them to death."

"Oh. Well, no. Horses are still relatively easy to come by. But you can go faster in a car than on a horse. And a car's enclosed, so if it rains you stay dry."

"Very good. Let's return to the Gap. What happened after the car?"

I went over the accident in detail as well as I could remember: the rain, the headlights (which I had to explain), screeching brakes (which I also had to explain), Lucy, the man in the car, then my strange flight. "Here's the weirdest part. I think I hit my head *before* I landed."

"Oh yes. The obstruction you hit was the armour of the Saxon you killed. It was quite a blow. You must have been going very fast. I'd say you're hallucinating from some sort of concussion but that wouldn't explain why *I* can see *you*."

"Nope."

"So. Rain, car, screech, horse, man, flight, bump. What else? Think hard. Might you have forgotten any details? Did you see anything in the Gap?" Myrddin's face leaned close to mine, his black eyes tiny gaps leading to deep, endless space. "Remember."

I let my eyelids fall. I found myself astride Lucy in the rain. A chaotic storm rampaged around us, though I was warm and dry. Then Lucy's shoes skidded on the pavement. Light flashed, silhouetting the man in the car. The man's mouth moved. I thought he wanted to talk to me, but I was already flying into the Gap.

"The reins. I'm holding Lucy's reins."

"Anything else?" Myrddin sounded like he was in the Gap with me.

"It was only a second. A puff of wind on my skin. Then, the blackness opened up. I saw King Arthur ahead and I was flying toward him really fast."

"Good, very good." Myrddin snapped his fingers. I was in his hut again. He smiled.

I rubbed my eyes. "You hypnotized me."

"A word with which I'm not familiar. More tea?" He sprang to the corner and filled our mugs from the cauldron.

"Is that how you turned Arthur into ants and fish and stuff when he was a boy? I read that in a storybook."

"Very much like that, yes."

"In the twenty-first century, we call that hypnosis."

"An invention of mine! Still used fifteen hundred years in the future!" He plopped flower buds into the steaming mugs. "Do you suppose my other inventions survive?"

"I wouldn't be surprised."

"Hmm." Deep in thought, he set my mug on the table and padded to his desk.

I took my tea and stepped to the doorway, allowing time for Myrddin's superior brain to work on the information I'd given him. The background noise in the dell, as opposed to the pounding work on Cadebir Hill, was birdsong, accented by Drostan's humming, and occasional laughter from the orderlies who played dice in the shade near the huts. Maybe the dell was a busier place at wartime, when the injured needed tending. But that morning Myrddin's staff had the place to themselves.

"We don't need a car." Myrddin's voice rumbled behind me.

I ducked back under the thatch. Myrddin wrote vigorously at his desk. "What we need is the power the car generated, in combination with the lightning."

I didn't know how we were going to generate such power, but I didn't interrupt.

"We may need to get you to the location of your arrival, or at least near it. Arthur won't tell us where it was because he doesn't want you to go, and his men won't give us the information against his wishes. But we know you were close to the Giant's Ring." He stopped writing. "That could work. We have Lucy and her reins. Lucy may well be the most essential ingredient. I, of course, am a man, and will play that role." He went back to scribbling. "Though we do not anticipate rain at the next full moon, the partnership of full moon and precipitation will happen in time and we'll need that time for creating our moe-tor."

I sighed. Silly of me. Silly to hope Myrddin's plan would send me back when it didn't make sense for me to be there in the first place.

Myrddin put down his quill and brought his hands to his chin. "The question may be, Casey: are you willing to put yourself through another concussion?"

Even if we could generate the power, which we couldn't, Myrddin was not the same man as the one in the accident. The Giant's Ring was not the same place. The circumstances would never be exact, if exactness was what we required.

But the problem was not accuracy, or my willingness to endure pain. I realized with a shock that the problem was I wasn't ready to leave.

TWENTY

Morning sun beamed through the high windows of the hall like light from an old-fashioned projection booth. The soldiers must have eaten and gone, their departure transforming the room from breakfast tavern to women's club. The zither player, so nervous a few nights before, stretched his languid legs along the length of a bench and strummed his tunes.

I wore Lynet's bracelet pushed up on my arm, and had tied my hair back with Elaine's ribbon in an attempt to look presentable. I wondered how the privileged women stayed so clean. The differences between them and the serving women were blatant: women of wealth wore their hair loose; servers tied theirs back out of necessity. Wealthy women had soft skin; serving women were ruddy and sunburned. Except the queen, who wore only white, elegant ladies wore tunics dyed in all colors; servants dressed in undyed browns and beiges. And the women of means were relaxed; servants always hurried.

For the morning meal the kitchen staff had converted the king's table into a breakfast buffet. Great portions of aromatic egg pies had presumably gone missing by the time I arrived, but plenty of food remained for the twenty or so women lounging throughout the hall. Ignoring the flies that feasted at the rims of jam pots, I loaded a trencher with a slice of warm bread, a piece of egg pie, and small, sweet strawberries from a bowl that spilled over with them.

Guinevere and Lynet had already eaten. They were sipping tea and cleaning their teeth with toothpicks when I joined them at one of the long tables.

I was beginning to feel more a part of things at Cadebir. I jabbed a bite of egg pie with Myrddin's knife. "No Elaine this morning?"

"She's gone to work," said Lynet.

"Oh," I said, "she was afraid she might not be able to keep up—"

"You must both stop worrying," the queen interrupted. "*I* will help Elaine."

Feeling scolded, I chewed my pie. The flies had probably been on it but I hadn't seen them and I was hungry enough to pretend they'd missed it. Guinevere twitched nervously beside me. Across from us, Lynet sat stiff and unsmiling. In the silence, I realized I'd interrupted their conversation, and it hadn't been a pleasant one. It would be awkward to pick up my trencher and leave.

"Thank you for inviting me to breakfast, your majesty," I said, trying to smooth the air.

"*Guinevere.*"

"Right. Sorry." I was silent for a few moments more while I ate, but I was compelled to placate when people weren't speaking to each other. It was my family role. "The kitchen sure does an amazing job."

"Heulwen's in charge. That's her, there." Guinevere pointed out the big-boned woman I'd seen Myrddin talking to in the kitchen. Heulwen moved up and down the center aisle carrying a clay pitcher in one hand and several mugs in the other. "I can't imagine how she feeds so many people every day," Guinevere continued. "Arthur loves her. We all do."

Heulwen's hair was pulled tightly under a bonnet, accentuating her round, red face. With one hand she hefted the pitcher and poured a mug of hot liquid while laughing with a boy who collected empty plates from a table. Her eyes were puffy.

"She looks tired," I said.

"Not at all," said Guinevere. "Heulwen's always jolly. It's good fortune to work inside the fort, especially to be a kitchen servant. Better than tilling fields or tanning hides. And she's the monarch of the kitchen, is she not, Lynet? Even Arthur obeys her there."

Lynet chewed a mint leaf, nodding.

"I wonder if she'd let me use a bowl or something," I said.

"Shh," said Guinevere. "Don't ask."

Heulwen arrived at our table and placed a mug before me.

"Good morning, dear," said the queen.

"'Morning, ladies," said Heulwen, one hand pouring while the cup hand rested on her broad hip.

"Mistress Casey was just saying how much she likes her breakfast," said Guinevere.

"Good," Heulwen grinned at me, her cheeks going redder. "I do like being appreciated." She strode off to fill other mugs.

Guinevere lowered her voice. "For what do you need a bowl?"

"Spells?" asked Lynet, her violet eyes wide.

All I needed was something in which to dump my money and credit cards so the stuff wouldn't be lying around loose in my hut. The tea smelled not of well water but of spices. I took a careful sip. It tasted of apples, and something like pepper.

"I'm not supposed to practice magic. King Arthur's orders. But..." I winked for effect, "...a wizard can always use a bowl."

Both women nodded in complete understanding. "Don't ask Heulwen," said Guinevere. "She'll never let you have one. She's too thrifty. She uses and reuses everything."

Lynet stifled a giggle. "It's true. From apple cores she can make a dessert so delicious that King Arthur is proud to serve it to King Cadwy of Cornwall."

"We had that last night," said the queen. "Cadwyr loved it."

"Owain of Corinium Dobunnorum had two servings," said Lynet.

"The priest took an entire bowlful to his lodgings," said Guinevere.

Their laughter made me hope that perhaps whatever tiff I'd interrupted was minor. I wanted another piece of egg pie but was too full to manage it. "Don't men eat in the mornings?"

"Yes, but early," said Lynet. "They're working already."

"What are they working on?"

We followed the previous day's walking route with fewer stops, covering only about half the circumference of the fort. Down the slope to the north wall we went, up the ladderway by the oubliette (they, graceful; me, clumsy), along the perimeter with the view of the Tor, around the corner above Myrddin's woods, through the southwest gate with a quick stop to flirt. Then we continued above the stream to the break in the southern wall where we climbed down and walked by the slaves at their labor. I couldn't help but watch as they bent to their sorrow, yet I was ashamed to look.

"They'd do the same to us if they could," the queen said.

It would have been nice to give her a speech about tolerance and freedom, but it was her century, not mine. And I knew she was right. I'd seen the fighting in the woods.

We didn't see Lyonel at the barn again. Nor did Guinevere make excuses to part with us there. Instead, she accompanied Lynet and me to the well. We found Elaine snoozing, one foot in the water and one on the dirt, while her women sloshed pants and shirts against the stones.

"Let's not disturb her," whispered Lynet.

But Elaine woke, eyes bleary. "How was the walk?"

I dipped my hands in the well to run wet fingers through my hair. I'd already gone days without a shower. Water soothed my scalp.

Guinevere sat beside Elaine and put an arm around her. "We missed you at breakfast. We're going further today. Casey wants to see the men at work."

Even the washing women laughed.

"Why, Casey?" Elaine asked. "It's not interesting at all. Though I wish I could go."

"Take the path," said Lynet. "Meet us on the other side of the yard."

"No, I'm tired. I might go in for a nap."

I thought that was a good idea. Elaine looked pale.

"You should," said Guinevere, stroking Elaine's hair. "You need your rest for the baby."

"But the work..."

"I'll see to it."

Guinevere was queen; the others let her have what she took. But the love in her touch was genuine and the trust in Elaine's eyes was real. Lynet's protective gaze hovered over not one or the other, but both.

I stepped onto the wall from the ladderway and looked out over the makeshift tent city that spread below us across the plains south of Cadebir Town. Smoke rose from campfires, browning the clear air. It seemed the tent village had grown since my arrival. Without fog or mist, the morning left nothing but distance and imagination for the number of tents to disappear into.

"How are you going to get past the armies if you go to town?" I asked the queen as she and Lynet topped the ladderway.

"They won't stop me," said Guinevere. "When I go down the hill, those below will assume I have permission from the guards. Visiting armies have no authority over Arthur's men."

"So many tents," I mused.

"We must be prepared," said the queen.

"Do we expect a Saxon attack?"

"No. We expect to attack the Saxons." The queen's lip curled with a touch of bravado. She and Lynet marched away from the gate to the west.

The Saxons I'd seen were no one I wanted to see again, whether we were the attackers or they. What if Myrddin didn't figure out how to send me back to the twenty-first century before the war started? What if he did? My friends would be left behind to fight. There had to be a third choice.

"Why do you stay here?" I asked, trotting to catch up. "Why aren't you at the coast where it's safe?"

"At the coast we risk being attacked from the water." Guinevere slowed her pace, then stopped. "Here at least we're with our men."

"Nowhere is safe, Casey." Lynet smiled and took my hand.

Guinevere must have taken my surprise for something else. "It's not your fault," she said, her earlier coolness forgotten. She held my other hand and we walked.

The breeze blew our hair from our cheeks. Inside the wall, men worked on the finishing touches of thatch on a new building below us. Outside the fort, a tiny bird soared along the ramparts, then flitted off to the north to disappear above the secret, forlorn marshes. I couldn't remember ever having done anything as recklessly girlish as holding hands with Guinevere and Lynet. Though to them it was an everyday gesture, I felt silly and elated.

At first I didn't notice the chaotic shouts, but soon the roar drowned out the camp's constant undercurrent of banging and clanking. We stopped and looked over a broad, dirt yard bordered on two sides by a wooden fence and on the third by the wall where we stood. A viewing stand enclosed the fourth side, creating a pit in which a hundred bare-chested men pushed and banged and bloodied each other, fighting and shouting, or throwing their arms around each other and laughing as if this were the most delightful way to spend a sunny morning.

"Okay," I said. "I've seen the work. Let's go help Elaine."

But Guinevere had already begun to glide down the ladderway near the viewing stand and, without hesitating, Lynet skipped after her. The volume of the melee below diminished when fierce fighters took notice of the feminine intrusion. I attempted my entrance with a wizard's poise but finally had to hold onto the sides and descend backwards into the pit. I bumped into Lyonel at the bottom.

"I beg your pardon, Mistress Casey," he said. The man could not speak without sounding like he was insinuating something snide, evil, or lewd.

"No, it's my fault."

He bowed and took my hand in his huge paw to kiss it, looking up at me with bedroom eyes. "A pleasure to see you again." I wondered if he'd received his scar in battle or from a lady defending herself.

"Casey, more stairs!" Guinevere called from the viewing stand. I pulled my hand away from Lyonel's grip and trotted after the queen, following her up a short flight to where King Arthur sat under a thatched awning, flanked by Bedwyr and Sagramore.

Guinevere climbed to the bench behind her husband and leaned over to kiss him on the cheek. "Good morning, my love."

He patted her hand. But like a coach on game day, his attention never left the fighting field. Bedwyr, too, was riveted. Behind them, King Cadwy, King Owain and the other visiting chieftains appeared to be placing bets.

Sagramore blushed and made way for us to pass. "How fares the Lady Elaine today?" I detected mint on his breath.

"She's only tired," said Lynet, "she'll deliver soon."

"Arthur," Guinevere adjusted her tunic around her, "Casey wants to know what the men do all day."

Like his wolf-dog, the king cocked his head at me. "Do you?" He patted the bench beside him and I took my seat.

Was it none of my business? "I'm interested in the work. Of protection." It was a lie; I found the spectacle unpleasant to say the least.

"Square on, Pawly!" shouted Lynet, making the queen laugh.

By the fence, which bore evidence of recurring violence, Medraut and Pawly made impotent slices at each other with short, broad swords, drawing blood but stopping short of stabbing. Directly before us Gareth and Agravain pounded away with their fists, hitting hard enough to bruise the family flesh. Agravain struck a blow to his brother's stomach and Gareth doubled over laughing, earning cheers from the ladies. Agravain helped his brother to his feet and they went at it again, this time hitting harder. Blood dripped from their lips.

"Tell me what you think of our exercises," said King Arthur.

I attempted to be diplomatic. "To my people, Your Grace, it's strange for brothers and friends to fight each other."

"One wants a sparring partner one can trust."

"But they're having fun."

"Oh, it's great sport." He watched me, assessing my distress. "Mistress Casey, you and I have seen some years."

I wasn't sure I liked that.

"We're in no need of speed. But these young men want action and plenty of it, in one form or another. For now I can offer them only the one." He grinned. "Perhaps you've noticed the lack of ladies in the camp. Fighting prepares the men for battle. Makes them strong." He looked out over the field. "It also occupies them."

Lancelot and Lyonel had removed their shirts and were putting on a cable TV wrestling show. Lancelot slung his cousin across his back like a mink stole and modeled him for the crowd, many of whom interrupted their workout to cheer. But Lyonel, a worthy opponent, reached down and grabbed Lancelot's leg, toppling them both in a heap of sinew.

The ladies screamed with delight. I glanced at my lap.

"You don't like it?"

A direct no to his majesty was too bold. "It's not to my taste, Your Grace."

"If you're to protect me in battle you'll see much more violence than this."

"Does there have to be a battle?"

"Most likely. Although," enthusiasm warmed his voice, "you give me hope that it might be a massacre in our favor."

"Yay."

"When you brought your saddle to me—eh, instead of taking it to your Saxon leaders—you gave us an advantage."

"I did?"

"The stirrups. They give a soldier height when he wants it. They add leverage to his stroke. Thanks to you, we shall be unbeatable."

"Didn't the Romans have stirrups?"

"Perhaps. They didn't leave us everything."

Beyond King Arthur's shoulder I saw Guinevere give a little smile to someone on the field. The king caught the automatic movement in my eyes. He looked to Lancelot, who returned the queen's gaze.

I tried to distract him. "I'm glad I brought the stirrups to you, Your Grace. I would have brought them to no one else."

King Arthur stared at the field, breathing hard. Guinevere and Lancelot must have been very certain of his protection. At the moment I thought that unwise.

PETREA BURCHARD

TWENTY ONE

I felt sorry for King Arthur, though I didn't think he'd want me to. My father had experienced the same thing—my mother cheating on him right under his nose—and I'd felt sorry for him, too. At least Guinevere didn't flaunt her relationship with Lancelot. She just wasn't any good at hiding it. My mom made no attempts to be discreet. Quite the opposite. When I was about ten, at a family barbecue hosted by the head of the history department, Mom flirted with the graduate students so outrageously it embarrassed not only me but the students, most of whom left early. But the one who stayed had his hands full behind the garage and everyone in the history department knew it except my dad, who didn't notice, or at least pretended he didn't. And that's just one example.

In her way, my mom was trying to get my dad's attention. There was an endless supply of grad students and faculty parties, and Mom kept repeating her experiments, expecting different results. Dad continued to ignore her. I wished she would lie, and I hated her for flaunting her affairs, if you could call them that. Maybe I should have hated my dad. Instead I felt sorry for him. Kids don't understand these things.

Whatever feelings my father had about my mother's dalliances he kept to himself. He was a smoldering, quiet drunk. At age nine or ten I didn't know enough to notice. I was accustomed to his smell of scotch and smoke and sadness. But about a year before he died it sank into my adolescent psyche that our family life was all her truth and his denial. What I didn't know was how to make either of them happy.

I wasn't naturally outgoing, but entertaining my parents got their minds off their misery and got me some attention. I was inferior at throwing the ball in gym and my short attention span wouldn't accommodate math, but I found a place in arts and letters. So everything I learned in history class became a performance at home. And screw the facts. I went for drama. I was the Roman army, advancing across the ancient northern Africa of our living room. I was Joan of Arc, getting too close to the fireplace in my religious fervor. I was Henry the Eighth and his six wives, chopping off lampshade heads while my dad cheered me on.

When he passed out I was Ulysses S. Grant's cleaning lady. I stashed the bottle in the pantry, noting how much less it contained than it had earlier in the evening. I washed his glass and returned it to the cabinet. In winter months I put a blanket over him and he slept in his chair. Mom slept in their bed on the nights she was home. None of us ever talked about it.

TWENTY TWO

I welcomed Myrddin's summons. I was glad to get off the hill, if only for an afternoon. Cadebir boiled with secrets, and every person there was a bubble I was afraid I'd pop.

Clouds loomed beyond the forest, but it had not yet begun to rain when Myrddin's mute, brunet page rode up to meet me and Lucy at the bottom of the hill. We followed him and his horse into the woods, enjoying the quiet noises of hooves on the path, creatures in the underbrush, and unseen life deep among the trees. When we came upon the ancient stelae that marked the entrance to the compound, I left Lucy with the page, confident of his care. I found my way to the stairs, making my precipitous way down to the dell. My soft shoes padded along the dirt path I'd followed the first day. It led me among high trees, then low huts. Wild chickens pecked for bugs along the path, ignoring my passing.

The garden appeared, misted in cloud. There, where lavender and yarrow shared space with foxglove and deadly nightshade, where sun, rain and Myrddin's gardener joined together to do their best work, where a small bench waited for an exile to take her place, I felt safe. I slowed my pace to cross the garden to Myrddin's hut, allowing my fingertips to drag along the tops of the herbs and stir their scents into the moist air. I thought to sit on the bench for a time, but a summons was a summons.

Inside the hut it was cold and dark. "Oh hello. Not quite ready for you yet. Here." Myrddin gave me two rocks, one with a sharp edge. "Make a fire for tea." He went off to shuffle amid the minutiae on the shelves, mumbling to himself.

I took my rocks to the fire pit in the corner and started scraping. I'd seen him do it. How hard could it be? I scraped and scraped, but made no spark.

"That is pathetic," he said, coming up behind me.

"The king told me not to practice magic."

"Flint and steel is not magic." He snatched the stones from my hands. "Watch."

He picked a clump of dried grass and leaves from the fire pit and held it against the paler of the two stones. A quick scrape of the dark stone against the light tossed a spark onto the clump. Myrddin blew on it gently, moved it carefully to the pit and added more tinder to it there.

"Put the tea on, then come to the table." He walked away, grumbling, "I've never met an adult, much less a wizard, who hadn't at least mastered the flint and steel."

I filled the cauldron from the water barrel and left the tea to brew. Myrddin waited for me at the table like a merchant with his wares set out before him. Odd wares they were, too: a fist-sized black rock, a clay jug and a length of wire. And Myrddin made a strange merchant: he wasn't going to attract many customers by glaring at them, and tapping the table-top with frustrated fingers.

"There will come a time, Casey, when you will be required to prove yourself."

I wished he was wrong. I was supposed to be Arthur's protector in battle, yet I couldn't protect anyone anywhere, and in a battle I'd be the first to die.

"I'm saving my strength."

He frowned. "Perhaps you're not afraid. But I am. And as much as I like you, I'm not certain I believe in you."

I wanted to confide in Myrddin but if I did, he'd either have to turn me in or lie to King Arthur to protect me. Knowing the penalty I didn't think he'd choose the latter, and I didn't want to put him in that position. I said nothing.

Myrddin sighed, and raised the jug from the table. He held it high, showing it off like I used to do for the cameras with the *Gone!* bottle. "Your moe-tor," he said smiling, his beige teeth glinting with pride.

Apparently I had not described it well.

"It runs not on gas-o-leen but on current. Like lightning, only not as powerful. With this moe-tor, I intend to make a car to send you back through the Gap."

Any current he could get from a clay pot wouldn't propel a mouse, much less an automobile. I didn't want to hurt his feelings so I kept that to myself. "You said it wasn't the car that sent me here, but the power."

"Correct."

"So maybe I was struck by lightning." That must have been it. I'd been hit by lightning and I wasn't really talking to Myrddin, I was in an insane asylum somewhere doing meticulous basket work.

"If lightning had struck you directly, you'd be an ember. It might have struck *near* you. We shall experiment with that later this morning."

Lightning struck at that moment, outside near the hut, lifting the darkness for a second and giving me cause for concern about the upcoming experiment. Rain began to fall outside, but Myrddin paid no attention. He lifted the black rock and coiled the wire around it, leaving the ends hanging loose. With a swatch of wadded cloth, he twisted one end of the wire around a strip of metal that poked out of the clay jar like a straw from a milkshake. Then he held the other end of the wire between his fingers with the cloth. "Observe," he said.

He extracted a dead mouse from his pocket and plopped it on the table. The mouse must have been newly dead, and I feared he'd killed it expressly for the experiment because it was still floppy. He tickled the mouse's pink foot with the end of the wire and the tiny body twitched.

I had been wrong about mouse propulsion. "Wow."

"It's an old trick," said Myrddin. Pleased with himself, he indicated the items as he described each to me. "You need a lodestone and a bit of copper. You also need some wine that's been sitting out too long with the cork missing."

"I think that's like a battery."

"You've seen it?"

"Yeah, we use that kind of power to run cell phones and laptops."

"Are they moe-tors?"

"Sort of. But Myrddin, it would take a thousand of those jars to move a car. Maybe more."

"That many? Hmm." He thought about it, but not for long.

Myrddin charged through the gloomy forest ahead of me, carrying the clay pot. Branches formed arches above us, heavy with rain, turning the path into a dark hallway. Trotting to keep up with his traveling stride, I carried the sodden folds of my tunic. My muddy slippers splashed in cold puddles and kicked up the scent of life swarming in the underbrush. When at last the woods thinned, the rain was free to make its freezing way to my skin. We'd barely cleared the edge of the forest when lightning flashed over the plains, renewing the storm's vigor.

"There!" Myrddin shouted, pointing to the split-second view of a crest of high ground a couple of hundred yards away.

We waded out into the downpour through grass as high as my hips. Grass tangled around our ankles as we crossed the open field, grass grabbed at our legs as we climbed the slippery sides of the rise. At the top we were just high enough to gaze out over an ocean of grass and more grass.

Myrddin thrust the pot at me. "Hold this!"

I almost dropped it.

"Hold it tight! Now raise it to the sky!" He took the lodestone from his pouch.

"Are you kidding? I'll be struck!" As if to back me up, the heavens chose that moment to shout down their loudest thunder yet.

"The lightning didn't kill you," Myrddin yelled, "it sent you here!"

"You said it wasn't the lightning!"

"I said it struck near you! I'm attempting to send you home! Do you not wish to go?"

I hugged the jug to my chest. Myrddin spread his arms, welcoming the rain like a priest welcomes the holy spirit. Black clouds poured forth, opening like overturned urns of ice water.

I craved hot coffee. I wanted that coffee in a civilized coffee shop with electric lighting and a flush toilet. I wanted soft, dry fabric against my skin. I wanted more than one pair of shoes and I wanted a decent, hot shower.

I also wanted Myrddin's respect, Guinevere's friendship and King Arthur's trust. And I wanted to live.

I held the jar out to Myrddin. "I'm afraid."

He reached for the jar. When his bony fingers touched mine on the clay a crunching blast of thunder smashed our ears, accompanied by lightning bright enough to blind us. The jar exploded in our hands, shards striking our skin like pelting rain.

I screamed. Myrddin roared. We tumbled down the rise.

TWENTY THREE

When I could see again, I noticed I was still there.

Myrddin helped me to my feet. Leaving shards of the broken jar behind, we slogged across the sodden grass and returned to the forest. I no longer cared how cold and wet I was until we got back to the hut. Drostan, Myrddin's hefty aide, tended the fire and brought biscuits, making the place feel more than civilized. As much as I wanted coffee, Myrddin's tea sufficed. I stood by the fire to let my tunic dry.

Myrddin went off to change, leaving me to wonder where his private quarters were. He soon returned in a dry robe. His long hair had become frizzy in the moist air, a detail he obviously cared nothing about. He stood in the doorway, arms folded. "They say wizards can't cross water."

"I've heard it said, yes."

"You did fine in the rain."

"I didn't have to cross it, did I?"

"Ah," he said. "You've got me there."

PETREA BURCHARD

TWENTY FOUR

"One must be physically the most powerful," said King Cadwy of Cornwall, a slim, elderly man whose lack of chin could not be disguised by his thin beard. He leaned back in his chair after dinner, satisfied to have ended the conversation with his pronouncement.

"Not necessarily," said King Arthur, raising his goblet to call for more wine. "A soldier may succeed by being deft even if he's the smaller man."

I avoided such conversations. It was easy to do at my end of the table. Rarely did Myrddin show up for the evening meal and as Elaine wasn't much of a talker, where I sat it was relatively quiet. I could watch and listen.

At the center of the table, Kings Arthur and Cadwy continued while the priest nodded agreement, no matter what anyone said, and Owain of Corinium Dobunnorum continued to drink as much wine as he could.

"But," said Cadwy, waving his hand so the jewel he wore on his finger caught the flicker of firelight, "one big soldier, like Lancelot for example, can crush two smaller, agile men. I've seen him do it."

"An unfair example, " said the king. "Lancelot is our champion. He's powerful, and deft as well."

"You're too kind, Sire," said Lancelot. He'd stayed out of the discussion for the most part, but he was nothing if not gracious.

"Let the wizard solve the argument," said the king.

For him, it was a bit of a brag. Among his colleagues, King Arthur was the only one to have two wizards and, for all we knew, I was the only female wizard in Britain. I enhanced his prestige. We both liked that.

"Mistress Casey, what's the best defense when fighting hand-to-hand?"

I thought about it. "I suppose it's ideal to be invisible, Your Grace."

King Arthur laughed, but Cadwy didn't like the joke. "Where's the honour in that? If your opponent can't see you, how can he strike you?"

I should have said, "I was only kidding." Instead, I said, "The honor's in protecting one's people from the enemy."

"I believe the wizard's got something," said King Arthur.

Cadwy said, "Hmmph." He opened his mouth to argue further but I pretended not to notice and rose to leave, thinking it best to quit the conversation before I got deeper into it. The queen had long since excused herself and it was time I sought my opportunity as well. "Thank you, Your Grace, for including me at your table once again." I bowed a little. I was picking up courtly manners, or what passed for such at Cadebir. The king nodded, his lids heavy with drink and argument.

The other women tended to excuse themselves early for the same reasons I did. Even when sober, the men loved arguing for the sake of it. Once they got drunk the logical next step was fighting or sex. On a good night they tore up the hall. On a bad night it was best to stay out of their way.

It was too early to go to my hut. Often I couldn't sleep, and with no books or magazines to help pass the time, all I ever did was sit in the dark and ponder my state. My presence at Cadebir and the stupendous unfeasibility of my return to the twenty-first century made it impossible to lie still most nights. I didn't know if it was reality or unreality I was facing and I couldn't sort it out. Restless, I often wrapped myself in Sagramore's cloak and walked the wall, gazing out over the blackness of Myrddin's woods or the twinkling candles of Cadebir town.

I left the hall and climbed the nearest ladderway at the southwest gate. I wanted to walk, and to think about Myrddin's lightning experiment. The rain had cleared, leaving a sparkling night. With the woods below me I walked, letting the plains and then the marshes beyond reveal themselves as I approached the northern part of the wall. I wondered what I'd do if Myrddin found a way to send me back to the twenty-first century. I'd thought it was impossible, but there I was in the sixth century, possible or not. If Myrddin could send me back to Hollywood, I didn't know if I'd want to go. Yes, I missed coffee and plumbing and electricity. But the future didn't hold much else for me.

The day's work had been put to bed, leaving the night quiet and clear, with stars bright enough to light the plains. The sentries noted my passing but left me to myself. Illogical as it was, I felt safe on the wall, though my life lacked logic. The future, Hollywood, was behind me and an ancient war was coming. The world I walked in was imaginary or at least tenuous, a bubble. I had to figure out what to do before it burst. I searched the sky but whatever gap I'd come through wasn't in the stars.

I pulled the cloak tighter and stopped to watch a small blaze atop the Tor at Ynys Witrin. The priestesses must have been having a bonfire. Their island existence was presumably more primitive even than life at Cadebir. How impossibly distant from LA I was. I hardly remembered it, though at Cadebir I was more of an actor than I'd ever been in Hollywood. Had the people there once meant something to me? They had, so much so that I'd run away from them, feeling—what? Grief? More like fear, or desperation, or shame. But those were feelings about myself.

I'd once had feelings about other people, especially as a child. Something had happened to my sympathy along the way. Maybe I'd given up on it when my dad died because I gave up on my mom then.

But sympathy was coming back. I felt it for Guinevere, though I could see her feelings for me ran hot and cold. For one so young, her pressures were great. When I was her age I was drinking my way through college. In my clumsy hands, the responsibilities of a barbarian queen would have been worse than bungled. Knowing me, if I'd been forced to marry an older man I didn't love, I'd have cheated on him, too.

My sympathy for Arthur was even stronger. He wasn't the handsome romantic of my fantasies, though he had a rough charm. But a cheating wife on his mind and the weight of Britain on his shoulders made me want to step in, hold him up, be more than a friend to him.

My fakery had alleviated his fear. That made me happy. It scared me, too. I couldn't protect him. Myrddin was already onto me. So far the only way I could imagine to get out of what I was getting into was to leave. But there were two things wrong with that: I had nowhere to go and—yes, I had my answer—I wanted to stay.

My walk brought me above the exercise yard. Any further would take me near the barracks, a dangerous neighborhood for a woman alone at night. I turned back toward the huts, to take the ladderway down and go home.

"Moonlight suits you, Mistress Casey."

I jumped, not expecting the sentry to speak. It was Lyonel, walking off his mead.

"Oh. Hello."

"You sound less than happy to see me."

"You surprised me." I tried to move past him.

He blocked my way, towering above me and trapping me atop the wall between himself and the ladderway. "You should not be here alone, mistress. You may be a wizard, but you are also a woman."

"I'm going that way." I tried to look him in the eye, to seem powerful, but I couldn't.

"I will walk with you."

"There's no need."

"I said, I will walk with you."

He allowed me to pass, then placed his hand on my shoulder and walked alongside me. I didn't know if, under Cadebir mores, I had somehow acquiesced to such familiarity or if Lyonel took it without my granting it. I only knew I wanted to ask the sentries for help but I wasn't sure I was in danger.

"This is my stop," I said brightly, when we reached the top of the ladderway closest to the huts. "Thanks."

I moved to go around him. He grabbed my waist while reaching his big paw behind my head to pull me to him. I stiffened, but he buried his face in my neck. His lips crawled across my skin, squirming their way up my chin to my face.

With my hands against his chest, I pushed. He was strong, as strong as the odor of alcohol on his breath. The only way I was going to get out of his embrace was if he decided it would be so.

"Let me go!" It was not a whisper, not a yell. I spoke it plain and clear. "I don't want you."

He grunted and released me, staggering back a step. I ran down the ladderway—not graceful, but not backward. I made it to the ground without falling and took off running, only to stumble and fall in the wet grass. Lyonel laughed, but he didn't follow me.

I pulled myself up and ran.

TWENTY FIVE

"Casey, sit beside me. Lance, you don't mind, do you?" The king did not wait for an answer. He turned to the servant to request more wine.

I thought Lancelot minded but he was too polite to say so. I took up my trencher. Lancelot and Elaine stood, both displaced by the inconvenience and embarrassment at what amounted to a public demotion. Most people were too busy gorging and drinking to notice, but Medraut's eyebrows lifted like Roman arches when we played our musical chairs at the head of the dining hall.

King Arthur relaxed when I took the seat next to him. He threw his arm around me. Guinevere, at his other side, seemed to find it amusing.

"Casey, can you make my men invisible?" His breath bordered on the Sagramore. Sometimes he drank too much wine. This was one of those times.

"Maybe one or two of them, Sire. Not the whole army. It's a very complicated process." I touched the wound on my forehead, where I'd run into the Saxon's armor upon my arrival.

"Of course, of course," he said. "We'll talk about it when you've fully recovered. Soon, I hope."

Cadwy leaned across Guinevere. "What if Mistress Casey is invisible while you're in battle? How will you know where she is?"

"We shall have to come up with a signal," said King Arthur.

Guinevere laughed. "I suppose a wave of the hand won't do."

"Perhaps a bird call," said Owain, sloshing his words.

"Tweet," said King Arthur. "Can you do that?"

I assured him I could, but if he couldn't distinguish me from a bird we weren't getting anywhere. They thought that was funny.

Lancelot picked at his food. The king pretended not to notice, but his chattiness made me think he enjoyed Lancelot's displeasure.

I thought the seating change was for only one night, but it stuck. After a day of sewing with Guinevere and Lynet or making batteries with Myrddin, I'd arrive at the hall to find the place between King Arthur and Lancelot reserved for me. It was an uncomfortable spot, hot on one side, cold on the other.

Lancelot was never anything but polite. He'd pull out my chair for me and see to it that the servants kept my glass full. He'd retrieve a piece of bread I dropped and return it to me. Not that I wanted it, but anyone else would have eaten it.

Ordinarily, Lancelot didn't speak to me unless he had to, but the night Elaine didn't come to dinner he drank heavily, which made him drop his guard.

"Is Elaine all right?" I asked.

"She is not well," he said. "The baby will come at any moment. Lynet is with her."

"Maybe we should get Myrddin."

"For what purpose?"

"To help. With the baby."

"Bringing babes is the work of women."

"Is there someone here who...specializes?"

He downed the rest of his wine and shrugged as if he didn't understand the question. "In the dell, yes. I know only that I shall stay away until the baby is born. And I pray God will give me a son."

"Sure. Good." There may be worse situations for lectures on feminism, but I haven't been in them.

Lancelot's unaccustomed chattiness made me nervous, especially coupled with his inebriation. When Guinevere excused herself, the king gave me permission to leave as well. I edged through the crowd of soldiers toward the front door. Gareth shouted, "Goodnight, Casey!" Bedwyr and Sagramore gave a little salute from their table near the fire.

Lyonel, lording it over the back of the hall with his Belgae friends, had obviously experienced no embarrassment over our encounter on the wall. "When will you drink with us, Mistress Casey?" He pounded the table with his fist. His scar glowed red from too much drink. "Come sit with me! Stay late for once, eh? Why don't you like me, Mistress Casey?"

I didn't answer. Drinking with Lyonel would be like drinking with Mr. Hyde. Fortunately there were several tables between his and the door. I turned to go.

"Stay!" Lyonel roared. The hall hushed. He pounded the table harder and spilled his mead.

I turned back again, not knowing what to do. The fear on my face must have looked like something else.

"Lyonel, she will put a hex on you!" said a Belgae soldier nearby.

Then it was all laughter and yelling in their Gallic tongue, and my chance to leave.

The torches still blazed outside the door. I pulled one from the ground to take with me, partly to light my way and partly to brandish at anyone who bothered me. Holding it before me like a standard, I started down the path into the Cadebir night. Within seconds I heard footfalls behind me. Immediately, I whirled and brandished.

"Mistress Casey!"

Medraut and his overfed shadow, Pawly, appeared and disappeared in the light of the torch I swung.

"Sorry. I thought you were someone else."

"Lyonel, perhaps?" Medraut's voice oozed like grease from between his lips. "We thought you might like an escort tonight, mistress."

Something about their skulking was wrong, though Medraut was too skinny for his violet breeches and Pawly was so awkward I perceived no physical danger. "Are you guys gonna protect me from Lyonel?"

"After one more glass of mead, Lyonel will fall asleep with his face on his trencher," said Medraut. "But Lancelot will lie awake tonight, plotting his return to the king's side." They fell into step on either side of me, Medraut slinking, Pawly lumbering.

"Lancelot's unhappy with me for taking his spot next to the king."

"Lancelot has a high opinion of himself. But I'm happy my father has found a friend in you."

It was my instinct not to take Medraut's offered arm. I switched the torch to my other hand.

Medraut's mustache fuzz twitched above his too-sweet smile. "I must admit, as much as I'd like to sit at the king's table, from below I'm better able to watch Lancelot as he squirms."

Pawly giggled.

"I don't mean to take anyone's place," I said.

"You've done right by my father." Medraut patted my arm, a touch I endured with discomfort. "You saved his life. You deserve his recognition. Yet it must have been so terribly difficult for you to kill a fellow Saxon. Did you know the man? Was he a friend of yours? Or was he of a different tribe? Did that matter?"

I didn't like this twist of conversation. "It mattered."

"How did you know about the raid on my father's party?"

"You mean—"

"When you saved his life. How did you know to find them in the forest near the Giant's Ring?"

"Well, I—"

"Your magical perception. Of course. Well, here we are. Good night, mistress."

Medraut gave a deep, respectful bow. His companion did a clumsy imitation and off they went.

I stood outside my hut holding my torch, wondering if I had time to wait for the coincidence of full moon, lightning and rain.

TWENTY SIX

Birds chorused in the branches high above Myrddin's dell. Bugs strafed the flowers, seeking nectar. While squatting beside a basket to gather tinder at the edge of the pulsing woods, I heard giggling on the path.

"Casey! I'm so glad you're here!" It was Elaine, obviously in high spirits. With the aid of Heulwen and Drostan, she hobbled toward me along the path from the huts. "I cannot see my feet!" she said, launching herself into more giggles. Her laughter continued until the next cramp.

"The baby's coming," said Lynet, catching up at a trot and scaring the chickens off the path. She was taking the situation seriously. "We need to find Beatha."

"I saw her earlier," I said, "she's—"

"Just here." The female orderly called from the doorway of the largest infirmary hut where she stood, arms open. She squinted her elfin face into a smile.

"Is Guinevere coming?" I asked.

"She's putting the cart in Myrddin's barn." Lynet sighed. "The servants would've done it for her."

Drostan helped Elaine to the threshold, where Beatha pulled the curtain aside.

"Thank you, Drostan," Elaine chirped, letting go of his arm. She and Heulwen disappeared into the hut, leaving the rest of us outside.

Drostan lumbered off to the garden. I wanted to follow him. "I'll go tell Lancelot."

"He knows," said Lynet.

"We'll need a birthing spell," said Beatha.

"I'm not supposed to practice magic."

Beatha's forehead wrinkled. "What kind of wizard doesn't practice magic?"

"King Arthur's orders," I said.

She sighed, exasperated. "Then I'll do it. Men know nothing about bringing babies. In any case, Mistress Casey, bring the herbs, if you will." She tossed the curtain aside and marched into the hut, calling, "Heulwen, water from the barrel, please." Within seconds Heulwen strong-armed the curtain, bustling out of the hut and across the garden.

I didn't know which herbs to bring. I leaned against the outside of the hut. With the exception of the business inside, the dell was quiet. It appeared to be empty, too.

A long, low "owoooh" came from the hut. It filled the air then trailed off, leaving the dell empty of sound.

"Oooh! Ow!"

Couldn't they give her something for the pain? Willow bark tea. Maybe that's what Beatha meant. But she'd spoken of a spell, not a painkiller. How often did women die in childbirth in the Dark Ages? As often as not, was my guess. I'd better find Myrddin.

I ran across the garden, passing Heulwen on her return to the birthing hut, disturbing the rosemary and rousing its pungence. I burst into Myrddin's laboratory and found it empty. Outside the door I climbed onto the bench to search the dell for him. The garden, lush in summer fullness, simmered in the sun. No leaves rustled. No bee buzzed the lavender. Even the rosemary I'd disturbed had settled back to stillness. There was not an orderly in sight.

I had no idea what herbs Beatha needed. Myrddin grew a hundred different ones for his medicines and experiments. The old man had vacated the dell. I was on my own.

"Do you want to know about it?"

Drostan squatted beside the bench, huge and squinting. I should have known he'd be there. He was a constant presence in the garden unless Myrddin needed him to move something large, like a wagon or a fallen tree. Drostan was like a bear—whether teddy or grizzly depended upon Myrddin's needs of the moment.

"Do I want to know about what?"

He pointed to where I'd been staring. A fuzzy plant. "Milfoil. For telling the future. And for healing wounds." He frowned.

"Oh. Would you know...? Beatha needs to make a birthing spell."

He pursed his lips and gave it serious thought, then stood and stomped away. I jumped down and followed him. He stopped to point at a plant with purple flowers and dark berries. "Belladonna." His heavy brow furrowed. "Not for birthing. Don't eat it. It can make you die." He pointed at a leafy bush across the path. "That's goose-foot," he said with a soft lisp. "Cleans you out." That made him giggle like a third grader.

"This. Lavender." Drostan picked a sprig. "When a baby comes, the women boil this. It smells good. If you chew it, you won't fart." He slashed off a thick bouquet with his knife, tied it with a stem and handed it to me. "Here," he said. He stooped to yank a fistful of tiny leaves on springy stems. "For you. Thyme. Put your head on it when you lie down at night for sweet dreams."

I took a whiff. It smelled of grass and wood. I tucked the thyme into my fanny pack. "Thank you, that's sweet of—"

Drostan gulped and stood at attention, instantly forgetting me.

A ghostly figure, dressed in white, emerged from the woods. Without turning its head, it strode past the birthing hut and floated across the garden to stand before us. Drostan bowed in reverence.

Guinevere failed to notice. "I had to see to the cart."

"They're all in the hut over there."

"I don't think I can go." She shrank onto the bench, expressionless.

I waved the sheaf of lavender like a sorry excuse. "I have to—"

"—Mmhmm."

Drostan folded and unfolded his hands in a chaos of veneration. "If...if you're not going to the birthing, would your majesty like to see the garden?"

The closest I'd ever been to a birth besides my own (at which, I understand, there were enough drugs for everyone) was playing Nurse #2 in the episode of the soap opera "Blanche's Family," when Blanche's daughter had her out-of-wedlock baby. Every bit of it was fake including the baby, the blood and the pain.

Heulwen had built a fire on the ground outside the hut. She squatted to stir the embers under a pot of water, unmindful of dirtying her tunic. Several yards away, Guinevere strolled with Drostan in the herb garden, creating what I knew would be the best day of Drostan's life. We had the dell to ourselves.

I hesitated at the threshold of the hut. "I wonder where everyone is," I said, not to Heulwen, but not to anyone else, either.

"The men have gone."

"They sure checked out fast."

She shrugged her broad shoulders. "We don't need them for this part, mistress. Mind if I ask, do Saxon men participate in the birthing?"

"No, they..."

A moan from Elaine momentarily relieved me of the remainder of the lie. But Heulwen waited for my answer.

"...they wait. Outside."

She nodded as if that reassured her that Saxon men were normal.

"I guess I'll go in." If my friends believed in the powers of lavender, they would have lavender.

Again Elaine yowled, then again, louder. I touched the curtain over the entryway, its undyed threads coarse against my fingers. This part of being a woman had never been part of me. The sex I'd had in my life had been unrelated to childbearing, at least in my mind. As fraught as it was with birth control pills, lotion and self-loathing, how could sex have anything to do with the life of someone else?

I pulled the curtain aside. With her back to me, Elaine lay heaving on a pile of blankets on the floor, gasping for a breath of what was mostly lamp smoke. Lynet purred at her side. A muslin rag covered the only window, letting the tiniest bit of daylight filter through.

"Good. You've brought the lavender," said Beatha, glancing up from her vantage point between Elaine's legs.

"Yes." I thought I should whisper. Beads of sweat trickled down my backbone. I took a seat on the bench by the window to let my dizziness fade. Wiping sweat from my forehead with my sleeve, I tried not to look at Elaine. Her breathing filled the room.

"Could we open the curtain?" I asked.

"She'll get cold." Beatha didn't look up.

I waited, hoping it wouldn't take long.

TWENTY SEVEN

Heulwen, Lynet and I took turns helping Elaine to sit up, which required one of us on either side of her. She struggled to squat as Beatha instructed her to do.

From that position Elaine would push and cry herself to exhaustion then lie on her pillows, soaked in sweat and the sticky liquids of herself. Sometimes she'd nod off. Then the wrinkles in her forehead would smooth and her powdery pink cheek would squish against the back of her hand. Those times were the least overwrought, the times when Elaine didn't hurt, or at least wasn't conscious of hurting. Heulwen would sleep then, too, snoring softly on the bench. Beatha would nap if and when she could, leaving Lynet and me to shoo away the tiny flies that hovered at Elaine's nostrils.

In the deep hours I stepped outside to a moonless night. The forest appeared black, as though the stars had decided it was too much trouble to light everything and had therefore concentrated all their efforts on the garden.

"Casey." In the shadow of the forest's edge, Guinevere beckoned from among the trees. I walked the path to her, listening for sounds from the birthing hut. She had borrowed a cloak, no doubt from Drostan or one of Myrddin's helpers in the settlement atop the stone steps. She shivered a little. "How is she?"

No one had said it, but the baby was fighting to escape and Elaine hadn't the strength to free it. "Things don't seem right."

"What's wrong?"

"It's just...I think it's taking too long and hurting too much. I guess Beatha knows what to do."

"She does." Glancing toward the hut, Guinevere patted my arm as if to reassure us both. "Elaine is made for motherhood. I don't believe I have any talent for it."

"Is that why you don't go inside?"

"No." She expelled a sharp sigh. "I'm afraid," she said, smiling in spite of herself.

"Childbirth scares me, too." Not that there was a chance I'd ever bear a child.

"Not of birth. Of mothering. And—" she blinked upward, deciding whether or not to tell me, "—and I'm jealous of my friend."

Her unexpected honesty warmed me to her at the same time it honored me. I had never enjoyed such confidences from anyone.

"I'm sure you don't mean that."

"She's having his baby." With her small fingers, Guinevere dabbed tears from the corners of her eyes.

She'd left me the opening. Arthur had ordered me not to speak of Guin's affair with Lancelot. But Arthur wasn't there.

Guin gazed at me, bright-eyed, stricken by a sudden thought. "Casey," she whispered, "can you help me get pregnant? I've got to conceive. I've tried," her cheeks reddened, "with both of them."

"Shh! Guinevere, we can't speak of it."

"It's the one skill required of me, other than looking pretty, and entertaining Arthur's allies. That is challenging work," she added with a wry smile, "but I find I'm able." Her hands gripped mine in a plea. "There must be a potion. Something."

"The king has ordered me not to use magic," I whispered.

She sighed and let her hands drop, her eyes filling with tears. "Then I'm lost."

"That can't be."

She wiped her eyes on her sleeve and waved me away. "I shouldn't have asked. It was dangerous. Please don't speak of it."

"Of course I won't."

The air stilled, as though the leaves were listening. The silence of the forest floated around us. I wanted to help her but I knew nothing of fertility. If there were a potion, Myrddin would know. "Though it might be possible." I should have consulted with Myrddin before saying so, but I was never one to stop my mouth from moving when words were on their way out of it.

"Oh, Casey!"

"Guinevere. I can't promise."

"Thank you for understanding."

She had a role to play and she was faking her ability to play it. Sure, I understood.

"And it's time you called me Guin, as the others do."

Permission to be her friend. I hadn't realized how much I'd wanted it.

She sniffled, feeling better. "You?" she asked, after a pause. "No children for the wizard?"

"No. I learned mothering from the worst."

"How so?"

"I just...wasn't a priority for her."

"But you're not like her, are you?"

I stabbed a toe at the underbrush. "I try not to be."

Guinevere smiled and leaned back against the nearest trunk. I did the same. We faced each other, dwarfed by the giant trees, our skin blue in the starlight. Even there, at the edge of the woods, the underbrush was so thick I couldn't see my shoes.

"My mother was good and gentle," said Guin, her eyes closed.

"You're like her, then. You'll be a good mother."

She opened her eyes. "With the help of your potion, I will."

"Casey!" Heulwen shouted from the hut. "We need you!"

I ran and Guin ran with me.

Inside the hut, the stink of armpits and breath struck us, as did the yeasty smell of the womb, the same smells I'd stifled all my life with deodorants, mouthwash and scented tampons. Elaine seemed to sleep while Lynet furiously patted her cheeks and Beatha rushed to clear the floor of rags and debris, throwing everything onto the bench. Guinevere, her skin pearl-colored in twilight, set her shoulders and took her place, dabbing Elaine's brow with a cloth. Beatha shoved Lynet aside more roughly than I would have thought possible for such a tiny woman. Her movements betrayed her anxiety but her voice did not. "Prepare the herbs, Mistress Casey."

"But I'm not supposed to—"

"You must!" Beatha pressed on Elaine's breastbone with one hand and pumped her heart with the other.

Heulwen rushed in, holding the hot handle of the pot with the folds of her tunic. "Here's for the lavender, Casey," she said, placing the pot on the table.

I didn't know what to do, only that I must do something. With my heart pounding, I clawed through the rags and stones and bits of animal skin Beatha had thrown on the bench until I uncovered the bouquet of lavender.

Elaine woke, coughing though her sobs. I hesitated by the window with my herbs until her coughing subsided into whimpers. She's all right, I thought. I don't have to do anything.

"Mistress Casey." Beatha was squatting between Elaine's legs, staring at the girl's vagina like a cat waiting at a mouse-hole. *"Now."*

I dragged myself to the dark corner where the pot sat steaming on the table. There, I turned my back to the room. I considered telling them I had no magic so they'd give me a real task, something meaningful to do. But my shame was too great.

With a movement one might use to rip the head off a doll one hates, I twisted and tore the tops off the lavender and threw them into the pot. For a second of steam, the earthy, sweet smell of hot lavender defeated the room's miasma. I sniffed and waved my arms in ways I hoped appeared mysterious. The word "abracadabra" came to mind but I kept my mouth shut. My arm-waving and head-bobbing were disrespectful enough. I gripped the rough edge of the table, hating myself for pretending when Elaine's life was at stake. Why didn't I run into the woods, up the mossy steps, shouting for Myrddin all the way? Running and shouting would be more useful than cowering in the corner of the hut and flapping my arms, even if no answer came.

I'd been just as helpless at my father's deathbed, but no one expects magic from a thirteen-year-old. My father and I were in his study when he collapsed. I ran for my mom, whose reaction was, "Shut up, I'm on the phone."

I told her he was dead but he wasn't. He hung on in the hospital for a few days, white skin against white sheets. I wanted to stay by his side every minute. I wanted to be there when he woke up. I thought he needed me more than her; I didn't know my mother would grieve because he had never loved her the way she wanted him to. While she waited for him to die I waited for him to live.

I went to the hospital when my mom had time to take me. While she visited with the nurses I held my dad's hand and waited. I had so much more to say to him. I don't remember where we were when the call came—the grocery store, the beauty shop, nowhere important. He died when I wasn't there with him.

I would be there for Elaine.

I wiped my eyes. Elaine lay motionless on her pillows, the rise and fall of her chest barely discernible. Lynet kissed her hand and Guin stroked her hair. Then she dragged in a breath and clutched Guin's arm, willing herself up to a squat where her friends let her use them for balance.

"Push now, dearie. Push hard," Beatha growled softly.

Elaine pushed. She strained, from dirty toenails that gripped the sweat-soaked blankets, through her fleshy, white thighs, naked from the waist down, where moisture gleamed but where no babe emerged. She bit her lip and panted. Wet trails, where tears had traveled, led from the corners of her eyes to her ears.

"The baby's coming," said Beatha, "just a bit more now, don't stop."

When Lynet let go for a second to wipe her nose with her sleeve I grabbed a rag and squatted to dab Elaine's brow. I could do that much.

Elaine's body convulsed. She moaned and pushed again, flailing her arms. I reached out in time for her to grab my wrist. She squeezed so hard the blood couldn't travel to my hand. She had such a grip on me I had no choice but to stay. I wouldn't have left her.

"Give her the rag to bite on," said Beatha.

I did, and Elaine bit hard, arching her back.

"Once more now, my girl!" said Beatha.

From deep inside Elaine came a groan so full and determined it sounded like she channeled it from the ground. "Nnnggghhaaaahh!" The rag fell from her lips to the floor. Beatha reached forth her slime-covered arms. A pearly, bloody bulb of baby's head appeared between Elaine's legs.

"Here's the little one, oh!" Beatha's small hands took gentle hold of the tiny head.

Elaine squeezed my wrist harder and bore down. Heulwen supported from behind, peeking around Elaine's head. All of us held our breath to witness a life's beginning in its mess and odor and pain. Like a velvet curtain, Elaine's womb opened. Small shoulders emerged, slick with watery blood, and the baby slipped onto the soaking blankets.

Elaine released me and collapsed onto Heulwen, who fell onto the pillows. Elaine's eyes closed but her hands reached out and found Lynet on one side and Heulwen on the other. She grasped their clothing, hung on and gulped for air. Lynet began to weep. My hand tingled with the return of blood.

"It's a boy," Beatha sounded more surprised than pleased, and I remembered she'd predicted a girl. She placed the babe on his mother's bulbous belly, his flesh-gray umbilical cord intact. Elaine made no move to hold him but Guin instinctively reached to balance him beneath his mother's breast. For a few seconds the only sound was Elaine's gasping while Beatha cleaned the boy's nose and eyes. Guin gazed at him, her chest heaving, her lips pressed hard together.

Beatha lifted the babe and gave his bottom a solid smack. The child himself announced to the dell that Lancelot's baby was born.

"Thanks be to the gods," Heulwen whispered. Nestled in Heulwen's arms, Elaine let her hands flutter, feeling for something. Guinevere lifted the baby to her and she cradled him at her breast to nurse.

Blinking fast and sniffing, I turned my face upward to prevent the tears from falling. But my eyes filled and tears fell, running down my cheeks until I forgot myself.

"Your birthing spell is like none I've witnessed before, mistress," said Heulwen.

"Truly," said Lynet.

We sat on the threshold of the birthing hut, watching the dawn turn pink above the trees. Heulwen had doomed one of the chickens that wandered the dell and we huddled by the fire to eat it. With Beatha as sentinel, Elaine slept inside, her baby in her arms.

"The Saxon spell's the only one I know," I said. "But please, remember King Arthur said 'no magic.'"

"Your secret's safe," said Lynet.

"Mmhmm." Heulwen tossed a bone into the fire. "Saved her life."

"And Lancelot's baby," said Lynet.

Guinevere gnawed at a bone and said nothing. But she smiled.

"I'm afraid not." Myrddin put down the clay battery with force, rocking the table.

"Uh-oh."

"What is uh, oh?"

"I kind of promised someone." Morning trickled into the dell from above the treetops. Across the garden, the women snoozed in the birthing hut.

"To whom did you promise a pregnancy potion?"

"Doesn't matter."

He frowned at me over his nose. If he'd had reading glasses they would have perched there, enhancing his scowl.

"You must be careful, Casey. It is perilous to promise what you cannot deliver."

TWENTY EIGHT

It was impossible to avoid being jostled in the tiny church. It wasn't so easy to breathe, either. Soldiers lined the walls and filled the tiny apses of the same building on which I'd seen workers completing the thatch a few days before, a building so new that when one did manage to breathe one smelled the cow dung they'd used to mix the plaster. Fine ladies squeezed together on the benches between farmers and servants. Everyone who lived at Cadebir must have been there, Christian or no. How often does one witness the christening of the first-born male child of Lancelot du Lac?

Lynet and I found seats at the back where the scarcity of oxygen was relieved by the occasional opening and closing of the wooden door. A tiny window at the front, high above the altar and barely big enough for a bird to perch on its sill, allowed a bit of sunlight, if not air.

I stretched my neck to peek over rows of hatless heads. Lancelot was easy to spot, glad-handing through the congratulators and glancing about to see who was seeing him. Elaine sat placidly in the front row beside Guinevere. King Arthur was seated on his wife's other side, his arm draped casually across her shoulder like a comfortable scarf, his unreadable back to the crowd.

The door opened behind us. Several bodies pressed against the walls to allow passage for a ceremonial procession consisting of Caius, lugging an iron bucket in his arms, and the sad-eyed priest, who pressed a vellum scroll to his lips. Caius bent his long legs to keep from jostling the water but he failed, sloshing and splashing himself with every step. The priest made smooth progress behind him, his pious nose lifted to the ceiling.

Cai placed the bucket on the simple altar before the congregation, receiving a final splash to his chin. He stood aside and bowed his proud head. The priest faced the room and looked us over, waiting for all stirrings to subside. Finding us worthy at last, he unrolled the scroll and cleared his throat. The collective body leaned forward. Soldiers stood on tiptoe. Lynet breathed in but not out. The people of Cadebir were not often read to.

"Hodie congregamus nos ut filium Lancelot du Lac, dux Belgae, inungere..."

Lynet let out the air she'd been holding. "This must be the holy part," she whispered.

"I wouldn't know."

The cleric droned on. His congregants relaxed into whispers and fidgets. After a while the new parents stepped to the altar. Lancelot's posture radiated pride. Elaine cooed to the infant as she reluctantly handed him over to the priest, who dangled the babe over the bucket. *"In nomine patris, filii et spiritus sancti..."*

I thought it a crime to dunk the poor baby with so little air in the room already, and the underwater interval seemed perilously long. When the priest finally raised the dripping child, the boy wailed his indignant protest. Everyone laughed, perhaps in relief, and someone said that, judging by the cry, Lancelot's offspring was as powerful as he was.

When the laughter died down, the priest spoke in words we all understood. "In the name of Jesus our Saviour, I christen thee Galahad."

King Arthur's back stiffened.

One little fact about Galahad, the purest and most powerful knight, the one who achieved the holy grail, had slipped my mind. He was the son of Lancelot.

The king dropped his arm from the queen's shoulder and turned to search the crowd. Guinevere looked up at him but by then he'd forgotten her and found me. He shook his head in joyful amazement. I wondered why. Then I remembered.

I had predicted Galahad.

"My lady wizard astonishes me!"

Outside the church in the blessed open air, King Arthur threw his arms around me. His enthusiastic embrace surprised me and even hurt a little. I rested my face against his chest for a second, letting my blush pass, engulfed in his smell of burnt oats and wood smoke. I hadn't felt so approved by a man since my father was alive.

But Arthur's smell was not my father's smell. His arms were not my father's arms. And pleasing my father was easy. "That's my girl," he'd say, and he'd be right. Pleasing Arthur was unexpected, "astonishing." Pleasing him thrilled me with a blood-rush like a first kiss.

With one arm around me and the other around his queen, King Arthur gabbed with his friends like a tipsy barfly while a crowd formed on the dusty path the way it does after a wedding. Caius, his shirt finally dry, ducked out from the church doorway with his elegant, gray-haired wife. Their arrival built anticipation for Lancelot's, which, when at last it happened, the crowd greeted with applause. Lancelot accepted his accolades with a deep bow, and allowed his wife to fade into his background as though she'd had little to do with the work of bearing the child she held in her arms.

King Arthur let go of me to be the first to shake Lancelot's hand. "Lancelot! Have you heard the prophecy?"

"Prophecy?"

"Mistress Casey prophesied the name of your son."

Lancelot squinted, his spotlight dimmed.

Elaine gazed up at her husband. "But even I didn't know," she said.

"Galahad is to become a great warrior." The king made certain to be heard above the crowd. "That's what you said, is it not, mistress?"

"Something like that." I regretted having mentioned it.

"I'm amazed," said Medraut. "You are protector as well as prophet." I detected sarcasm, but King Arthur didn't seem to notice.

"Casey saved Elaine's life, Your Grace," said Lynet. "And Galahad's."

"How so?" asked the king.

"She did it with—"

Lynet stopped herself and I held my breath, trying not to glare at her.

"—her womanly knowledge." She hooked her arm in Gareth's.

"Wizard, prophet, and midwife," said the king, apparently not caring to know the details of childbirth. "Are you a physician, too?"

"Not really, Your Grace."

Lancelot tried to smile but his face pinched. "I am at a loss as to how to show my gratitude, Mistress Casey."

"There's no need."

King Arthur hugged me to his side again, making me trip over his feet in the dust. "Mistress Casey, I treasure you more each day."

"I'm glad, Your Grace."

"So great a wizard must call me 'Sire,' as my closest friends do."

I felt a rush of joy, like someone had poured a bucket of it over me.

I could only bow my head to hide my blush. Lancelot called him "Sire." Bedwyr, Sagramore, his son Medraut—even Myrddin called him "Sire." They all did, in a way acknowledging him as "father." I wanted that, too. Would he someday allow me to call him by his name? Even in my private thoughts I'd never dared think of him as simply "Arthur."

Guin reached across her husband to take my hand.

"Are you three not a pretty picture?" said Lancelot. "Felicitations, Mistress Casey, on your promotion to 'close friend of the king.'"

"Don't be jealous, Lance," said Arthur. "There's room in my heart for an infinite number of friends. Loyalty is all I require." He smiled at his disloyal friend and turned to me. "Casey, I'm filled with hope. How do you feel?"

"I feel fine, Sire," I said, inhaling the thin air of the inner circle.

"Good! Sagramore, prepare the saddles. Tomorrow we ride. We have Saxons to kill."

TWENTY NINE

Smoke rose from the smithy behind the barn. I hunched my shoulders against the pre-dawn cold, seated astride Lucy and bundled in Sagramore's cloak.

Myrddin's small, gilded knife, supplemented by the largest dagger I could manage, couldn't protect me in battle against experienced soldiers twice my size. Bedwyr hadn't issued me a sword because I couldn't lift one. Magic was the only thing that could save me, and where was I going to find that?

King Arthur cantered up to me on his chocolate-brown stallion, Llamrai, the one horse at Cadebir who came close to Lucy in size. "What do you think?" he asked, stroking Llamrai's new saddle.

"Very nice." Sagramore and his men had made a fine copy of Lucy's tack. The stirrups were not as sleek but every bit as serviceable as Lucy's.

"You see, we have more." The king opened his arms to direct my eyes to the barn. Horses stamped and snorted outside its doors, their nostrils steaming in the early morning cold. I watched Sagramore cinch a new saddle onto Bedwyr's muscular pony. Gareth and Agravain were already aboard their saddled horses amid the group of soldiers by the pasture fence.

Near the barracks, half a dozen of Lancelot's men mounted up. Their steeds were outfitted with the usual small blankets in apparent defiance of this new way of riding. Either that or Lancelot was low on Sagramore's priority list.

With darkness still upon us, Bedwyr's shout came. "The carts are ready!"

The king's excitement was evident in the flare of his nostrils. "You're my protector," he said. "You ride with me."

Good, because I liked him. Bad, because I couldn't even protect myself.

Before we felt the heat of the rising sun we turned north, leaving the main road for a lesser path across the plains. We also left behind the tent city south of the road, and the hundreds of soldiers there.

"Why don't we take the army, Sire?" I asked. No matter how strong our men were, no matter how fierce they looked in torch light or how excited they were to kill Saxons, fifteen of them was insufficient for my taste.

"That is not my plan." King Arthur threw his shoulders back and breathed the morning air through his nostrils.

"What is your plan, Sire? If I may ask."

"You must, for you are to protect me." He glanced over his shoulder, checking. The others were several horse-lengths behind us. "My plan is stealth, surprise and destruction. Keep it to yourself. The spy may be among us."

"Sounds good." It sounded vague.

"The Saxons we seek are mere stragglers, left behind from the incursion we were fighting when you appeared. If I'm correct, they're caught between Poste Perdu and Beran Byrig and cannot return across our border to their people. They're likely hiding in the woods north of the Giant's Ring, not far from where we left them, hunting for food and robbing travelers on the road."

"Why don't the troops at Beran Byrig take care of this?"

He smiled as though I were the simplest child. "Because revenge is mine."

"But you already killed the Saxon who tried to kill you."

"You may recall I killed two. You killed a third. But they shall all die, every one." The king shook loose his hair. "The world will know what happens to those who breach my borders and seek to murder me."

To think I'd killed a man, even King Arthur's enemy, turned my stomach. What grief had that meant to his intimates? What, if anything, had it done to the future? I preferred to think I'd accidentally run into a Saxon and accidentally forced him onto the king's sword. I patted Lucy's neck and kept silent.

The Tor of Ynys Witrin glowed pink in the west, sponging up the sunlight. Maybe the life of a priestess would be more suitable for me than the life of a wizard. I lacked faith in gods and goddesses, though I had a better chance of finding that than I did of finding magical powers. I was beginning to think I needed both.

Our route took us straight north, leading us west of where I'd originally landed instead of directly to the spot. To maintain secrecy we avoided roads and towns, using paths that were all but overgrown. At times we created our own path, single file, our shoes brushing the high grass. Late in the day we entered untraveled woods so thick our legs scraped moss off the trees as we picked our way through.

My movie riding experience had consisted of short takes for the camera. Never before had I been on horseback long enough for the ache in my behind to surpass merely uncomfortable and become downright painful. I tried leaning forward to take the weight off my posterior but there was nothing else to sit on but my own derriere.

To make things worse, Lancelot and his menacing cousin rode near me all day. It was to be expected, as Lancelot was King Arthur's close confederate. Although Lynet's announcement that I'd saved Elaine and Galahad had delighted the king, it served to make Lancelot like me less, and he wasn't much enamored of me to begin with. When the king's attention was elsewhere, Lyonel found opportunities to casually sideswipe Lucy with his horse, or to steer around and cut me off in front. He even tried "accidentally" reining right up to Lucy's hindquarters. Any other mount would have thrown me, but being a rental horse, Lucy was accustomed to trail riding and comfortable with other horses nudging at her personal parts.

Lancelot found ways not to notice. He occupied himself in conversation with King Arthur. He rode behind to check on his men. He examined the trees. I wondered if he'd put Lyonel up to it, but I couldn't know.

At midday we came to a place in the forest where the trees stood straight and sparse enough to ride two and three abreast, though there was no path. We found no clearing, nor did we need one. A stream was sufficient, with tender shoots growing alongside for the horses to munch on. When Bedwyr called a halt to eat I was overjoyed, though my thighs were so stiff I embarrassed myself with a clumsy dismount.

I found a place far from Lyonel and Lancelot where I could sit in peace and eat my hard, dry bread and dry, hard meat.

"Sit over here, Lyonel!" called a soldier.

"If I wanted to hear from an ass, I would fart." This got Lyonel a big laugh. "He thinks he's Caius," he continued, "keeping everyone organized."

"You mean Gassius Assius?" Gareth's response got an even bigger laugh, which Lyonel didn't seem to mind.

They continued roasting Cai with fart jokes, most of which I swear I'd heard in Hollywood if not junior high. I moved off to find a private place to pee. "Don't leave without me," I told Bedwyr, tapping his shoulder as I slipped into the trees. He winked a crinkly-cornered eye.

I walked away from the warriors, keeping the stream beside me so as not to get lost. At a distance from the men I stopped. Kneeling at the shore I cupped my hands and drank. Then I drank more. I'd been avoiding the well water, and as much as I liked wine and mead it surprised me how delicious the stream water tasted.

The forest's quiet quenched a different thirst. Before coming to Cadebir I'd been accustomed to being alone. As much as I liked my role in the camp's small spotlight I sometimes felt the need to steal minutes for myself. It was especially true after being dogged all morning by Lyonel.

I walked further, slowing my stride to listen. My shoes crunched the bits of leaves and dirt that made up the forest floor. My palms read the texture of each tree I passed, this one rough and so hard a hammer wouldn't dent it, this one smooth, with bark that came away like candy wrappers and smelled of gin.

Something large splashed in the stream. A thick trunk served as a good blind for peeking, and there I hid. A man sat on the bank in shadow, his back to me. To get closer I stole from tree to tree, taking time to place my steps for silence.

It was King Arthur, seated cross-legged on the shore, a pile of stones arranged in a circle beside him. He took up a stone, held it in both hands, and spoke to it. Then he closed his hands over it, thought for a moment and tossed the stone into the stream. He selected another rock and repeated the ritual.

I didn't want to disturb him, but I'd never seen this ring of stones thing before and I wanted to hear what he said to the rocks. I tiptoed closer to watch from behind the nearest tree. Hugging the trunk as close as I could, I leaned forward to listen.

With a sudden pounce he leapt behind me and drew his knife against my neck. I believe I said, "Whup!" I had never experienced a choke hold before.

King Arthur let go. I stumbled to a fallen log and sat to catch my breath while he laughed, loud and long.

"I hope you're a better wizard than you are a spy." He stood over me and sheathed his knife.

"Me too."

"It's rude, you know, to listen to my prayers."

"I didn't know you were praying, Sire."

"But you knew you were spying."

"Yes."

"Never do that," he said, suddenly angry. "I might have slit your throat."

"Yes, Sire."

He calmed his temper with a deep breath. "I prayed to the gods for victory."

"Not...God?"

"Bah. The people may worship as they choose, but I pray the old way. There may be some good in this new god. But the ancient rituals have muscle. They give me power to reach across the centuries and touch my ancestors." The king's forehead wrinkled and his lips opened and closed while he reached inside himself to come up with the words he wanted. "We were once a wild people of poetry and art. Every tribe had a bard. Magic lived in the forest." He looked to the treetops, remembering. "That is my disappearing world. I am but a remnant of it. That is why you mean so much to me. You are proof that magic lives in the future."

He offered his hand.

It was my chance to tell him the truth. It was wrong to lead him on any further. But the truth would break his heart. And he would kill me.

I let him help me to my feet.

"Sire, my magic is nothing."

"It's everything," he said. "You've returned my hope to me."

King Arthur reined Llamrai to a stop. He sniffed the air and smiled. The sky, a soft gray in the forest's diffuse light, was beginning to darken to a cooler blue. The stream we'd been following, full from the previous week's rain, bubbled nearby and the ground was soft with decaying leaves.

The king sent the order back along the line to dismount and make camp. I slid down from Lucy's saddle and fell. After riding all day, my legs were too wobbly to hold me. Maybe some of the men saw but no one said anything. I had righted myself and was picking leaves off my tunic by the time Bedwyr found his way to Arthur.

"Bedwyr. Good, good," said the king to his sergeant. "Medraut will camp to one side of me and Lancelot to the other. They may tent with what companions they will. The others may suit themselves."

Bedwyr nodded and strode off to carry out the king's orders.

"Keeping close your best men or your enemies, Sire?" I asked.

"To do both is wise." He tossed me a heavy rope. "Do as they do." He indicated with his chin.

I followed his gaze. Across the clearing Gareth and Agravain tied a rope taut between two trees at about chest height. They threw a blanket over it and tied down the ends. In minutes they had a tent.

After watching the brothers for my instructions, I found a likely tree and wrapped the rope around it, fumbling. The rope's thick fibers splintered my fingertips and I couldn't tie it tightly enough to make it stay.

"Have you never tied a rope?" The king watched me, arms folded across his chest.

"I haven't done much camping, Sire."

"That's the weakest knot I've ever seen." He smiled, almost flirtatiously. "I'll tie the knots. You get a blanket from Bedwyr's cart. He should have saved a large one for me."

I felt my cheeks blush hot. I liked the way he smiled at me. I smiled back.

Medraut and Pawly offered to hunt for our dinner. But Bedwyr had already sent Hew, the soldier from the wall, and the red-haired boy who'd driven my cart the first day. Instead, Bedwyr ordered Medraut and Pawly to gather dry brush for camp fires, fires Arthur allowed because we were still far enough west not to alert the enemy.

Sixteen men and one woman settled in as night rested on the forest. I felt safe as long as I stayed near the king. The tall trees surrounding our campground hid from view a forest as yet untrammeled by the likes of us. Tomorrow we'd push further in. For the night, the men stayed by the fires, perhaps as much in need of a safe haven as I was. Animals crept near but not too, clicking and chirping outside our periphery of light.

Bedwyr, a good supply sergeant in any century, had brought extra blankets. I used one to cushion my sore behind. The small creatures we roasted were a welcome change from our dry lunch. We sat in a circle around the fire and picked at their sides, leaning across the flames at our peril to pluck a piece with a knife or grab with blistering fingers.

"I will tell you nothing of my strategy," said King Arthur when asked, his voice low so only those nearest us could hear him over the crackling fire. "You will await orders."

"But Sire..." Lancelot's mouth was full.

"I do this for your safety, my friends. This way if there's a spy among us, as well there could be, our plans cannot be leaked to the enemy because I'm the only one who knows them." The king leaned across me to spear another piece of bird.

"I think it's ingenious, father," said Medraut, wiping his sleek chin. "How many of the enemy do you think we'll find?"

"Not as many as on the River Douglas," said Bedwyr.

"Thank the gods for that!" Gareth laughed out loud.

"Quiet, cousin," said the king. "Let's not alert the entire woods to our presence."

Gareth covered his mouth.

"How many did you take on at the River Douglas, Bedwyr?" asked Hew.

"Thousand."

"No!" The red-haired boy gaped in awe. I reminded myself to ask his name as soon as I got the opportunity.

"It wasn't a thousand," said Sagramore. "Perhaps eight hundred."

"Eight hundred, then," said Bedwyr, flipping a blond braid over his shoulder, "and we had not five hundred men. It was slaughter." He let the word hang in the clearing like an overripe plum, dangling from a bough. "They hadn't a chance."

Everyone laughed, covering their mouths to suppress their noise.

"They'd need more than double to best King Arthur's men."

"Saxon bodies *everywhere*."

"The river ran red!"

"Lancelot's army was there, too," said the king. "You haven't seen Lancelot fight, have you, Hew?"

"No, your majesty." The young soldier flushed, suddenly awkward, leading me to think he'd never before been addressed directly by the king. I knew that warm feeling of being singled out by his majesty.

"Watch him when we meet our enemy. Watch your back first, son, but when you can, learn from the greatest fighter I've ever known."

Arthur and Lancelot shared a look of mutual admiration, maybe even of love. I recognized my reaction: jealousy.

"I follow the greatest leader Britain has ever had," said Lancelot. "That is enough to make any man great."

"Hear, hear." The men raised their flasks and drank a solemn toast. I drank, too.

"Now, off to sleep," said the king. "We've another day's ride tomorrow, and I want all of you to be as good as Lancelot when we fight."

In a shuffle of leather and clink of knives, the men picked up their blankets and saddles and moved off. I didn't think the king meant me, so I stayed. Lancelot and Arthur lingered, sipping from their flasks. My flask, issued from the supply wagon, held stream water.

Bedwyr tossed dirt on the fire. "What about the lady, Sire?"

"Hmm?"

"Where shall Mistress Casey sleep?"

"In my tent, of course."

My stomach took a leap and refused to land. I reminded myself the king thought of me as his protector and would keep me close.

"Yes, Sire," said Bedwyr, keeping his reaction to himself.

Lancelot corked his flask.

I squatted behind a bush, away from camp in the black woods but close enough to keep the fire in view. I was less fearful of the unknown among the blue-black trees than I was of what awaited me in King Arthur's tent.

What did the king expect of me? Was sex required? What if I didn't want to give it? I had sworn off married men. Could I refuse King Arthur?

What if I didn't want to refuse?

My mouth hadn't had the benefit of toothpick or mint since the night before. My most recent bath was a distant memory. I should be clean. No matter what was about to happen.

It wouldn't do to remove my clothes so near to camp. But if I stayed with the water I wouldn't get lost. I hiked up my tunic and underdress and waded along the edge of the cold stream, following it as deep into the woods as I dared. My passing made little waves on the shore and sent small-footed creatures skittering. Their noises crawled across my skin and made me jumpy. I told myself not to fear. I could brave a mouse or two to be clean for the king.

I tiptoed to where the stream burbled away from the dim campsite into absolute darkness that sounded like water caressing rocks, creatures crawling in mud, and gods of the ancient, wild unknown whispering in a language long forgotten. There, the forest canopy broke and revealed a sliver of moon. No rabbit or deer or fiercer creature appeared in the thick of trees, though their scurryings betrayed their presence. I climbed the bank, removed my clothes and draped everything over a branch. Naked, shivering, and with mud squishing between my toes, I hung my shoes high up, because I didn't want to find spiders and mice in them later, and

I hurried, because I didn't want the king to worry and send someone to find me.

The stream was cold but I forced myself in, wading to the center where I was able to stand but it was deep enough to swim. The water lapped quietly against the banks with a soft *fwap, fwap.* I stood, shivering, and listened to so much animal activity in the underbrush I wondered if I'd ever be able to sleep in the tent. But I was too nervous to sleep.

I held my breath and went under. No sight. Muffled bubbles and groaning brook, no animal scratchings or tiny footfalls, my senses altered for the cold, rapturous instant of fresh water flowing through dirty hair. I stayed under as long as I could and came up with a gasp.

"...wonder if barbarians make the mating like we do."

I knew Lyonel's voice, stilted with that stiff, Gallic accent. He was close. I wiped the water from my eyes and made a frantic search but couldn't find him. I could see the dim outline of my clothes where I'd left them hanging on the branch near the shore.

A splash. The furtive movements in the underbrush had stopped.

"It is an odd question." Lancelot's voice came from further downstream. I didn't know whether to be relieved or more terrified.

"But aha!" said the nearer voice. "Here is a Saxon. I shall ask her."

Lyonel's voice came from between me and my clothes, but I couldn't see him in the dark. I didn't like the idea of returning to camp naked and besides, conditions looked bad for my getaway.

The water moved and I heard Lancelot swim toward me. He emerged from the woods with head and shoulders white against the black murk of the stream. What I had thought was a boulder became Lyonel when he stood, not ten feet from me. The water didn't quite cover all his pubic hair and the triangle of his pelvis glistened wet. "Tell us, Casey," he said, his eyes hot beyond flirting. "How does a Saxon woman, a wizard, mate? Do you have magic to please a man?"

"Of course not," I said, outrage beating my heart as much as fear. "We're all the same."

"Oh? Will you test that tonight?"

Lancelot, still mostly submerged, said, "Cover yourself, cousin. You are rude." When Lyonel did not obey him, he went on. "Perhaps she is not a wizard. She takes well to the water."

My teeth chattered. I glanced past Lyonel's shoulder at my clothes.

"Don't worry, Casey," said Lancelot, "no one will touch you. You are the king's property."

I stared at him, more shocked than afraid.

"You have done service to me and my family. I would not allow even Lyonel to hurt you under any circumstances, except those you and I have discussed."

"Which—?"

"Do you not recall? I must make myself more clear." His voice was calm, sweet. "Pose a danger to my king or my country and I will kill you."

I remembered. By a different stream on a different day, he had threatened something like that.

"Get your clothing."

I stayed in the water.

"Turn away, Lyonel."

The two faced away, Lancelot submerged and Lyonel standing, brashly naked in the frigid stream.

THIRTY

King Arthur knelt at the edge of a circlet of embers outside his tent. Around us, the camp was dark.

"I almost sent Bedwyr to find you."

"I wanted a bath."

"It's cold. Come in under the blanket."

I stooped under the rope. No fancy traveling pavilion for the king; the space was the size of a pup tent, with barely enough room for the two of us. King Arthur crawled in behind me.

"Here, face this way."

Clumsy, I scooted and bumped. It was impossible to lie next to the king without touching him, though I tried. With Sagramore's cloak to cover me I finally squirmed to face the fire, lying on my stomach.

King Arthur rose on his elbows. "Do not stray again without informing me. It's your duty to stay close and keep me safe."

"Yes, Sire. I'm sorry."

He picked dried leaves from the ground and tossed them out of the tent into the fire, sending up sparks. "You seem to like bathing. Is it popular in the future?"

"Where I come from it is, Sire."

He faced me squarely, sizing me up. "Are you truly from the future, Casey?"

I'd been at Cadebir three weeks and already Los Angeles seemed not future but past. I pictured traffic backed up in the Cahuenga Pass along the Hollywood Freeway, jets taking off from LAX over the Pacific Ocean, and my iPod, for which I'd never downloaded a note of music, hidden amidst the detritus of my purse on a soft bed in a cozy B&B in an English village. "All my memories before you are of someplace different," I said. "It's the future. I'm pretty sure."

"It must be fantastic."

"It's...busy."

"What is this land like in the future—my land?"

"Well, I haven't seen much of it. But there are more people, more towns, more roads. It's beautiful, though."

"Peaceful? Prosperous?"

"Yes, Sire."

"Who is king?"

"Uh, it's a democratic government, elected by the people. There's a queen, but she's not really in charge."

"A queen. How modern. And is it still called Britain?"

When I'd said "England," Myrddin had bristled. "Britain. Yes. Or the United Kingdom."

"Oh!" He threw his head back with a short, incredulous laugh. "How many years in the future, did you say?"

"About fifteen hundred."

He shook his head in cheerful disbelief. "I must pray thanks to the gods. 'United Kingdom.' My dream fulfilled." He returned his attention to me. "But your family must be worried about you."

"I don't think so, Sire. They're not expecting to hear from me any time soon."

"You don't live with them?"

"In my time it's common for adults to live on their own."

"No husband, no lover?" His lips formed a slight smile with the word "lover."

An image of Mike and his cheekbones flitted through my brain and was gone. "No one, Sire. I'm my own master."

His eyebrows went up.

"In my time, Sire."

"Woman as master, and Britain with a queen. The future is indeed strange." King Arthur thought on that while he gazed at the fire. "I wish... well. I feel awkward asking."

A rush started near my nose and worked its way down my torso, through my groin and along my legs, not stopping at my feet but turning around and heading up again, shaking me so hard I was afraid King Arthur would see it in the dark.

"You can ask me anything, Sire."

He threw a handful of dust on the embers, dousing a corner of the fire. "I wish to speak of the legend."

I gulped, glad he couldn't see my embarrassed blush. Lying beside him, awkward and speechless, was like living in Hollywood, where stardom was always in reach. I'd never known how to reach for it and I was terrified of what would happen if I did. "I'm sorry I don't remember all the legends in detail, Sire."

"Do you recall anything I've left out, anything I should do that the stories say I did?"

"Well. They say you championed chivalry."

"And that is...?"

"It meant the Knights of the Round Table—your men—were merciful to the enemies they defeated. They treated ladies with respect. They were nice to servants. Slaves, too, maybe."

"Sounds outlandish."

"I guess. But that's what the legend says. And the table was an interesting idea. You and your most trusted men supposedly sat at a round table so everyone was equal."

"Hm. Equality for my allies and mercy for enemies. I wonder if you tell me these things because they're true or because you're a Saxon spy?" He smiled, waiting for a comeback.

The fire outside spat a spark that landed close and made me jump. Having King Arthur's smile to myself unnerved me with pleasure. I had to look away.

His voice softened. "No. It's truth you bring, more directly than my 'most trusted men' would dare." He sighed and rolled onto his back. "Perhaps we can build a round table during the winter, after we fight."

He lay quiet for a time. I watched the flames die, and he was still awake.

"Whom do the legends say are my most trusted men?"

He needed to know that, maybe more than anything else the legends had to say. I pictured the large print of my storybook and wished I'd read further on the subject.

"I remember Bedwyr's name, and Sagramore and Kay. I'm guessing that's Caius. Gareth and his brothers, I think. I'm pretty sure. And Galahad."

"And Lancelot?" He rolled onto his side, bringing his face within inches of mine.

"He's loyal to you, Sire, in all ways but one."

"Thank you. You've been discreet." The wrinkles at the corners of his eyes came as much from worry as from years. "What about Medraut?"

"He sits at the Round Table, too, Sire. But..." I wasn't sure how to phrase it.

He waited. The honor of his trust inflated me. It was my knowledge that made me valuable, not some imaginary magic I wielded.

"Sire, the legends say Medraut is your downfall. He must never have proof of Guinevere and Lancelot's affair."

"I told you never to speak of that."

"And I haven't, Sire."

"Not even to me."

"But Sire, your life depends—"

"I'll not hear it even whispered. There is no proof."

I hung my head. Why didn't he have the lovers arrested, or banish them? As soon as I thought the question I knew the answer: because he loved them, because of his pride, and because if his allies knew his wife was unfaithful it would damage his PR and diminish his power. He was a king, but his position was not unassailable.

He heaved the kind of sigh you heave when you feel cornered into explaining. "I can force them not to see each other," he said, staring into the fire. "I cannot force them not to love each other."

The pang in his voice crumpled my heart. At the same time it made me bold. I believed I understood him. This was why he'd brought me along, why he'd tented with me, why I'd braved the woods and Lancelot's unruly cousin for a bath.

He allowed me to stroke his hand. His skin was leather-tanned and rough.

"I am your property," I said.

His breathing changed, deepened.

"We don't do that where I come from," I continued, "—I mean, people don't own people." Too shy to face him I watched in firelight while my fingers moved across his skin. "But I like you. So if you want to... mate—"

He stopped my hand with his. "Casey. You're my wizard, not my woman."

I looked up to see his amused but compassionate eyes. "Being king does not privilege me. Quite the opposite, it restricts me. I must be better than the others."

"I'm sorry. I misunderstood." Feeling patronized, I blinked away tears of embarrassment and stared down as though my cloak were the most riveting thing in the tent.

"I'm sorry as well. I haven't had so tempting an offer in a long while." With that mixed message he released my hand, pulled his cloak up to his square, stubbled chin, and turned his back to me.

The sensual warmth that had pulsed up and down my legs was

replaced by a rush of angry adrenaline. What sane man turns down sex? No man I knew. Why did the king flirt with me if he didn't want me? It's not like I was in love with him. He was a sexist, for one thing, and his face was too square for my taste. "Being king doesn't privilege me." What an evasion, what bullshit. He was privileged enough to toy with me.

I huddled in my cloak and turned away.

I had never been so insulted in my life.

He was right.

He was right to turn me down.

With Lancelot and Lyonel out there in the night, maybe even listening to our conversation, he had to be prudent. And worse, Medraut, who, at least according to legend, would prove lethal to King Arthur if he got hold of the least bit of dangerous information.

But even if there were no danger of discovery, King Arthur wouldn't have made love to me. He would not cheat on his wife. He was righteous, virtuous, a man of his time. There was nothing wrong with King Arthur.

There was something wrong with me.

PETREA BURCHARD

THIRTY ONE

I awoke in darkness to the clank of metal upon metal. Arthur was gone. I peeked out of the tent to see warriors donning chain mail in the blue light of pre-dawn.

Wrapping Sagramore's cloak around me, I shuffled to the supply wagon. Bedwyr saw me coming. "Didn't bring your magic hauberk?"

I'd left the chain mail sweater folded neatly on top of my cargo pants beneath the bench in my hut. "I guess I didn't think of it."

"I'll see what I've got." He dug around in the wagon and came up with a small pile of steel that turned out to be a shirt of mail, probably made for a boy. He raised it over my head, and I held my arms up while he dressed me like a little kid. The mail weighed so much it forced my arms to my sides and it was a chore to lift them.

"I suspect you'll need your arms," said Bedwyr.

"I'd better go without chain mail."

"Try a helmet." He offered me one. My breathing echoed inside it, muffling other sounds. When I turned my head I lost full range of vision. I would need years of training, like the soldiers had, to feel anything but claustrophobic inside that little prison.

I returned the helmet to Bedwyr. "Thanks, but I'll need all my senses for the king's use."

He frowned. "Magic must suffice then," he said, with a solemn pat on my head.

We knew east by where the sun punctured the forest canopy. Keeping the light ahead of us we rode on, with but one incident: Medraut and Pawly, who seemed never to do anything separately, somehow became disengaged from the group.

"We do not need them," Lancelot told Arthur.

"I'll have him where I can see him," was Arthur's terse reply.

Assuming Medraut couldn't have gotten far, the king dispatched men in pairs to search in four directions. The rest of us waited an agitated hour, staking out a central location in the thick of the forest. I napped against a moss-covered boulder, taking what sleep I could get. There had been almost none for me the night before.

Lancelot and Hew dragged back the strays. Medraut and Pawly looked like a couple of scared runt puppies who'd escaped from the yard and knew they'd been bad. The episode made Medraut even more unpopular than he already was. He and Pawly waited astride their horses with shoulders hunched, as though expecting the whip. But, without asking their excuse, Arthur merely shot Bedwyr a look and we set off again, our pups now trained to stay.

In late afternoon we left the wagons and horses at a rocky area abundant with small caves. I found a strong branch and tied Lucy's reins to it before kissing her nose and begging her to stay put. Dread began to close in on me like a helmet with no breathing holes. I wanted Lucy's reassuring presence beneath me, or at least at my side. Leaving the horses behind meant we were closing in on the enemy. If Arthur thought stirrups would make us "unbeatable," then why leave the horses behind? I knew the answer. It was silence he wanted, in a forest too dense for riders.

When the king ordered his soldiers to "be invisible" my stomach squeezed with guilt. But the men understood the metaphor. From that point we moved more quietly than I would have imagined sixteen people could maneuver through underbrush, wearing chain mail. Arthur grabbed my hand and pulled me with him. For a while we followed the others. Stealth and armor did not slow the warriors' pace. Keeping up with them winded me, though I was unencumbered.

Upon some signal I didn't see, the company fanned out among the trees. The more isolated from the others Arthur and I became, the more my terror grew. Even holding the king's hand didn't reassure me. Arthur was unafraid. His sense of direction certain, his steps light on the ground, he was adept at silence and speed. He was never out of breath, whereas I feared the sheer volume of my panting would broadcast our location.

The late sun deepened to gold. Scattering its filtered beams, we scurried along behind the brush paralleling a path. I was watching Arthur's feet, trying to mirror his steps, when he froze to listen.

The message came in a chirping sound. At first I thought it was a bird, but the repetition was too rhythmic, too precise. Arthur led me down into a crevice where we looked out from behind a fallen log. He pointed upward with his eyes.

A scruffy man sat perched high in a gnarled tree, unaware of us. A Saxon lookout, I guessed. He'd parked himself in the elbow of a branch to put his feet up. The tatters of his pants hung in ragged strips on his legs. His dirty, blond hair fell across his face. None of that seemed to bother him. He hummed, intent on his work. In the fading light I saw the quick gleam of a knife flick. He was carving.

Arthur tugged my arm, pulling me to sit beside him in the crevice. "We'll await the dark," he whispered.

"What'll happen to him? Slave?"

Arthur put his finger to my lips. "No," he mouthed. His eyes glimmered. Nothing of the previous night's bemusement remained. He was on the job and this was his vocation.

At first the only sound was the man's oblivious humming. As darkness grew, an owl joined him. Eventually the hum stopped and became snoring. My fear pounded around inside my chest as though someone had gotten locked in there and was desperate to get out.

The air cooled, heightening the damp forest scent to pungency. Arthur ate the dried meat in his pouch. I tried to eat the rations in my pack but my stomach wouldn't stay still. I could only listen to that infernal owl, the terrifying flapping of wings, the crunch on leaves when an animal came sniffing, the *pound pound pound* of my heart.

After what seemed like hours but couldn't have been, Arthur whispered, "Make ready your powers."

I hung my head. The gesture must have looked to him like concentration. He gave me a moment.

"Ready?"

I nodded. I was not ready.

"Shadow me. You know the rest."

We peered out over the edge of the crevice. The moon was the tiniest bit fatter than the previous night's sliver had been. The Saxon lookout's rhythmic snores filled the forest, adding bass notes to the symphony of owl and trickling stream.

King Arthur whistled.

Fwomp!

The Saxon in the tree jerked forward as though awakened by a sudden thought. His hands opened and he released an object to the air. Moon-flash glinted as his knife tumbled from the tree, landing somewhere in the brambles. The Saxon followed in a forward dive, his body bouncing against the tree trunk, cracking branches on the way down and finally thudding to the ground a few feet in front of us, with a British axe buried in the back of his head.

Hew appeared out of the black night and retrieved his axe, making a soft, crushing sound when he pulled it out of the dead man's skull. Two of Lancelot's men dragged the body into the underbrush to loot it for weapons, while Hew climbed the lookout tree to take the Saxon's place.

This was where I had come in: blood in the forest, revulsion, fear. I was stiff with it.

"No crying," Arthur whispered. He pulled me from the ravine with a jerk.

I followed him from tree to tree, him crouching and creeping, me wiping my eyes and stumbling, wishing I had something to blow my nose on. Twice more I heard the *fwomp!-crack-thud* of a Saxon lookout being removed, to be replaced by one of ours. I dogged Arthur's heels, hoping proximity would keep me safe. But I knew better. The Saxons knew him. They wanted him dead.

I had known the battle was coming but, typically, had put no realistic thought into what "battle" would mean when I was confronted by it. I'd thought only that I'd figure it out when I got there. I'd hide or pretend, as usual. And now I was stumbling through the woods toward doom. I could pretend I had magic but an axe was an axe.

Such thoughts only made it harder to keep up with Arthur, to slide down a slope after him or to crawl behind the same log he crawled behind, to crouch among thorns with him while the air around us hissed with British warriors speeding through the forest.

After hour-long minutes, I followed Arthur up a rise. A bird called. The red-haired boy whose name I kept meaning to ask perched in the black branches above us. All around us, British and Belgae warriors peeked from behind tree trunks and boulders above a fire-lit clearing.

We had surrounded the Saxon camp.

Our victims had no inkling of us. Their fires blazed like beacons and they conversed in full voice, though I didn't understand a word. A slim man stirred a pot over smoking embers. Three others squatted around the fire, their clothes as ruined as those of the lookout. More men stood talking beside a huddle of sagging huts. I counted eight men, no women. More could be in the lean-tos, but not many. We had fifteen strong, well-fed warriors, and me. It was going to be a massacre.

Arthur scoured the camp. He was counting, too, strategizing—noting where the weapons were, judging elevations and low places, casing out the hiding spots, choosing what to use. When he raised his arm and whistled I cowered, furious at myself for not having used my precious time the same way he had.

It was too late. The king donned his helmet and charged into the clearing. With wild shouts, my friends descended on their victims in an avalanche of flashing weapons. I stayed on the rise, digging my fingers into the ground as if to bury myself.

The red-haired boy leaped past me to take on the first Saxon he met. That Saxon may have been a starving straggler but he was also a veteran, and he saw a rookie coming. In a quick motion he pulled off the boy's helmet, tossed it aside and slit the freckled throat.

The nameless boy twirled. I gasped, and tasted his blood on my tongue. He seemed to see me in his last moment, then all knowledge left his face. His legs gave out and he fell, blood pouring from his neck and soaking into the ground.

The killer didn't have time to see me. Two of Lancelot's men immediately set upon him. More interested in victory and revenge than honor, they each stabbed him once in the back and moved on.

The boy's death released me from the panic that had gripped me. Death took seconds. I had to move. I had a job: to protect the king. My eyes watered, making it difficult to see across the clearing. But there was no time for crying and Arthur had ordered me not to. I sought him amid the chaos of fire and fighting, and finally found him crossing swords with a big, unarmored Saxon who was holding his own.

Creeping outside the reach of the clearing's light, I crawled bloody patches into my knees and brought myself to crouch behind the trees nearest the king and his opponent. The enemy staggered. The king was tired, too. Their battle was winding down. One or the other would end it soon.

I would end it. I would throw things at the Saxon. I would distract him. I would protect King Arthur. I would keep my promise, even though my promise had been a lie.

The nearby rocks were too big to lift, much less throw. Sticks wouldn't deter a warrior. I had to be careful. I had to distract the Saxon without distracting the king. I found my opportunity in the campfire. A fallen branch had caught fire, leaving one end cool enough to handle. I crawled to it through the forest floor decay, staying out of the ring of firelight and ducking behind a lean-to.

Arthur and the Saxon moved around each other, stalking. The king came so close to me I could hear his jagged breaths. The Saxon was beyond him, but still in my view. Though wearing no armor he was a younger man, stronger than King Arthur. A couple of weeks of deprivation had not weakened him much. He panted through his nose, glaring at the king, determined and ready. He raised his weapon and began to circle. In seconds the men were clashing swords again.

When the Saxon came close to me I pushed the burning end of the branch toward his feet, dislodging a rodent who ran squeaking. I stiffened, but the fighters carried on. The branch was too heavy to lift so I inched it toward the Saxon's legs, hoping neither warrior would notice. When it scraped the ground at the Saxon's feet, he stepped into the flames and yelped.

Hands covered my eyes and mouth. Someone grabbed me from behind and swept me up over his shoulder like a sack. I struggled but he had my legs in a tight hold. The beating I gave his back didn't deter him. He carried me for several circuitous yards. When he put me down, something like a cloth sack went over my head. Someone held my arms behind my back. I made the beginnings of a noise. A hand stuffed the sack into my mouth.

Frantic whispers. I guessed we were inside one of the huts. They laid their hands on me. I didn't think they would rape me, not yet, not in the midst of battle. But they wanted to tie me down, control me. I kicked and scratched. I tried to shout, and I kept on trying until I finally managed to free my mouth and let out a grunting noise before losing my breath when one of the Saxons threw his crushing weight on top of me.

Then the hut, or something, came clattering down on us. A thump, a moan, another thump and I was swept up again by a single, swift runner who carried me off under his arm like a bundle of laundry.

The sack over my head came away but I was in no position to turn around and see my courier's face. The forest floor blurred beneath us as he ran away from the camp, deep into the woods, with desperate speed. I flailed my legs but to no avail. His grip only tightened and my legs scraped against the trees we passed.

This one was crazy. This one would kill me. His strength was a thousand times that of the others.

He threw me to the ground. I hit the dirt head first, and came up dizzy. But I recognized the slits on his visor. He pulled off his helmet and waved it in the air, his blond curls falling around his shoulders.

"This is your magic?" said Lancelot. "You protect my king with a burning stick while allowing the Saxons to capture you?"

"You saved my life."

"If I had thought they would kill you I would have left you there. But they would have him ransom you and I will not put him through it. You have no such value."

"I'm grateful to you, Lancelot."

He spat. "You are selfish. I do not care for your gratitude. If you survive tonight you must go. Return whence you came."

"I can't."

"Were you banished?"

"Sort of."

"This does not surprise me. Well. I have no sympathy. If you stay in Arthur's lands I will kill you."

"But I'm not your enemy," I said, pushing myself to my feet.

"You know things others do not know."

"Medraut knows—"

"He knows nothing!" Lancelot slammed me against the nearest tree. My shoulder felt like it came apart in his hand but there was no time to think of that. He drew his sword and pointed it at my chin. The whites of his eyes gleamed in the dark. "Arthur will never have his damned proof. That does not worry me. But you knew the name of my son *before* I named him!"

"That's because I'm from the fu—"

A victory shout arose from the Saxon camp, of voices both British and Belgae.

Lancelot shoved me to the ground and jammed his sword into its sheath. "Leave or die," he said, and stomped off into the night.

PETREA BURCHARD

THIRTY TWO

I ran, stumbling, toward the battleground. I couldn't miss it because the forest was on fire.

"Casey!" Arthur called as he helped Agravain carry a body away from the flames and lay it on the ground. "Heal Gareth!" He ran off, but Agravain stayed, kneeling beside his brother.

"A dire wound," said Bedwyr, arriving with clothing and rags to pillow Gareth's unconscious head. "He must be tended quickly. Help me, Agravain."

The two raised Gareth's arms and removed his mail shirt. His blood-soaked tunic had been slashed above his abdomen.

Bedwyr ran off, leaving Agravain to watch while I did my magic.

I guessed I should clean the wound. Men ran past, shouting. Flames crept closer. With Agravain watching I didn't dare take a rag from beneath Gareth's head, so I tore a swatch of cloth from my underdress and began to daub. It wasn't enough, it would not be nearly enough. The cloth was immediately soaked and the wound still bled. I tore off another piece.

The shouting receded but the fire did not. I hoped the soldiers had gone for the horses. The recent rain had soaked the land and I didn't think the whole forest would catch fire, but flames cracked and spat at my back. It wouldn't be wise to move Gareth again.

My tunic was getting shorter. I reached for a rag from Gareth's pillow. Agravain glared. I hesitated, then took it. I was the wizard, damn it. I wished Agravain would say something.

I continued to dab at the wound and the flow finally stopped. Whether it was my doing or not I didn't know.

Our wagons could not travel through the dense forest, so Bedwyr sent Hew back with a stretcher. He and Agravain had obviously moved bodies before; a pair of experts, they laid the stretcher flat and carefully lifted Gareth so I could slide it under him.

We were to meet the others on the road. It wasn't far; the fighting had taken place near where I'd first found the king upon my arrival through the Gap. We had little to guide us but the fire we left behind, the fire that must have ignited the trees around the clearing when a soldier either kicked the campfire or tripped on a stupid branch trick.

When we climbed the rise to the road it was still dark. Our troops approached us from the south, their torches lighting the way. According to Hew, with the exceptions of Gareth and the red-haired boy our casualties had been minor injuries and the men were able to move quickly. They'd carried the boy's body through the woods, loaded the wagons and ridden out onto the road.

King Arthur himself led Lucy by her reins. "Mistress Casey," he said, dismounting and handing the reins to me, "you will attend my kinsmen Gareth and Agravain to Beran Byrig, to heal Gareth with the help of the physician there."

I couldn't go to Beran Byrig. What would I do there? Tell the physician I was Arthur's wizard? Then what? Make up some fake spells? I'd be found out in minutes. I could do nothing for Gareth but dab his sweaty forehead and carry out a real doctor's orders, and I was safer doing that with Myrddin than with anyone else. At least when Myrddin figured out I was of no use he wouldn't kill me. At Beran Byrig I might not have such luck.

Lucy tossed her head, jerking the reins in my hand. My shoulder ached where Lancelot had shoved me against the tree. I followed the king to the wagon where Hew and Agravain waited with Gareth on the stretcher.

"Sire," I said, "as Gareth is your kinsman and his wound is severe, I ask you to give me Myrddin's help."

"Hold that torch up and give us some light, will you?"

Wincing at the jab in my shoulder I moved Lucy's reins to my left hand and pulled the torch from its bracket on the wagon's side with my right. "Two wizards are better than one," I said.

"Beran Byrig is closer," said the king.

Agravain jumped aboard the wagon. King Arthur and Hew lifted Gareth onto the bed and Agravain guided the stretcher into place.

"But Sire, Myrddin's healing is the best there is."

"The trip is arduous for a wounded man. Gareth needs care as soon as possible."

"What about Ynys Witrin?"

"It's farther and the road is not good."

The king helped cover Gareth with blankets. "That's fine. Agravain, you'll want to drive."

"Yes, Sire."

"To horses, then!" The king jogged toward the front of the company, where he'd left Llamrai.

I returned the torch to its bracket. I knew how to sell. I'd been doing it for years. Leading Lucy, I trotted after King Arthur, made him my target audience and sold him my wish like it was a bottle of *Gone!* "Aren't the priestesses known for their healing, Sire? Send us to Ynys Witrin and Gareth will have Myrddin, me and the priestesses to take care of him. Three in one! It can't fail."

The king stopped with his foot in the stirrup. His shoulders sagged. "Why do I argue with the healer who saved Lancelot's wife and baby? Bedwyr—"

"Yes, Sire."

"Send whoever you can spare to ride apace and tell Myrddin to meet Mistress Casey at Ynys Witrin."

I had a hard time climbing aboard Lucy; my shoulder hurt more and more where Lancelot had slammed it.

The two leaders, Lancelot and the king, led their tired but triumphant troops south, away from the woods. I recognized the curve of the route. We must have gone that way the day I was captured, the last time the king's men had been out killing Saxons. I wondered if we'd been fighting in Small Common just then, and if the Saxons we left behind took their final rest where a livery stable would be one day.

I clucked to Lucy to catch up to the wagon where Gareth lay covered in furs, jostling whenever the wheels hit a bump. Agravain drove in his usual silence, staring ahead, avoiding eye contact and conversation.

"Hurt yourself?" Bedwyr reined his horse alongside mine.

I held Lucy's reins with my right hand and kept my throbbing left arm close in front of me. "Yeah. In the battle."

"Priestesses can take care of it if you can't, I expect."

"I expect."

"Could've been worse. You with no armour."

There were some for whom it had been worse. "What was the boy's name?"

Bedwyr kept his eyes on the road. "Crewan. Parents came from the north and stayed. Father died in Arthur's service, too."

"What about his mother?"

"Works the fields. She and her daughters."

Morning dawned for us even as it did not for others, a fresh day with a scent of late summer in it. The forest thinned and soon we rode on open road, the plains widening as the day became new. This time, though they were tired, the men did not seem so wary.

I felt myself warming as the sun rose. When I reached to loosen Sagramore's cape, pain shot up and down my left arm. I suppressed a moan. No one noticed.

Bedwyr tugged on his reins. Though no order was given, the party slowed to a stop. Ahead, King Arthur and Lancelot leaned across the short distance between their horses to confer. The company had stopped at Stonehenge, the Giant's Ring.

Arthur dismounted and led Llamrai to the roadside to graze. He left the horse there and walked slowly up the road, away from his troops toward the Giant's Ring. One at a time the men dismounted. Bedwyr and Sagramore followed the king.

"We will be here for perhaps an hour, no more," Lancelot called out to the ten men who remained with the wagons. "You may rest or go with the king. The time is yours."

I stayed in the saddle. Arthur had reached a place up the road where a bridge of land spanned a wide ditch, leading across to the standing stones. His friends caught up to him and together they crossed the bridge with eyes uplifted. Their heads and torsos moved through the high grass. They were the older men among us. The young ones played dice on the road and peed in the ditches, forgetting, or not caring, that there was a woman present. Some napped in the grass like kids at the edge of boredom. Belgae and British were polite to each other but kept to themselves, uncomfortable with their foreign languages. Lyonel scratched his back against a tree like a big bear. He caught my eye and grinned.

I decided to dismount and go with the king, to walk among the stones as he did. But when I put my weight onto my arms and leg to dismount,

I began to understand what kind of damage Lancelot had done to my shoulder. I wouldn't be able to get down from Lucy's back without help.

"How is the patient, mistress?" Lancelot strode across the road to me.

"Ah. Time to check on him."

"Yes. Check on him."

Aware of Lancelot's scrutiny, I reached down from Lucy's back into the wagon to tug at Gareth's fur blankets and feel his clammy forehead. These were not easy moves to make. The pain in my shoulder had seeped through my back. It crept along my arm.

"He's stable," I said.

"Good. I trust you have not forgotten our exchange last night." The early morning light accentuated the shadows under his eyes.

"I haven't." The words "leave or die" were going to stick with me.

"You may stay until you have healed Gareth. Then you will go." Lancelot glanced at Gareth and frowned. I thought he might say something more, but he turned his back and walked away.

Up the road, King Arthur, Sagramore and Bedwyr paced among the stones, their heads bent. From time to time one of them would stop, pick something up, hold it, speak to it, pause, and throw it.

When the three old friends returned to ride again I was glad to move on. Though it hurt to guide Lucy by the reins, each step got me closer to Myrddin, closer to the priestesses, closer to healing for my unresponsive patient, and closer to help for me.

We came to the tree-lined intersection marked by the stone cross inside its circle, where the road split southeast for Poste Perdu, south for the coast and west for Cadebir. The company halted to let the horses drink in the stream, and Lancelot's men took leave of Arthur's soldiers, shaking hands and saying adieu.

"I would not part with you, Lance," said Arthur, leaning toward Lancelot and making his new saddle creak, "but you have earned your rest." I detected no guile in the king's tone, yet it struck me that he might like to have his wife to himself for a while.

With a quick glance to me, Lancelot said, "I require no rest, Sire."

"You would return with me, then?" I couldn't say if the king was glad about that or not, and I wasn't to know. The two steered their horses away from the group for a private discussion.

While we were stopped I used Gareth's medical needs as an excuse to ask Sagramore to tend to Lucy and help me into Gareth's wagon. Any one of the soldiers could have done a better job of caring for Gareth than I could, but I could no longer hold the reins.

The decision was made. Lancelot would accompany the king to Cadebir and his men would rest at Poste Perdu before returning for the festival of Calan Awst in a week's time. The company split up. Lancelot's men headed southeast, waving goodbye. King Arthur's party, accompanied by Lancelot, turned west for Cadebir. I'd have been glad to see the last of Lyonel, but he remained always at his cousin's side.

Beside me Gareth lay on his back, pale and shivering under the furs. A closer look gave me reason to worry. Gareth's condition appeared more grave than I'd originally thought. I held his hand but he didn't grip mine in return. The others may have thought I was saying spells over him but I was scolding myself. We should have taken him to Beran Byrig. If we didn't get to Ynys Witrin soon my lies could cost him his life. I was lucky they hadn't cost mine, and they might still do so.

By the time Agravain turned our cart north, splitting off from the others to take us to Ynys Witrin, Gareth's forehead was hot to the touch and my left arm felt like it had been torn away from my body.

Agravain was his usual, chatty self.

THIRTY THREE

When our small barge landed on the island's shore I was more than relieved to deliver Gareth into the hands of the priestesses. I drank something delicious, administered by a silent young woman in a muslin robe, then slept.

Deep in the night, Myrddin woke me.

"Bite this."

"What is it?"

"Doesn't matter. Cloth. Bite."

I bit. Before I could ask more questions he slammed my arm up into my shoulder almost as hard as Lancelot had slammed it against the tree. The tears that spewed from my eyes were less from pain than from surprise, yet I gave full voice to my shock.

Myrddin waited for me to finish yelling.

"Someone tore your arm from its socket," he said.

My shoulder ached but the searing part of the pain was gone.

"Did you put it back?"

"Sleep now," said Myrddin, and I did.

A barefoot priestess, her robe the color of a mushroom, stepped in under the eaves of the small hut where I sat. "Vivien sends this," she said, handing me a steaming cup. "Medicine. It's strong."

It would be, coming from Vivien. The high priestess, Vivien was the island's ultimate power. I took the cup with my right hand because my left arm was in a sling. The priestess stepped aside to wait by the door.

Agravain and I sat in chairs, facing each other across a cot. Gareth lay between us, barely conscious and so weak it took all his energy to breathe. Agravain's expression was unreadable, as usual. He had bathed, as I had, and like me he wore a muslin robe much like those of the priestesses. Though he and I had spent most of the last five days together he rarely made eye contact. Now, he watched with interest to see what magic I would exert over the cup.

I glared at the vessel. Gareth's improvement had been slow to nonexistent. I was exhausted of my pretense and anxious for a way to stop it. But the intensity of Agravain's gaze told me this was not the moment. I moved my lips in silent incantation, to whom I didn't know: *Please help Gareth, please take care of him, bring him back to health, save him, please!*

I nodded to Agravain and he lifted his brother's head. Gareth, who looked like Agravain's ghost, took only a tiny sip of the medicine. Agravain laid Gareth back on the pillows. He folded his strong hands in his lap to wait for the next time they might be of use.

Gareth's injury had turned out to be a hole, the size of my fist, above his abdomen. When I finally saw it in daylight I almost fainted, something I thought only happened in old movies. Myrddin had snapped at me, insisting I collect myself and assist him as he treated it. At first my job had been to bring clean materials and wring the blood out of rags, but later Myrddin had me hold the skin together while he stitched.

"How's the patient?" Myrddin peeked in from the sunny out-of-doors, letting his bass tones curl softly across the room.

"The same," I said.

"Wait for me outside." He'd been chilly toward me since we'd arrived on the island.

Agravain, his patience infinite, remained at his brother's side. "Can I get you anything?" I asked him.

He shook his head. I knew from experience he wouldn't leave Gareth, not even to eat. I'd send him something from the kitchen.

The priestess still waited by the door. Together we stepped out onto the threshold overlooking the broad meadow at the center of the settlement. A flock of grazing sheep took no notice of us.

"Your healing magic is a blessing for Gareth," said Morgan le Fay. She smiled. The crow's feet and square jaw made her Arthur's half-sister. She had handed down her long, slim fingers and high cheekbones to their son Medraut.

"I don't think it's helping."

"You've done well by him," she said. "I can see it strains you." On her the square jaw was as noble as Arthur's, but elegant, too, and the gray eyes were more calm than sad. "I know you're wounded, too," she said, "but Gareth needs all you can give."

"I can only do my best."

"Of course."

I had nothing to offer. I was near the end of my vast store of pretense. The pressure of it tightened the muscles in my neck and shoulders.

Myrddin emerged from the hut, running his fingers through his thin, white hair. "He's resting," he said. "Morgan, may I leave your cousin in your charge? I'd like to walk with Casey while we still have the sun."

He strode away with his usual purpose of step, scattering sheep in his wake. I trotted after him across the grass toward the dominating Tor, leaving behind the huts that circled the meadow's lower edge like brown jewels around a green throat. Above us, on the Tor's terraced flanks, priestesses harvested grain, the fullness of their robes pulled up between their legs and tucked into their belts. Wide-brimmed, cloth hats shaded their necks from the sun. We reached the lowest terrace of the Tor and began to ascend. Myrddin slowed to a stroll, his hands resting comfortably behind his back. I trudged and panted, only one arm free to balance me.

When I caught up to him, Myrddin said, "You are well enough now to tell me what happened to your arm."

"Oh. Well, it was pretty chaotic out there."

"Of course. It was a battle. Did your injury occur while you were protecting Arthur with the magic branch?"

"No."

"Because it appears," Myrddin barreled through my answer, "that either your arm was caught by something and you pulled it harder than I would think possible, or someone powerful was helpful enough to shove it out of the socket *for* you."

I didn't answer right away. We gained height, walking the terraces and circling the Tor above the meadows, looking out over the apple orchard to the small lake beyond. The way continued upward to where the terraces ended and a dirt path began, encircling the conical hill. The incline burned my thighs and made my lungs hungry. Morning walks around the Cadebir perimeter hadn't exactly gotten me into athletic shape. Breathless as I was, from that height I could appreciate the poetry of the eastern plains. Their grasses flowed in waves to the mossy edges of the lake that made Ynys Witrin an island. To the north, more sun-gold hills rose above the wetlands, and when we rounded the Tor's western side the shining opulence of the marshes undulated toward the distant sea.

I had to trust someone.

"Lancelot says I have to leave or die."

"Ah. Where will you go?"

I hadn't expected that. "I was hoping you'd know what to do."

"You're the great wizard from the future. I should think the answer would be clear."

It was clear I had only made things worse for myself at Cadebir. I'd thought it through in my few days on the island: if I told Arthur I had no magic he might have me killed for lying. He'd at least exile me. And if he knew Lancelot had threatened me it could jeopardize their alliance, so for Arthur's sake I didn't want to tell him. I might find a place among the Saxons if I discovered the spy and allied with him. But I'd have to be a traitor to Arthur to do it. Even if I could stomach that, which I couldn't, I wouldn't be safe with Arthur's enemies. There weren't a lot of options and they were all bad.

I followed Myrddin up a flight of steps that looked like they'd been carved into the hillside in a previous century. They brought us to the top of the Tor. There, a stone wall encircled two small buildings that flanked a blackened hearth scorched by the fires of thousands of years and big enough to barbecue a mammoth.

We sat on the wall and watched over the tapestry of Arthur's world. Below us, hats bobbed along the rows of grain. Sheep floated on the meadow like tiny cotton clouds in a dark green sky. In the orchard, branches quivered, ceding apples to the harvesters' hands. Beyond, the lake's dark waters lapped at the quiet shore. And in the distance, a last glimpse of Cadebir rose above the southern plain before the mist rolled over the water, closing us off from the outside world.

"I'm not a wizard, Myrddin," I said. "But you already know that."

He sighed and put his arm around me. "I understand lying to protect one's self in fear. But you haven't time for it anymore."

I began to cry because he was right on both counts: I was scared and it was too late. I hated to cry. I never had anything to blow my nose on. "Could I stay here?"

"At Ynys?" He patted my sore shoulder gently. "For a time, perhaps. No man but the king enters here without permission from Vivien. But if Lancelot is determined, he'll find a way. You've usurped his position as Arthur's closest friend."

"He's afraid I'll disclose his affair."

"You wouldn't."

"I would never do anything to hurt any of them."

"Except Gareth?"

I sniffed. "I didn't make him worse, did I?"

"There's a perfectly good physician at Beran Byrig. You were mere hours away, yet you insisted that Gareth jolt about in a wagon for an entire day to come here instead. That day was precious time."

Guilt ran through my veins, slowing my blood like lead. "You've done everything you could for him, haven't you?"

"Of course I have. But his condition is grave." He pressed his lips together. "If he dies you could be blamed. Arthur expects great things from you. He knows my limitations, but he doesn't know yours."

I hadn't thought of Gareth. I'd thought only of myself. Maybe Lancelot was right. I had to leave. "I could head south, try to find passage to Gaul." Gareth had been the first person in the Dark Ages to give me a smile. If he died it would be my fault. Of all the people there, he'd be the first to forgive me. "But I don't think I'd make it. And that's just running away."

"There is one other option," said Myrddin. "There is the Gap."

I half-laughed. "It's not possible."

He straightened. "I've made twenty-five batteries."

Twenty-five thousand batteries couldn't do the impossible. Leave or die. Those were my only real choices, and they were what I deserved.

"I've done everything wrong, Myrddin. I wish I could start over."

Myrddin's black eyes flashed with something like a scold. "If you should ever get a chance to start again," he said, "do begin with the truth next time."

THIRTY FOUR

Vivien stood on the topmost rung of the ladder in the dusky light, picking apples with the vigor of a teenager. When I told her I'd like to stay at Ynys Witrin she said I'd have to become a priestess and worship the goddess. I said I'd try.

"We accept no false worshipers," said the elder, eyeing me from where she towered among wizened branches. "You must seek reverence in your heart or the goddess will find you out."

"Okay."

"You will work the fields and orchards as well." She handed her basket down the ladder to me. A full basket of ripe apples weighs about as much as a person.

Vivien climbed to the ground, then lifted the ladder with one hand. "Dance with us tonight in the sacred grove. The young ones will anoint themselves with mandragora. You and I shall not, as we must remain alert for the sake of our charges." She winked. My charge was Gareth. I was on call.

We each took a handle and carried the basket through the orchard toward the kitchen. Gnarled old branches hung heavy and low. There was plenty of work to do on the island. I could learn to pick apples.

Vivien's veined arms swept up to grab at the stars in the treetops. No fabric bound her small breasts. No ribbons tamed the long, wild hair that flowed away from her upturned face in shades of white to ash to slate. The shadow of her slim, strong form floated inside her robe, giving the impression she could bend like a willow one minute and uproot it the next.

The younger priestesses raised their arms, too. Palest moonlight filtered into the grove and dusted their bodies, glinting on the greasy spots between their breasts where they'd rubbed the mandragora ointment. Most had thrown their robes aside because the night was warm. Muslin swayed like ghost faeries in the branches of the surrounding grove.

Their toes digging into earth and leaves, the women danced a pattern among the trees, chanting, "Rigantona, Rigantona, Rigantona..." I followed a beat behind, waving my free arm while my sore one rested in its sling, my chant not exactly earnest, but hopeful. Beside me, Morgan sang to the goddess, letting her head rock from side to side. When I fell out of step I watched her feet to find my way back into the pattern. We moved forward and back, side to side, a simple sway with the chant as we progressed through the grove. I closed my eyes and tried to let the chant overtake me as it had Morgan and the others, but I fell out of step again.

When I opened my eyes I found Vivien watching me, her expression receptive and warm as the embers of the bonfire we'd made on the beach. She knew what I knew: while the priestesses grew more serene in their song, I grew more certain I could only imitate it. I was going through the motions. It would never be otherwise.

Whether or not the goddess Rigantona would find me out was irrelevant. I had found myself out.

An hour later I walked back to the settlement, leaving the priestesses to dance until the mandragora visions subsided. Upon the black lake, the reflection of the waxing moon rocked with the water's gentle undulations.

I picked up a stone and held it. I could pray—for Gareth to get well, for Lancelot to let me stay, for King Arthur to care about me. But no god or goddess could make others do what I wanted them to do.

"Help me know what to do," I whispered to the stone.

I aimed for the moon's reflection and threw. The milky disk split into twenty moons, shivering on the water.

An oil lamp burned in the kitchen. Someone, perhaps a novice, was at work. The rest of the settlement slept. In utter darkness, I crossed the meadow to the huts. Sheep huddled together at the base of the Tor, murmuring in a contented, woolly drift.

A lone figure sat silhouetted in moonlight at the doorway to Gareth's hut.

"Is Gareth sleeping?" I asked Myrddin as I came near.

The old man raised his weary head to gaze past me to the orchard, the Tor, the stars.

"Young Gareth of Orkney is dead."

PETREA BURCHARD

THIRTY FIVE

During the dark hours when I wasn't lying awake on my cot, I paced the dirt floor of my hut. Surrounded by a ring of huts with fifty priestesses snoring in ecstatic oblivion, two grieving men in their sad tossings, and one corpse in irretrievable slumber, I had no one but myself to ask, over and over again: had my selfishness caused Gareth's death? Or would his wound have killed him regardless of my actions?

I'd never know, and the answer didn't matter. Gareth was dead, and I had been so concerned with my own fears that I had made his death more probable. I could rationalize one Saxon death as a necessary accident. I could not rationalize Gareth's, no matter how hard I tried.

I told myself I had no way of knowing if the physician at Beran Byrig was as skilled as Myrddin. But King Arthur had wanted to send Gareth there. That should have been enough for me. I should have trusted him.

My shoulder had been severely injured.

Yes, but I wasn't dying.

Lancelot's threat was real.

Yes, but at Beran Byrig, I'd have been further from Lancelot and perhaps safer.

No. I'd insisted on dragging Gareth to Ynys Witrin because I was afraid I couldn't fake wizardry with the physician at Beran Byrig. I had not insisted on Ynys for the sake of my life, but for the sake of my lie.

Was I willing to spend other people's lives to save my own? How dark would I become before I realized I wasn't worth what I'd spent on myself? Dying terrified me, especially out of time, where I wasn't meant to be. But letting an innocent person die so I could continue lying made a guilty hut to live in, a dirty place not only without baths or tissues, but without light or love or air.

I cried all night. Crying hurt my throat. I wept for Gareth, because he was good and innocent and lost. I hoped, begged and pleaded with Rigantona, or whoever would listen, that it wasn't my fault. But I couldn't let myself off that hook. I cried for myself, which infuriated me because I didn't even know how to weep for Gareth without getting some tears in for me as well.

I must have slept some. When I woke, puffy-eyed and thirsty with the dawn, I knew what I had to do.

"You can go directly west then down the coast," said Myrddin. "I have friends in the south."

The sun had barely risen, tinting the lake mist a soft lavender. Because most of the priestesses were sleeping in, Myrddin, Vivien and I had the wide kitchen almost to ourselves. The few island denizens who hadn't partaken of mandragora ate their breakfasts seated on indigo linen pillows at low, scattered tables.

Myrddin broke off enough bread to feed a Saxon for a week, dropping crumbs so huge they left shadows on the table. "It's an easy ride."

I sipped tea from a clay mug. "You mean travel alone?"

"Mmhmm." His mouth was full.

"I've made the trip many times." Vivien rested her smooth, old cheek on Myrddin's shoulder. More than mere colleagues, I realized. If this woman was to imprison Myrddin in a tree as legend told, clearly he'd be happy about it. "The coast isn't far," she said. "You can see it from the Tor. It's a lovely ride."

Sure, if you're not a fugitive in the wrong century.

"Most of the villages along the coast are friendly," said Myrddin, reaching for a bowl of dark berries and popping several into his mouth.

"That's reassuring," I said. "But I'm going back to Cadebir."

Myrddin stopped eating in order to give full energy to a frown. "You won't survive."

I leaned on my good elbow. "I know I have to leave, but before I go, I'm going to tell Arthur the truth."

"It's a bad idea." He pouted as though the berries had gone sour.

"You said I've become his closest friend."

"And he told you he brooks no lies."

"That's why I have to—"

"Send him a message from Brittany."

"I'm going back with Agravain this morning." My voice was as shaky as my resolve.

"Oh my." Myrddin sighed and rubbed his chin, staining it with berry juice.

Vivien raised a slender finger. "Is Agravain ordinarily a late sleeper?"

"I gave him a sedative," said Myrddin. "Otherwise, I couldn't have moved him from his brother's bedside."

"He's hardly stirred from there since he arrived," said Vivien.

Myrddin reached across the table to place his hand over mine. His black eyes glistened with something like pride. "Casey," he said, "We do not expect rain at the full moon. But if there is lightning I'll meet you, with batteries, at the Giant's Ring."

THIRTY SIX

The first person who'd smiled at me in the Dark Ages wore a death grimace. Gareth's body lay on a low bier in the center of our small barge. I avoided his empty gaze and sat at his feet, swatting persistent flies.

Young priestesses sat posed like warriors at the vessel's flanks, dipping oars in the silent water and occasionally wiping their brows. Rowing a body across the lake wasn't what they'd planned to do on the day of their ritual hangover.

Agravain's mourning was wordless but not silent. He stood at the head of the body and gazed at his brother's face. His lungs pushed forth forceful sighs. The moans he heaved came directly from his broken heart. His tanned brow wrinkled with questions and aggravation. I worried, wondering if his questions would lead him to me.

We made our crossing under an overcast sky. Black water lapped at the barge and the mists closed behind us like a curtain. We arrived on the opposite shore in a fog so thick I'd have thought there was no island at all.

The wagon we'd left there a few days before had been cleaned and prepared by the priestesses, who seemed to do much of their work invisibly. I sat in the rear of the cart with the body rather than ride with Agravain while he drove. I could tell by his unsmiling nod that my choice was his choice as well.

But neither brother was my first choice of traveling companion. Agravain refused to cover the body—a priestess told me this would leave

Gareth's spirit free to rise when it was ready—and during the two hours' ride I couldn't avoid the void of Gareth's blue-green face. Sometimes I could believe for a moment that I wasn't responsible for his death. Then I'd think of Agravain or Lynet and be shocked again by my selfishness.

I wished desperately for magic, and in strange moments I felt as though Gareth would, at any second, smile and make a joke. He was obviously dead, yet even with the evidence before me, death's finality was hard to believe.

I exhausted my good arm fanning flies. I brooded on whatever subjects willed themselves to plague me. Agravain's unreadable back, above me in the front seat, raised constant questions. Did he blame me? Did he blame the Saxon who had wounded his brother? Did he know I had lied? With no one to converse with, my mind chattered away. Arthur had trusted me. I'd judged Lancelot and Guinevere for taking advantage of his trust but I had done the same. Worse. Myrddin had said I was Arthur's closest friend. Poor Arthur, to have such awful friends. I was finally ready to be honest with my friend but I had already botched it. Before me lay my grimacing guilt, and it would not be assuaged simply because I planned to come clean.

Bedwyr waited inside the gate atop the zig-zag path, twisting his blond braids with his big fingers.

"You're wanted in the paddock, Casey," he said, peering into the cart. Shock widened his eyes when he recognized our cargo. "Good gods." He helped me down then looked to Agravain, blinking. "Lynet's in the workroom, friend."

The two gripped hands, then let go. Agravain drove off toward the hall, the question mark of his back bending low, the cart rocking in the ruts of the path, now that jostling Gareth was no longer a consideration.

"What happened?"

I wanted to tell Arthur first. "He died of his wound."

"Hm." Bedwyr chewed his lip. "More bad news," he said. "There's been another death."

The smith was paying far less attention to his hammer and tongs that morning than to the group of men across the dirt yard behind the barn.

King Arthur stared down over a plump body that lay sprawled

where the paddock fence met the vine-covered fortress wall. Pawly's neck twisted wrongly opposite his torso, his empty eyes facing upward as if to watch the smoke from the forge twist toward the sky.

I leaned against the wall for support. I should have been accustomed to such horrors by then.

"He's been dead since quite early this morning or late last night," said Cai, rising from beside the body and wiping dirt from his knees.

"Poor lad." The bags under King Arthur's eyes made him look like he hadn't slept in the five days since I'd seen him. I had missed him. "Was there a struggle?" he asked.

Cai examined the ground around the body. "I see no evidence of one."

"The killer must have erased his footprints," said Medraut, tugging at his father's arm.

King Arthur jerked his arm away. Medraut backed off.

Cai pretended not to notice. "The vines are undisturbed as well," he said. "Had there been a fight this close to the wall, Pawly might have clutched at them." He paused, his eyes sweeping from the wall to the body and back. "Or so I imagine."

The three of them looked to the wall, searching for a clue. Along the length of it, inside the paddock, thick vines dangled from the copse like a dusty curtain no one had bothered to open for as long as anyone could remember. Behind me, clinging to the growth I blocked from their view, a small piece of torn, white cloth had become caught on a broken vine. Only one person at Cadebir wore white. That person had left this place in a hurry.

"He didn't have a chance to fight," said Medraut.

"How do you know?" King Arthur pounded the fence with his fist. "What's your evidence?"

"His killer lay in wait for him."

"You were here?"

"I was in the copse. Pawly was in the paddock. We were looking for something. But I heard—"

Medraut barely had time to grunt before his father grabbed his shoulders and shoved him against the fence.

"Stop your looking, idiot! You see where it's got you! You had one friend. One! Now you have none."

The king released his son, who fell to the ground like a handful of crumpled refuse. King Arthur stomped to a bench in the shade of the barn and threw himself down beside Bedwyr, who'd been watching the proceedings with hunched shoulders and grim visage. I wondered where Sagramore was.

"Mistress Casey," sighed King Arthur, his head in his hands, "what insight do you bring?"

"None, Sire." I rose from my kneeling position by the wall. With the king in such a temper it was bad form to keep him waiting. "Except I think Caius is right. Pawly must have been attacked from behind and killed pretty fast."

Cai pursed his lips in what for him was his gratified face.

"Then we have a murder," said Arthur. "I wish it were not so. But a man doesn't strangle himself." He sat up and inhaled a deep breath, taking a pause before taking command. "Caius, allow no one to leave the fort. You may have the body removed if your investigation is complete. Go now. I'll watch over him. Mistress Casey," he said, in the same tone he'd used to give orders to Cai, "sit beside me and tell me the news from Ynys Witrin." He gave no orders to Medraut.

Cai took his opportunity and left through the barn. Bedwyr, too, thought it best to depart from the bench at that moment and help Medraut hobble away. The smith returned to pounding at his furnace. Soon, with the exception of the smith, Arthur and I were the only ones to share the paddock with Pawly's desolate body.

I wished Bedwyr would stay. I began to second-guess my resolve, wondering if my purpose in telling Arthur the truth at that moment was to serve him or to serve me. Serving my friends had become my purpose, yet with so little experience at it I wasn't sure what was best.

"Sit. Have you rested well? How is Morgan? Did you like my aunt Vivien?" His questions were clipped commands.

His aunt. I should have known. Cadebir was a small world. "Yes, Sire, very much." My stomach growled. Not hunger. Nerves.

Arthur stared ahead. "I envy you your time there, even your wound. If I'd had such an excuse I could have gone with you. Ynys Witrin is the only peaceful place I know. I'll be buried there one day."

The legend. "Have you heard of Avalon, Sire?"

"No."

He waited, so I spoke. "The legend says you were taken by barge to the Isle of Avalon. You lie beneath it still, to return when Britain needs you again."

He emitted a sharp breath—a shortened, bitter laugh. "How sentimental. It sounds like Ynys. But I won't return. That's something a god would do. I'm a man." He continued to gaze ahead and I was free to watch him, to want to ease the worry in his forehead and the sadness in his eyes, to admire how he held the weight of his dying tribe on his shoulders.

"Sire. Gareth is dead."

He blinked. His mouth worked in tiny movements. I couldn't know what he felt but I hoped it wasn't anger.

"Nothing you could do, eh?" The gravel tumbled in is throat.

"No, Sire." Which was true.

I meant to tell him then that Gareth might have died because I'd refused to go to Beran Byrig. I was sure it would be the next thing I'd say. But the grief and disappointment that overtook Arthur's face defeated my courage. One blow at a time was enough. Honesty wasn't going to be a simple matter of telling the truth. What if the truth didn't serve the king? What if it meant more anguish for him? When would the things I wanted to say be the things he needed to hear?

We remained on the bench with a space of quiet between us, a quiet punctuated only by the blacksmith's hammer, until Cai and his helpers returned carrying a stretcher and muttering about logistics. I silently thanked Cai for having the respect to bring the priest. Even simple, squirmy Pawly deserved a blessing.

Arthur left when Cai's men came. I stayed to think things through. I had long suspected Guin and Lance met for their trysts somewhere in the barn, taking romance where they could get it even if that meant making love on a pile of straw amid the smells of animal and human industry. Apparently Medraut suspected something similar—not in the barn, but near it. This I guessed because he'd been searching the copse outside the wall when Pawly was killed. I also guessed the killer had seen Pawly get too close to the lovers' hiding place.

Medraut had heard something. He must have hurried around through the gate and arrived at the paddock too late to save Pawly, but not too late to interrupt the murderer. Otherwise why would the killer have left the body in the open, so easy to find?

Had Medraut and Pawly found the lovers' hiding place without realizing it? From my seat on the bench I searched the paddock's wide space of black earth muddled by hooves and muddied by rain. Beyond the smithy to my right, the ground opened to the southeast corner of the pasture. In the opposite direction, a log fence separated the paddock from the main path and the northeast gate, with its guard shack and potential witnesses. Directly behind me, the barn might have held a hiding place. But Medraut and Pawly didn't think so, and they'd gotten close.

I saw nothing but dirt, wall and vines.

Maybe the trysting place was beyond the wall. I'd seen the lovers enter the copse weeks before, when Myrddin had toured me around the hilltop that early day at Cadebir. But Medraut had been searching there, and he wasn't the murder victim.

Maybe the hiding place was between copse and paddock. On the wall. Or in it.

I'd never walked that part of the wall. On our morning walks we climbed down the ladderway at the construction site and walked around the pasture to the gate, never traversing the section behind the barn. The wall was made up of stones and dirt below and the timber walk above. But what if a breach was hiding under that walk, behind those vines? Such a spot lay open on the south wall, where the slaves worked. It was possible.

The one person who would know was Sagramore. The barn and paddock were his domain. Where was he? No one had remarked on his absence, making me wonder if he was a suspect.

But I suspected Lancelot. Lancelot had threatened me. He could as easily have threatened Sagramore, whose domain was the barn and paddock. *Keep the secret or die.*

With that thought I saw Sagramore's perpetual sadness in a new light. Pawly's murder was proof that Lancelot was capable of making good on his word.

I had to find Sagramore.

When Cai and his men carried the body away I went with them. I didn't know what I was going to do with the swatch of white cloth in my pack, but I thought it might come in handy.

THIRTY SEVEN

No fire burned in the workroom fire pit. Laundry and mending lay untouched on the floor, strewn like bodies after a battle. When I backed away from the window the dogs scattered behind me, barking and yipping.

In the kitchen, the workers were as busy as the flies. Carcasses for the evening meal dangled from the ceiling like bloody chandeliers.

"She's with Agravain," said Heulwen, when I asked about Lynet. "They're guarding Gareth's spirit. You won't see her 'til after they've put him in the ground this afternoon."

"Guarding his spirit?" Heulwen frowned as though I'd uttered a non sequitur, then shook her head. "Ah. Sometimes I forget you're a Saxon. It's what we do. Gareth's spirit will not be left alone 'til he's safely in the ground."

"Oh. A good custom. Are Elaine and Guin with them?"

"I suppose the queen's there. Elaine's gone." Heulwen pounded a heap of brown dough, sending clouds of flour into the air. "Her husband thought it best. A woman with a babe's no use 'round here."

I noted her sarcasm. "Where'd she go?"

"The coast. Tintagel." Heulwen flipped the dough. "She and Galahad will be safe there."

Tintagel. The poster I'd seen, so long ago. The luxurious castle Lynet had mentioned. The coast might not be so bad. "It must be a dangerous trip for a lady and a baby."

"She has an escort." Heulwen's strong hands rolled the bread.

"Sagramore will see her safely to the castle." Her cheeks went red.

"Well. At least that went right."

"Aye," said Heulwen, winking. "It's high time something went right for Elaine."

Alone in my hut I combed my hair with my fingers, pulled it back from my temples, and tied it with the ribbon Elaine had given me. I chose the blue tunic, hoping it would set off the color of my eyes. Perhaps there would be a chance to speak to the king that night, when he was full of roasted meat and wine.

When I reached for Lynet's bracelet, I saw on the table a plain, red clay bowl that hadn't been there before. It was just a bowl, but even mundane items were scarce at Cadebir. The queen must have secured it. A gift in exchange for a potion.

At a restaurant in North Hollywood, a certain salad on the menu was said to make a woman fertile. I'd always avoided that salad and ordered the individual pizza instead. I couldn't remember the ingredients, except lettuce.

I scooped up the loose bills and coins I'd left on the table and put them in the bowl.

Myrddin said there was no pregnancy potion. That was the truth I would tell Guinevere.

THIRTY EIGHT

Night poured down on the mead hall like a hard rain. Smoke drifted from the fire pit, seeking escape through the clerestory windows. Finding comfort in their numbers, warlord kings, soldiers of rank, and a few women crowded into the hall to fete Gareth. They would stay late, fortifying themselves against events foreseeable and unforeseeable, with glass after glass of mead.

I steered my trencher out from under a bird that perched in the rafters waiting to swoop at the scraps. Agravain, Lynet, Medraut and Guinevere were late. Perhaps they'd stayed long over the grave. King Arthur had been at the burial, too, yet he managed to be present at his nephew's funeral feast. Lynet and Agravain could be excused in their grief. Medraut might be too humiliated to show up. But it was bad form for the queen not to be prompt. Drinking wine and more wine, the king watched the doors for her, brooding.

I thought his anxiety unnecessary until I considered who else was missing. Where once Lynet had brought order to the masculine chaos of Gareth, Agravain, Medraut and Pawly, nothing but shadows moved along the benches at the empty corner table. Now Hew sat across from Bedwyr, his slim shoulders hunched where Sagramore's broad back had once blocked my view. The tables at the rear, where the Belgic soldiers feasted and drank, were sparsely populated. Fewer than a dozen of Lancelot's men had remained at Cadebir instead of returning to Poste Perdu to await the festival of Calan Awst. Among them sat Lyonel, hulking over his mead.

Myrddin was still at Ynys Witrin. Besides his and Guinevere's, two other chairs at the king's table sat empty. I knew where Elaine had gone. But Lancelot had no reason not to be there.

Before I could trap myself in worries, a murmur arose near the door. I sought Guinevere's white tunic in the shadows. Instead, a man I didn't recognize strode into the hall under the flicker of torchlight, followed by Agravain and Lynet. If the man's confident entry hadn't made him stand out his height would have done so, as would the mud on the heels of his boots and the hem of his black robe. His dark hair hung loose to his shoulders. When he strode down the center aisle toward King Arthur, Lyonel and the other Belgae stood and drew their knives. Arthur's men greeted the stranger warmly and Lyonel's gang sat again, but the mood of the crowd remained wary.

King Arthur stood, opening his arms in welcome. "Forgive my surprise, Gaheris. How could you have known to be here so quickly? Join me and drink to your brother on this sad day."

The resemblance was there, in the dark hair and dark eyes. The stranger was one of the brothers Gareth had bragged about.

Gaheris skirted the fire pit and knelt before his kindred king with a swift motion more insistent than beseeching. "Sire, it's by accident that I've arrived in time for my brother's funeral feast. Only hours sooner I'd have seen him laid in the ground."

"You are welcome in any case," said Arthur. He glanced at Lynet. She looked as though she'd fall into a heap if Agravain were to ease his grip on her. But like a second backbone, the young soldier held her up. "Come," said the king. "Take some food."

"I'm on a different errand, Sire." Gaheris rose, but made no move toward the table. He lowered his eyes from the challenge but his urgency could not obey. "I've brought my army because you have not sent yours. Why have you not responded to my brother Gawain's request?"

The king stiffened. "I've had no word from Gawain."

"He sent a messenger at the last full moon, Sire. Did the man not arrive? Saxons gather in the north. Gawain needs your armies to help to hold them off. He hasn't supplies for a siege. His stores are low after the fires."

Agravain's body straightened to alert.

"No messenger has been here," said King Arthur. "I know of no fires."

No one moved. King Arthur took his seat one muscle at a time, taking short breaths through his nose.

"Sire. Two granaries went up in flames at Beran Byrig last month."

Gaheris spoke more gently, in response to the king's shock. "Gawain sent to you for help, but when he could wait no longer he got a dispatch to me at Essa. I'm only stopping on my way."

Agravain screwed up his nose like he smelled something rotten. Something about the story seemed wrong to me, too.

"Sire—" said Agravain.

"I've caught them!"

Agravain whirled around to see who had shouted.

Medraut charged into the hall. "I've caught them in the immoral act!"

Benches toppled at the back of the room, setting the dogs to barking. A torch clattered from the wall and someone stomped out the fire. Medraut shoved his way toward the front of the hall, pushing people aside. Half a dozen soldiers followed him, hanging their heads and shuffling their feet. They herded two glassy-eyed prisoners. Guinevere and Lancelot were leashed like dogs, with leather collars around their necks and hands tied behind their backs. They stared at the floor like criminals, which was what they were.

The king shot from his chair, overturning it. "Seize him!" Every soldier in the hall rose to his feet if he wasn't standing already. I stood, too, instinctively wanting to reach out for Guinevere. One by one, King Arthur's men drew their weapons. Outnumbered as they were, Lancelot's warriors drew as well, ready to fight. Lyonel puffed out his chest, daring someone, anyone, to start it. No one knew whom to seize until the king said, "Seize my son!"

Bedwyr was close enough to grab Medraut's arms and strong enough to hold on. Medraut wriggled and cried out his innocence. "What's to hold me for? I've brought the traitors before you!"

"Peace!" said the king. "Put away your weapons, all of you!" He waited for his order to be followed. No one wanted to be first. It was a standoff until Gaheris sheathed his knife with a flourish. Agravain followed, Lynet still shielded behind him. Then the others quickly put up their weapons. Lyonel held out until last, finally stowing his blade with ostentatious deliberation.

"Now," said King Arthur, "We shall rule with law, not swords." All eyes turned to the king when he shouted, "Medraut! I accuse you of the murder of Pawly. You used your friend as bait to trap these innocents and when that failed, you killed him."

"These are no innocents, father." Medraut writhed in Bedwyr's clutches, more to express himself than to attempt freedom. He pointed his chin accusingly at Guinevere and Lancelot. "They are lovers. I caught them together. Lancelot killed Pawly to prevent him from discovering their hiding place. Who else is strong enough to kill a man with his bare hands? When I suspected he and the queen were together—on Gareth's funeral day of all days, Sire!—I took these soldiers with me to protect my life. They're witnesses to the lovers' treason."

Lancelot's shirt hung open, an apparent admittance of guilt. Guinevere's white underdress was torn at the hem where I knew it would be. Surrounded, the two of them stared at the floor.

No one said a word. A servant girl bit her lip to stop tears. A soldier hung his head and sighed. Lancelot and Guinevere had lied to them all.

"Proof," King Arthur demanded.

"If the testimony of these witnesses and your own son is not enough," Medraut sniffled, "ask your friend Mistress Casey for proof. I saw her take it from the barnyard and put it in her pack."

Everyone inched forward.

I hadn't made a plan for the scrap of white cloth. I thought no one had seen me pluck it from the vines. I thought its destiny would be my choice. I figured I'd show it to the king when I finally got to tell him everything. Or I'd give it to Lancelot, to prove I meant him no harm. Or I wouldn't show it to anyone.

Arthur turned to me, his expression unreadable. "Reveal it." Low flame and shadow flickered across his eyes.

I could not have moved more slowly had both my arms been restricted by slings. I touched the zipper on my pack. Fearing magic, a few people stepped back. I wished their fears were true. If only I could pull a rabbit from the pack, or a dove, or a magic wand, anything but a scrap of white cloth.

Watching Arthur, I unzipped the pack slowly, to give him time to change his mind. I thought I discerned the tiniest nod.

He wanted me to show it.

I extracted the scrap and raised it high. The evidence that damned the queen dangled before the crowd like a bone held up to tempt a pack of hungry dogs.

The low flame in Arthur's eyes flared, and he turned away.

"Ha!" said Medraut. But his defiance fell like a thud in the silent hall.

Guinevere blinked and would not look at me. Lynet moaned, burying her head in Agravain's chest. I wanted to put the scrap away and pretend it didn't exist, had never existed. Agravain, his cheek against Lynet's hair, seemed to be thinking about something else entirely.

Everyone else stared at the white scrap except Lyonel. Lyonel watched me. His mocking smile disturbed me, but most unsettling was the way he gazed at me with carnal eyes while gripping his throat and pretending to strangle himself.

"Sire." Agravain broke the silence. "Ask Medraut why he didn't tell us about the fires at Beran Byrig."

I tore my attention from Lyonel as Caius stepped forward and took the scrap from my hand. Agravain had hit on what was wrong with Gaheris's story.

Medraut ceased his squirming. "Why ask me?"

"Be silent, both of you," said the king. "We must deal with the prisoners first."

"If you please, Sire, it may be relevant," I said. "The morning after I got to Poste Perdu, I overheard Medraut at the gate. He told Gareth and Agravain he'd just come from Beran Byrig."

Agravain looked at me as though seeing me for the first time. "Yes. Mistress Casey could have heard. Medraut said the granaries were full. If he'd been at Beran Byrig he'd have known of the fires."

"They lie," said Medraut. "I never said I was at Beran Byrig. I haven't been there in months."

"If you were not at Beran Byrig," asked King Arthur, "where were you?"

"He was with the Saxons." Agravain faced the king squarely, standing beside his big brother Gaheris. The two of them, their dark eyes gleaming with earnest fire, made a formidable pair. For the first time I noticed how tall Agravain was. "Medraut is your spy," he said simply.

"I am no spy!" shouted Medraut, his anguish clear but not convincing.

"Someone led the Saxons to us in the forest last month near the Giant's Ring," said Agravain. "They knew you, and they'd have killed you, Sire, if not for Mistress Casey. The spy is responsible for that, as well as the lives of Tore and Fergus and Dynadan." He picked up steam, his voice deepening and getting louder. "You require proof, Sire. I don't have it in my pouch. But if we were to scour the roadside between Poste Perdu and Beran Byrig, I suspect we'd find the body of the messenger Gawain sent to you. That might be proof enough."

Lynet released Agravain's arm and stood back to look up at him, as surprised as I was at his sudden verbosity. The people began to murmur. The king pushed against the air with both hands, as if to soothe the pressure in the room by patting it. "I'll send a search party."

Agravain gritted his teeth against his anger, but it came out fast and hard anyway. "How much more proof do you need, Sire? You have two witnesses to Medraut's lie about the fires. The third is dead of a wound got in a battle we would not have fought but for Medraut's treachery! Even then, he and Pawly became 'lost' in the woods trying to find their allies and warn them we were coming. Those allies killed the boy Crewan and our brother Gareth!"

Agravain's chest heaved. It was the most anyone had ever heard him say. Awed by his monologue, the soldiers were slow to react when he leaped atop a bench, dove across a table and locked his hands around Medraut's throat shouting, "Murderer!"

Bench and table overturned, sending to the floor not only diners, but all those crowded around Medraut. Someone rushed in front of me— Caius—and leapt across the king's table, knocking it over. Below the table Lynet, bereft of her usual pluck, was being buffeted about by charging soldiers and screaming servants. Everyone had something to shout and no one was heard, which made everyone shout louder. Even the dogs growled and yapped from their corners, their tails between their legs.

I clawed my way down the steps, dodging elbows and sword hilts, to retrieve Lynet before chaos engulfed her. A panicked servant bumped my injured arm as he ran by, forcing me to stop and wait for the pain to subside.

Lynet allowed me to usher her up the steps behind Caius, who had snatched Guinevere from the bedlam. I led Lynet to kneel with me behind the overturned main table while Cai moved Guin further off. Lynet covered her ears against the shouting and clack of swords, but I couldn't do the same; I had only one free hand and I needed it for holding onto her.

Bedwyr had lost his hold on Medraut. The younger man wrestled himself free of the mass of bodies and benches to escape Agravain. Lyonel and his cohorts took advantage of the confusion to fight their way to Lancelot, and Medraut saw his chance; he leapt sideways to join the small, oncoming army of Lancelot's men. They slashed and hacked their way toward Lancelot, spattering blood in their wake. Though a few of Arthur's men tried to stop them, most were still grappling under the furniture.

I had read this. It had happened before, would happen again, had always happened in legends and in books. I was witness to the inevitable in real lives, real hearts, real screams and blood. I watched, mesmerized, as Lyonel sliced Lancelot's ties and thrust the hilt of a sword into his cousin's hands. Free and armed, Lancelot had little trouble chopping his way to the exit, where he shielded himself behind a support post and surveyed the battle. Light from burning torches on the wall glinted off the sweat on his hair and skin. Breathing heavily, he took a precious second to search across the sea of clashing swords until he found her.

Cai had moved Guinevere to the door near the king's quarters, as far from her lover as she could be and still be in the room. With a hundred men between them, Lancelot had no hope of rescuing her. The realization swept across their faces. Restricted by her bonds, Guinevere reached out to Lancelot with her eyes. She sent not fear to him but love and forgiveness. And Lancelot accepted.

I knew the legend. They didn't. Things were about to get worse for them. They had given everything for love. What would I give everything for?

Lyonel touched Lancelot's arm. After one more longing look at Guinevere, Lancelot followed his cousin out the door. Cai whisked Guinevere out the back.

The fighting spilled out into the night and the melee moved off toward the barracks. Lynet and I listened for what seemed like a long time. Horses came and went. Inside the hall, we heard the moans of the wounded. Some began to pick themselves up off the floor. The hall smelled of bodies, blood, snuffed torches and spilled venison stew. A few timid servants crept in from the kitchen to survey the damage. Arthur had long since disappeared, whether in the fighting or elsewhere, I didn't know.

Lynet yanked her arm from my hold. She stood and staggered to the steps, bracing herself with a pale hand.

"Let me help you," I said.

"I don't need your help." She meant it to sting. It did.

"It's not safe out there."

"I'm going to help the wounded," she snapped. "Are you? Or do you lack the power to so much as clean a wound?" Disgusted, she tottered down the steps to navigate through the shambles of the hall, carefully choosing her steps over capsized benches and shattered mugs, a tired nurse picking her way across the battlefield.

THIRTY NINE

My friends and I had beaten a path from the promontory down the slope to the wall, but the route was invisible in the dark. The ladderway we usually climbed to start our daily walks had been moved, rendering it useless as a reference point. I picked my way through the grass to the pair of armed guards who stood beneath a smoking torch.

"Your business, mistress?" A soldier I didn't know, missing a few teeth.

"I'd like to speak to the queen."

He and his cohort exchanged a look. "Raise your arms."

I obeyed. The second guard, fearing my magic, backed away and spat out the blade of grass he'd been chewing.

The toothless man waved his knife at me with his left hand and cautiously patted my sides with his right. I'd expected scrutiny and had left my fanny pack in my hut, tucked under the bench with Myrddin's knife.

"No tricks."

"I only want to comfort her."

Guin must have heard me. She waited beneath the oubliette's iron cover by the tiny opening, where she could receive fragments of sound and light. "Casey," she whispered as I knelt beside the little, black hole. "No one else will come. How is Arthur?"

The guards could probably hear me, but I felt the need to whisper, too. "I don't know. I haven't seen him since the fight."

"I've shamed him. I'll burn for treason."

"He won't let that happen."

"He has no choice. It's the law. The trial will be held tomorrow."

"Who can try you? No one's impartial enough."

"Cai will find fair judges. And I'll be found guilty. There's...evidence."

"Oh Guin." My chin went into spasms. I must not cry, not while her eyes were dry.

"I want to die. I deserve it."

"No!"

She changed the subject. "How is Lynet?"

I cleared my throat. "Upset, angry, grieving."

"Good. She has her spirit."

"Can I bring you anything?"

"It's not allowed. I won't be here long, thank God. It's awful." She lost her breath for a second. "God's mercy will come soon after the trial."

I dug my nails into the dirt. I wanted to tell her I wouldn't let it happen. But I had learned my lesson about making promises I couldn't keep. "How will you bear it?"

"God will give me what I need to face the fire."

Above us the torch belched smoke. Nearby, the sentries drifted back and forth. Grass swished against their legs. I couldn't imagine a faith strong enough to carry anyone, no matter how devout, through the ordeal of burning alive. I leaned close to the oubliette's small opening, though I couldn't see Guin in the blackness. "I can bring you poison from Myrddin's garden."

"No. One death at the stake is enough."

"Then what can I do?" It came out like a guilty plea, my tears spilling with it.

"Forgive me?"

"Me, forgive you? Oh Guin." She was just a kid who had followed her heart through territory too big for it to navigate. I'd behaved as badly as she had—worse—when I should have known better. I wanted to tell her I'd lied about the pregnancy potion, but the purpose would have been to cleanse my soul, not hers. And the scrap of cloth, my terrible mistake in showing it..."You don't need to be forgiven, Guin. But of course. If you want—"

"Then there's nothing else." Belying her words, her index finger rose from the void like a pale crocus to beckon me closer.

I lay on the ground, blocking the oubliette from the guards' view. Guin's finger disappeared then returned. Finger and thumb held her silver ring, the one that matched Arthur's, with the Giant's Ring etched on its surface.

"Give this to Arthur," came her unwavering whisper. "Tell him I'm glad to die for my sin, and I beg him to forgive me in his heart."

"I will." My voice broke. The ring fit tightly on the pinkie of my right hand.

"I know you love him, Casey. Take care of him."

I thought to say I wasn't in love with her husband. I started to promise I wouldn't let her die. But I would make no more promises I couldn't keep. I would tell no more lies.

Instead I held her hand and kissed her fingers, knowing what she and Lancelot had felt an hour earlier in the hall. They'd wondered—no. They had known. That look, this touch, could be their last.

FORTY

As Guinevere had predicted, Caius recruited the most impartial judges he could find. Presiding over the hall from the high table were the allied warlords King Cadwy of Cornwall, King Owain of Corinium Dobunnorum and Marcus of Lindinis, a newly-arrived military chieftain from the near west. They summoned everyone who could give evidence, from the smith who worked the forge behind the barn to the soldiers who had arrested the lovers, to me.

Most of the trestle tables had been dismantled and stacked along the walls. I stood before the judges in the early, gray morning. Guinevere faced them too, standing in the center aisle, forced to listen to witness after witness with no opportunity to sit down. Her tunic had become soiled during the night and I wondered if she'd slept. No redness or puffiness encircled her eyes, no sign of tears streaked her cheeks, but in the bleak overcast her skin was as pale as the white cloth she wore.

King Cadwy wasted no time in his interview of me. "Tell us where you found the cloth," he said in a voice as thin and elderly as he was.

"It was caught among the vines on the paddock wall." I couldn't think of a lie to help Guinevere.

"Why did you take it?"

The truth was I'd taken it because I wanted to protect Guinevere. But admitting that was admitting I knew of the affair, and despite my promise to myself I was still capable of lying. "I thought I should return it to the queen."

"Did you not suspect?"

"I suspected only that the queen had been in the barnyard, perhaps to see a favorite horse."

The judges conferred. Apparently they believed me. Guin and I had only the briefest second to share a burdened glance. Cadwy nodded to Caius, who waited at the end of the king's table. Cai ushered me briskly to the door, where he would call the next witness.

Until then I hadn't noticed King Arthur sitting in the shadows of the furthest corner. The comforting hand on his sagging shoulder belonged to Myrddin, who must have risen before dawn to travel from Ynys Witrin to his master's side. Myrddin's eyes glowed, bright as ever.

Servants gathered outside in the fog, clutching their threadbare shawls against the cold and gossiping in whispers. Above the gate, sentries stopped pacing to share suppositions about the proceedings inside the hall. Ladies and soldiers perched along the wall to have the best vantage when each witness emerged, and, ultimately, the accused. I knew the verdict. I hoped history would prove legend wrong.

In need of distraction, I ventured to the kitchen and to beg Heulwen to give me something to do "besides butchering, if you please." If it wasn't the worst day of her life, she said, that would have made her laugh. Most of the kitchen workers had gone out to join the vigil. Heulwen had given up on keeping them at their work and was glad of my company, if not my help. Up to my good elbow in greens, I sorted and chopped vegetables while Heulwen hacked away at some poor, dead critter, shaking the table each time she struck, and killing it over and over again.

We heard the hall's front door burst open. Heulwen ceased her slashing.

We waited. No further sound came.

"I can't bear it," said Heulwen, wiping her hands on her apron.

I followed her outside. We came alongside the kitchen garden and stopped.

Guinevere floated by in the lifting fog, flanked by half a dozen soldiers who held their heads high, more like somber grooms than prison guards. In her isolation Guin seemed to see nothing. But with her concentration forced on each inevitable step, her pace took on a measured grandeur, her skin a hint of the sky's blue.

Captivated like fans at a celebrity sighting, Cadebir's hundreds watched, some in dismayed silence, others whispering and wondering. It was too soon for the trial to be over. The whispers reached us: Guinevere, unable to bear the strain, had confessed. Heulwen buried her face in my shoulder and shook with tears.

Guin and her guards made funereal progress down the slope toward the oubliette where, anything but forgotten, she would await her death.

I leaned against the splintered wall in the cool quiet of the hall. The pounding of hammers and the crew boss's shouts receded into background noise. Cai had wasted no time in directing Rufus to set the slaves to work building a pyre. The exercise yard was the perfect place to burn a queen because it already had a viewing stand.

The hall had been set to rights for the evening meal; now it was empty of diners and servants. Even the dogs had abandoned the place. No torch burned, no rats chittered in the corners.

A sentry blocked my way at the entrance to the king's quarters. "State your business, mistress."

Was it my business to ask the king to pardon his wife? "Tell his majesty Mistress Casey is here to talk truth."

The sentry gave a slight bow and clumped off through the antechamber. Sighing, I sat on the steps to wait. When I considered what I was about to do I felt as much fear as I'd felt the first time I waited outside the king's quarters, chained and caked with mud, not sure whether the next minutes would make me prisoner, slave or corpse.

I couldn't have changed the course of events if I'd tried. I'd had no choice but to show the evidence. Yet I couldn't escape the feeling that Guinevere's plight was my fault. Even if it wasn't, I had to do what I could to save her. Yet I didn't know where to start with King Arthur, and what scared me most was that I had no control over the results.

My life's early confrontations had brought such painful consequences I'd long since avoided such encounters. My last one was when I was about thirteen, and I'd figured out what was wrong with our little family. It wasn't only my mother's cheating that made us unhappy. What set our icy table was the silence. My parents never spoke of infidelity. There was no discussion, no disagreement, no confrontation. No lies, even, because my father never forced my mother to tell them.

One afternoon, with daylight reflecting off the snow outside onto the stacks of books at my father's elbow, I sat across from him in his study, pretending to read. The green blotter under his papers was patterned with rings from a hundred highballs. I became bored with the book in my lap and began to toy with the pencils and pens in the clay mug on his desk. Already awkward with other kids, I was suddenly awkward with my dad, my best friend. Searching for the words I wanted, I tried my youthful best to do the confronting I wanted him to do, by broaching the subject that was the undercurrent of our lives.

"Please make her stop acting like an idiot."

My father closed his book. He downed his scotch, replaced the glass on the blotter and looked at his hands.

"I can't change her."

"King Arthur would defend his family." My dad's hero. Dirty trick.

The muscles churned in his cheeks. "King Arthur didn't have a kid." He stared out the window. "You can defend yourself. Her I don't care about."

"He did so have a kid."

He shook with what I took for anger. Then he fell, because what shook him was not anger at me but at everything else: the lies my mother had not told, the lie he lived and the lie he had just told me.

As a kid I believed our conversation led to his seizure. As an adult I knew better. But since then, I hadn't had the stomach for confrontation.

"His majesty will see you, mistress."

I pulled myself to my feet with the help of the post I'd been leaning against, and followed the guard. Precious little light made it through the single window into the black corners of the tiny antechamber. Hesitating by the faded red curtain, I wondered if I should announce myself.

"Enter." Arthur's voice came from deep within.

I pulled the curtain aside. Arthur brooded at his desk, slumped in his chair. Late afternoon light shone through the tall windows, glinting gray-gold off the Saxon helmet that hung on the wall.

"Sit."

Cavall lay curled on a pillow by the cold fireplace. As I stepped past the dog he sniffed my ankle, dampening my calf with his nose and stamping his approval of my passage. I took one of the chairs facing the desk.

"Do you bring comfort?"

"She asks your forgiveness, Sire."

"I have always forgiven her."

"There must be something you can—"

He raised his hand to halt my speech. "They broke the law."

"You're the king."

He slapped his hand on the desk, raising a cloud of dust. Apparently I wasn't the first to make that protestation. "I am *war* king, *dux bellorum,* not emperor. The law decides."

Cavall stood and shook himself, then circled his pillow and sat again with a sigh. I waited for the dust to settle.

"Is there hope for a judges' reprieve?"

"No." The king rubbed his temples. "Why did you take the evidence, Casey? What was your plan?"

"I didn't have a plan. I just didn't want anyone to see it."

"Then why did you show it?"

"You demanded it, Sire."

He threw his head back and moaned. "Come away from the door." We stood and he took my hand to lead me to the open windows. Outside, dutiful servants lit torches against the twilight. Arthur closed the shutters, then the curtains, cloaking us in darkness. He pulled me near to him, his callused fingers touching my elbow, careful of my sling.

"Did you not understand my signal?" he whispered. "I wanted you to make the cloth disappear."

"But you said never to—"

"I've changed my mind. Save her. If you don't, she burns at dawn."

My stomach rolled. I thought we'd have a day at least for prayers, plans, something. "Won't Lancelot come?"

"He'll be too late. Casey. Friend," he put his lips to my ear so the guard wouldn't hear. "My Guinevere loves her Lancelot. I can't change that. I will give her happiness if I can. I rescind my order. Perform your magic."

"Sire, I—"

"Call me Arthur."

"Arthur." Speaking his name felt like breathing for the first time. "I'm Cassandra."

"Ah. An exotic name for a prophetess." His gray eyes brimmed with trust.

"No. It's just a name." I inhaled deeply and reminded myself the truth would not kill him. What it would do to me I didn't know. "Arthur. I have no magic."

His grip on my elbows tightened, hurting my wounded arm. "Are you ill?"

"No. I've been wanting to tell you, needing to. I never had magic. But I was afraid you'd kill me."

"I might." His smile was gone. "Are you the spy?"

"No, Agravain was right. Medraut is the spy."

"But the protection..."

"You and your men did that, not me."

"Did you not kill the Saxon and save my life?"

"Saving your life was the only good thing I've ever done. But it was an accident."

He released me and fell back hard against the wall. "I could have caged you or killed you. Instead I gave you friendship. You've repaid me with falsehood."

"I'm sorry. It's true I'm from the future. I'm just not a wizard. I lied to save my life."

His laughter surprised me. "You charged into battle unarmed. You risked your life to lie." Mirrored in his incredulous gaze, I saw how strange I looked to him.

"I can't lie anymore," I said, and I meant it. "I'll do anything to save Guinevere. I'll beg the judges. I'll help her escape. I'll ride to Poste Perdu and tell Lancelot to come!"

"You'll die in the attempt." He wasn't laughing anymore.

"I got through the battle in the woods."

"A single traveler will be attacked by bandits. And Medraut is at large."

"But he went with—"

"You think Lancelot will take him in? No. You haven't a chance."

"Let me take Lucy. She's fast."

Arthur pushed away from the wall and strode to the desk. His fingers traced the rounded head of the horned helmet. "Did you lie about the legends?"

"No. I told you what I know."

"Then I will save Britain? I will be victorious?"

I had fudged the part that mattered most to him. History said his people would be defeated by outsiders. Britain would become an Anglo-Saxon country in the end. Angle-land, Myrddin had called it. England.

"Well...for now. But ultimately..."

I didn't have to finish. The knowledge crossed his face like clouds crossing the moon. Britain was already lost.

"Traitor!" He dashed the helmet to the floor and charged. Cavall growled. The few feet between Arthur and me disappeared in a second. As easily as if I were a pebble, he picked me up and threw me across the room. I hit the wall and landed in a heap at the foot of the ladder, with pieces of Guinevere's mirror raining down on me. Arthur loomed over me like a storm. At the last second he controlled his fists, shivering with the lust to beat me. Cavall continued to bark.

"Your majesty?" the guard called from the antechamber.

"Hold!" Arthur crouched over me, saliva seething from the corner of his mouth. "Do the Saxons win?" he growled. "Or do I die and return from Ynys Witrin to save Britain?"

I had resolved to give him the truth. "They win."

His words tumbled over each other. "Mistress Casey, at dawn you will witness as the queen receives her punishment. Then you will stand trial for treason. Guard!"

The soldier rushed in, searching the room with anxious eyes. His chest heaving, Arthur strode to the desk and tossed a look in my direction. "There's your prisoner. Ask Caius where to put her. Do not house her with the queen." He sat, took up a quill and, with fervent strokes, pretended to write.

The guard pulled me to my feet without considering my bandaged arm, which had come loose from the sling. I struggled for footing, stumbling among shards of mirrored glass. The guard dragged me past the king's desk.

I whispered, "I'm sorry, Arthur." My words felt weightless.

Arthur didn't look up. "Call me 'your majesty,'" he said.

FORTY ONE

I landed face first on the cot. While the soldier who'd shoved me swiped the oil lamp from the lopsided table, his partner tore my make-shift curtain from the window, letting in the night. The two made a cursory check of the hut. Their bulk took up most of the room.

"What's this?"

"A bowl of parchment, looks like."

"Written on already."

"Spells."

The soldier dropped the bowl, spilling English coins and bills.

"Get the money." They squatted to pick up the coins. "Won't do her any good where she's going."

The door slammed when they left. I heard pounding as they nailed it shut.

I grabbed a spare tunic from the pile under the bench and hung it on the window. In seconds a fist thrust in from outside, followed by a head. "We've orders to watch you," said the guard. He threw the tunic on the floor. I left it there.

My shoulder throbbed. The guard walked away but soon passed my window again, peering in to make sure I wasn't making magic. He was circling. The camp being a convention of chieftains and officers, Cai had no choice but to jail me in my own quarters. A lot of good it did me.

I sat on the floor by the cot to give them a clear view. Let them watch me. I had nothing left to hide. Truth was my big solution to my problems but I hadn't thought it through. I didn't know what Arthur's reaction would be, but I'd harbored a secret hope that he'd love me for my honesty. If I'd thought about it I might have remembered what century I was in and which king I was talking to. Falsehood might get you somewhere in Hollywood, where life was made of bright lights and scenery. But Arthur lived a reality of dirt and blood and fire. Lies existed there, but they couldn't endure. The Dark Ages were not exactly an enlightened time or they would have called them something else. It was unrealistic, to say the least, to expect King Arthur to say, "Thanks for telling the truth, Casey. I'll let Guin go. She and Lance can have their happy ever after and you and I can be in love. Maybe you'd like to be queen."

What a fool. Arthur didn't love me. And what if he did? Look what good his love had done for his wife. Cadebir was a barbaric place and Arthur was a man of his time. I should have known better than to play tricks on such a man.

It was too late to wish I hadn't lied. And telling Arthur the truth had been the right thing to do. The problem was that now he was going to kill me. He had called me "traitor." I knew what happened to traitors at Cadebir. In Arthur's eyes, death at the stake was fitting punishment. I deserved punishment, but no one deserved that.

A different soldier looked in to check on me. I lowered my eyes so as not to appear defiant. The soldier moved on but in lowering my gaze I had caught sight of my fanny pack under the bench. The guards had missed it in their haste. And I saw something else I hadn't noticed in a while. A small pile, long forgotten: my clothes. Not the tunic and underdress of a Dark Ages wizard but the chain mail sweater and cargo pants of a twenty-first century woman.

They meant to burn me. But I wasn't any use to them dead.

From one end of the bench I could peek out the window and see the path that led through the promontory village. Soldiers huddled by Cai's hut, the knives at their belts flashing in torchlight, their voices an indistinct rumble.

From the other end of the bench, near the door, I could watch people pass behind my hut on their way to the evening meal at the hall, their eyes flitting toward the soldiers, their quick mouths flapping in speculation.

If I squatted by the door I couldn't see out the window at all, which meant unless someone stuck his head all the way in, he couldn't see me.

I lay on the cot, huddled in Sagramore's cloak. From there I counted. The intervals between soldiers were more than thirty seconds but less than a minute. I counted them over and over again. I decided on thirty, to be safe. When I was sure, I waited for a soldier to pass. Then I ran to the bench for tunics and underdresses and took them back to the cot to stow under the cloak with me. On my next trip I grabbed the muslin gown and leggings Lynet had given me when I first arrived.

I bunched the clothes and stuffed them under the cloak at each opportunity. Then I lay still, marking my breath while the next man walked by. I watched through my eyelashes and tried to ignore the pain in my shoulder. The guards didn't look in every time they passed, but I couldn't predict when they would.

Under cover of darkness, between passings of guards, a fake Casey was taking shape on the cot. Soon there wasn't enough room under the cloak for both me and my twin, so I hid by the door when the guard passed. Only once did I lose my concentration and my count. Still at the cot when the soldier came by, I rolled underneath it, clutching my arm and hoping the light from the window couldn't reach there.

I waited as the guard passed, grabbed the bowl from where the soldiers had dropped it, and scooted back to the hidden place by the door. When all was clear I crawled to the cot and put the bowl under the cloak for fake Casey's head. I took a second to appraise my work, silently thanking Guin for procuring the bowl from Heulwen's kitchen. In the dark, it might be enough.

On my next forays I gathered money and credit cards, and even found my passport in the shadowy corners where my things had fallen when the soldier dropped the bowl. I left the visible bits where they lay so as not to arouse suspicion. Back by the door I squatted and removed the sling. I would leave it behind. My arm hurt as much as it had the day Lancelot tore it from its socket, but the sling marked me.

I breathed softly against the pain as I dressed. Modern, synthetic fabrics chafed my skin. My cargo pants felt like tents around my legs. The Rodeo Drive boots I had once thought of as fashion necessities were as comfortable as boards strapped to my feet.

I was ready.

I wished I could leave a note for my friends. I had missed my chance to tell them I loved them. Whether my plan worked or not, I wouldn't return. When they discovered I had escaped or died trying, would Sagramore know how grateful I was for the use of his cloak? Would Bedwyr find the remains of his charred brooch in the ashes and know what his kindness had meant to me? Lynet and Elaine had shared clothes, a ribbon, a bracelet—precious things they'd brought from home. I placed the ribbon and bracelet on the table, next to Drostan's sprig of thyme. Guinevere couldn't know the bowl she'd left in my hut had become Fake Casey's head and, if my plan worked, helped to save us both. Their generosity had changed me. If I succeeded, the evidence of their gifts would be lost.

And Arthur. I would take with me the gifts he gave—lessons to sort out when I had time to think.

They wouldn't know I thanked them. They might not know I loved them, nor would they know I had tried to save them. But that couldn't figure into my plans.

Myrddin's knife would not be found in the rubble. He'd understand why I took it with me.

FORTY TWO

I'd found a use for paper money at Cadebir. With straw picked from the walls for tinder, and coins I found in the corners for ballast, I wrapped a little package with a couple of five-pound notes and tied it together with threads pulled from the sling. From the fanny pack I drew the flint and steel Myrddin had taught me to use.

The flint looked like a plain chip of rock, but it was the right size for my hand. The steel, designed for the purpose, was a flat piece, one half with a thin edge for scraping against the flint and the other fashioned with a curved handle to make it easy to hold. After the next soldier passed I scraped, quick and sure, until I raised a spark. I breathed on it, just a little. The money burned well but it was smoky. That would call attention. I'd have to be quick.

When I scurried to the other side of the window my cargo pants made a synthetic swish. I reminded myself to be careful of that when I was out among the people.

The fire was already burning hot in my hand when the next guard came. I had one chance. I had always been lousy at softball or tennis, or anything where you had to aim a projectile. But I refused to intimidate myself with old truths.

The guard ambled by the window. Fingers almost burning, I gave him enough time to get around to the side of the hut before I threw the flame ball to the left. It rolled past the feet of the soldiers who loitered at Cai's hut. Then it fizzled and disappeared. I waited, but the fire didn't catch. It was just as well. I hadn't thrown it far enough.

I waited too long. The guard came around again, surprising me. I plastered myself against the wall. It was only luck that he didn't see me. When he was gone I darted back to the blind spot by the door. I had enough bills to make two more fireballs. I didn't have a plan B.

I wrapped more bills around coins and straw, tying it with threads. Hurrying made my fingers clumsy. My left hand and arm were already swollen with pain. I couldn't move fast enough.

A commotion outside sped my heart. The sweet smell of smoke burned in my nostrils. Someone ran by the window. I crawled over to dare a peek.

Across the path from Cai's, a smaller hut had caught fire. My fireball had worked after all. People arrived between the huts to watch, filling my view with their backs. Above their heads ran flames as big as men, scampering up the dry thatch like they had a deadline to meet.

I pulled up the hood of my sweater and stuffed the remaining money and credit cards into my pack, zipping it. My only egress was the window. There would be no waiting for the perfect moment. I'd be grateful for an imperfect second when no one glanced my way. I squatted at the end of the bench, ready to spring when my second came. While servants and soldiers pitched in with buckets, women gathered between the huts to chatter and worry. In the excitement, all eyes were on the flames and no one gave a thought to the wizard.

Their shouting covered the thud of my landing, the pound of my heart, and the swish of my pants, as I walked away from the fire.

FORTY THREE

The full moon's beam followed me across the camp like a spotlight across a stage, but thanks to the fire, I had no audience. Servants ran past me on their way to see what the ruckus was about. I recognized faces from the kitchen, but they took no notice of me. Walking with my legs apart to keep from swishing, I took on a masculine gait. Tightening my hood, I hunched my shoulders and settled into a new role: an anonymous, bowlegged man who loped across the camp. I no longer played the part of the king's wizard.

Clouds pestered the moon. I walked alongside the pasture fence, checking over my shoulder. Behind me on the promontory two lines of torches still blazed at the hall door. Shadowy spectators moved back and forth among them, watching the fire from a safe distance. In the huts closer to the fire no lamps burned. Farther away, toward the barracks and the gate, golden light warmed snug windows.

At a moment when the path was clear of stragglers I grabbed my chance to lie on the ground and roll under the pasture fence. Inside I staggered to my feet and held my left arm to my belly. If that arm still worked by the time I finished what I set out to do, I'd be lucky.

The moon was a bother when I wanted to hide but it came in handy when I propped the barn door open a crack to allow in a shaft of light. I found a rope and took it with me when I stepped out to the pasture. Lucy snoozed in the shadow of the barn beside the king's stallion, Llamrai. I approached on bowlegged tiptoes. Arthur's warhorse, alert to enemies, woke in an instant, wild-eyed and snorting, which woke Lucy. But Lucy recognized me as a friend. While Llamrai trotted away to find a safer place to sleep, the mare allowed me to rope her and lead her to the barn.

Lucy's saddle and bridle were easy to find where Sagramore had displayed them. But with my damaged muscles it took a bench, Lucy's willingness, and all my strength to get the saddle onto her back and cinched beneath her belly. The bridle was easier but I was impatient and nervous of discovery, and my fingers still felt a burn from the flaming ball I'd thrown. At last I led Lucy to the barn's back door and peered out across the paddock to the wall. After all the hurry, Lucy and I were forced to wait the interminable time between patrols. Maybe I should have counted heartbeats, but though it pounded insistently, my heart was unreliable. I tried to count seconds, losing count and starting over as my nerves overtook me. I finally guessed the delay between patrols to be perhaps two minutes or more. That was good, but it wasn't perfect: the paddock could be seen from the guard tower at the gate.

And there was one other thing. I wasn't sure there was a way out.

I had only guessed at the existence of a breach in the wall, hidden behind the vines. Its location was supposition on my part, a theory. I believed Lancelot and Guinevere had met there to make love. Even if the breach existed I didn't know exactly where it was, or if it went all the way through from paddock to copse, or if it was big enough for Lucy.

A sentry emerged from the gatehouse and ambled toward the paddock. He stopped for a moment to watch the fire on the promontory. Finally, heaving a sigh, he continued, approaching the copse. I pulled the barn door closed and watched through the tiniest slivered opening. The sentry stopped again, directly across from me, and scanned the paddock and barn. Lucy nuzzled my shoulder. The soldier placed his hand on his sword hilt and moved on.

Just as I'd found no perfect second to leap from the window of my hut, the right time to cross the paddock would never come. The sentry continued his leisurely stroll to the south wall, but at least one man occupied the guard tower at all times, with a view of the paddock. Lucy and I had to hope the night was dark enough, the fire diversion enough.

I pulled the door open bit by bit, stopping when it creaked, waiting, listening, then opening it further and waiting again. At last I led Lucy into the open, remembering to walk bowlegged and wishing Lucy could tiptoe.

I couldn't remember exactly where I'd plucked up the white cloth. The shadow of the wall darkened the vines, making it impossible to see where they'd been disturbed. Hoping to find the opening I punched my fist through the leaves, scraping my knuckles on stone. The woody vines scratched and bloodied my arm, revealing nothing, again and again. I pulled and scraped. Again nothing.

At last my hand found empty air. The vines came away like a curtain, revealing a black abyss with a shaft of gray light about fifteen feet away at the opposite end. I raised my hand to feel the ceiling but couldn't reach it. To test the width of the tunnel I reached out my good arm to touch one wall then, silently cursing the pain, turned to touch the other. Each minute spent working around my injury was a minute of Guinevere's life.

Lucy would fit.

I led her into the darkness, relieved to let the vine curtain fall behind us. We stood still, and I breathed fully for the first time in minutes. Between us and the light a pile of old blankets lay rotting in the damp. In peaceful times the lovers might have found better ways. At Tintagel, which I could only imagine, a romantic nook could be fitted with soft furs and flowers. Cadebir camp was not a palace but a castle, and I had come to know the difference.

I started when a rat scurried across the other end of the lovers' refuge. A month before, a rat would have stopped me. Gripping Lucy's reins, I groped my way forward along the rough wall, fingering dampness and stones. I was grateful for Lucy's trust. One loud neigh and my escape would be my death.

When we stepped out to the fresh air we were hidden by heavy foliage. With no path to follow we crunched through tangled underbrush, our noise covered by shouts on the other side of the wall. A fallen log marked the edge of the copse. I climbed onto it to mount Lucy, throwing myself across her saddle and pulling up to sit. The saddle creaked, but with all the commotion inside the fort, no one heard. The fire must have grown. I regretted the destruction, but huts could be rebuilt.

It was time to march out into the open and onto the zig-zag path. There was no other way down the hill, not for a horse. Noise was our only cover now. I steered Lucy below the well, as far from the gate as possible, and for the sake of quiet started her down at a walk. My back felt like a center of fear, a naked target crying out to be hit.

We completed a full zig and half a zag.

"You there!"

I reined Lucy to a stop and turned toward the guard tower, keeping my hood over my face. Two guards stood silhouetted in torchlight, aiming their spears at me. I was reining with my right hand so I patted my chest with my left as if to say, "Who, me?" The shock of moving that arm staggered me in the saddle.

"Some old drunk from Cadebir village," said one of the guards.

"Don't loiter about, old man," said the other. "Get on home."

I waved weakly. Good. Free to zig and zag, I played the "old drunk" character the guard assigned to me, slumped my shoulders, and kept Lucy to a walk. At last we reached the bottom of the hill where the Roman road lay ahead like a racetrack. But against my instinct to run, I kept Lucy to an easy canter for the mile into town.

I didn't anticipate problems from the camps south of the road. The soldiers there had no jurisdiction and would assume I had right of passage, coming from the fort. The townspeople, gearing up for the festival of Calan Awst, wouldn't inspect travelers too closely. Chimney smoke there told me people were still awake and it was early, a relief because it meant I had time. Still, I had to be cautious.

I hadn't considered what effect Calan Awst would have on the village. Carts full of people lined the roads. Any soldiers with money hung about in town to drink. Each little alcove harbored a camping family or a dice game. Lucy remained calm and determined, taking careful steps along the busy street. I was glad I hadn't traveled to the sixth century on a skittish show horse. If they didn't look closely, to all I passed I resembled nothing more than a farmer on his way home from an errand.

"Good evening, Felix." Two well-dressed gentlemen wobbled drunkenly outside the lamp light of a noisy hut that might have been the pub.

I turned away and pretended not to hear. What if I had to talk to them? I couldn't let them hear my voice or see my face.

"Silly, that's not Felix. His horse isn't nearly that large."

"Beg pardon, friend."

I saluted, keeping my face in shadow. I should have skirted the town altogether, but I didn't know any other road. Lucy plodded on. I knew I mustn't rush, not yet. But the urge for speed snatched at my breath, stiffened my back and clamped my thighs to the saddle. What little time Guinevere had was wasting away.

Lucy felt it, too. She tossed her head as we came to the edge of town. I tugged her reins to hold her back just a bit longer. Finally, the last oil lamps in the last windows glowed softly at our backs. With the road before us, Lucy was ready to run. I reined her in. I, too, had been itching for haste, but I shivered at the eerie sight of moon shadow outlining the lumps of burial mounds across the plains. For a time, adrenaline had given me a fire to light, sentries to hide from, even pain to combat. Ahead was only running. Just me and Lucy in the nowhere, all the way to Poste Perdu.

"Okay, Lucy," I whispered. I clucked to her, tapped her flanks with my heels and gave her full rein.

First she trotted, then cantered. When she realized I wasn't going to hold her back she picked up speed and soon lost herself to running and road. I trusted her enough by then to let her take charge as she had done long ago in that other century, when I'd lost control of her. This time we were both in power.

For the first time since I'd arrived in that darkened world I was under no orders but my own. The land lay wide awake and naked before us and we overtook it, letting the moon light our way. With only a vague comprehension of the landmarks we passed, I sensed rather than saw them fly by in a landscape where I had little history and no future. Wind rushed unchecked across the treeless plain behind us, browbeating the grass and trying to chase us down. Lucy outran it. I laid low and hung onto the reins and saddle with my good hand, giving myself up to speed and hope. We went like that as long as Lucy needed to, then she slowed to an easy canter and I sat up in the saddle.

I had been counting time in breaths and heartbeats. Now I counted hoofbeats, and they couldn't be fast enough. To ask Lucy to run at full speed all the way to Poste Perdu would be too much. Her smooth lope was plenty, and it required little of me. I had what I didn't want: freedom, and time to think.

Rushing toward Lancelot was my last resort. I had no other plan but to tell him he must go to Cadebir and save Guinevere. Upon arrival at Poste Perdu I could send him a note, but he couldn't read it. I could relay a verbal message but I could trust no one to deliver it but myself. I had no choice but to face him.

Unless I changed my mind. I could turn north at the crossroads and steer to the Saxon border, or turn south and head for the coast.

Clouds gathered, no longer just pestering but bullying the moon until they shoved it behind them. Lucy slowed to a trot, then a walk. Without the moon to light our way, the road disappeared twenty feet ahead, and kept on disappearing as we continued our slow pursuit of it. In the distance the plains were a silver carpet upon which legendary characters might tread, but closer around us, all was darkness.

Loneliness had once suited me, but no more. I wanted to counter the emptiness of the plains by chattering to Lucy but thought better of it. If Arthur was right the darkness might be filled with enemies. I would not let them hear a woman's voice.

For as long as the clouds chose not to release the moon, Lucy picked her way slowly. This was good, I told myself. This was fine. Lucy needed to rest and I needed her to last. But when the moon was revealed again I urged her to gallop once more. The cloud-moon fight continued to rage above us, making our pace erratic. Sometimes it forced us to slow down because Lucy couldn't see to run, sometimes it allowed her to surge forward with refreshed power and what I believed was an instinctive understanding of our mission.

Thunder rumbled far away. We had eased into a rhythmic canter when the moon disappeared again and something ran across the road. Lucy neighed and reared. Unprepared, I fell off, landing hard on the stone. That was bad. Worse, Lucy ran.

Whatever had scared her skittered down the muddy embankment. I heard Lucy's hoof beats retreat. Disoriented, I didn't know which direction she'd taken in the dark.

"Lucy!" My voice ran up against emptiness. No hoof beats answered. Lucy was gone. I'd brought her to this place and now she was lost in the wrong century just as I was. I couldn't get to Poste Perdu without her. I waited, but she didn't come back. I heard nothing except the gurgle of a stream.

I didn't bother to get up. Everything hurt. Even my hope was mortally wounded. Lucy had been an integral part, perhaps the main ingredient, of something I hadn't allowed myself to think about until then—my return to the twenty-first century. Though I'd told Myrddin it couldn't happen, the foolish side of me must have believed Lucy was essential to the magic that would take me back. But if there was a way of crossing the Gap, I didn't know it. Myrddin had come up with a list of ingredients he believed had led to my arrival in his time, but I didn't have those things anymore. All I had were impossibility, ignorance and ineptitude. I didn't even have a goddamned tissue when snot burbled out of my nose and tears erupted from my eyes and all I could do was cry.

I sat in the middle of that road and sobbed like a frustrated toddler until the thought of flames at Guinevere's ankles pushed me to my feet. Maybe I'd never get back to where I belonged. Maybe Lancelot would kill me. Maybe I was already dead. But Guinevere didn't have to die.

The water sound came from my right. That gave me direction. If it was the river, I was more than halfway there, but whether it was a lot more or a little, I didn't know. A light far out on the plain might have been a farm. It was too late to find out. The wind found its way to my skin through the adorable links in my chain mail sweater. I cradled my arm to my chest and hobbled on, sniffling, lonely for my soft leather shoes. They'd be ashes by now, along with the rest of Cadebir's gifts.

I should have stayed in Hollywood. At least I knew my way around there. It wasn't Hollywood's fault I'd failed. Hollywood is a place. A place doesn't have intentions or opinions. I was the one who'd arrived clueless and lied my way to the middle. I was the one who had never bothered to do what it took to move beyond so-so to okay.

Something straight ahead startled me—a pale, man-sized thing. The road ran directly to it, where it stood still, a specter in the dark. I stopped and waited for it to make a move. It didn't. I took a step toward it. When it still refused to move I recognized a stone cross inside a circle. The marker at the crossroads. A left turn would take me to Saxon territory. A hard right would take me to the coast. I stopped whimpering and froze. Only one choice lay ahead of me: the southeast curve of the center road.

With a *whump*, something struck me from behind and knocked me, airless, to my knees. I gave in to pain as clumsy hands wrenched my arms to hold them behind me. Someone pressed a blade to my neck.

"Get his pack."

Another man held me. A third fiddled with the pack, apparently unable to figure out the zipper.

"He don't have nothin'." A pock-marked face leered close to mine. He pulled his stringy hair away from his eyes to get a good look at me, then whistled inward. "He's a she."

"Izzat so?" The speaker angled around to share his sour breath. "Let's get her off the road."

"There's no one goin' to come," said the guy behind me, shoving me face forward onto the stone.

He was right. No one would save me.

"We're at the crossroads. Could be a patrol."

"This far? Coward."

"I've seen them."

Someone heavy sat on my buttocks, making a bench of me.

"Shove off her, I want a go!"

"I saw her first."

"Let him at 'er, he'll be quick!" They laughed.

My heart hammered against the road. When they finished, they'd kill me. My squatter stood and his friends helped roll me over. One undid his pants and the others were busy trying to figure out how to get mine off me when he stopped and looked up.

"What? She smell bad?"

"Shut it. I hear something."

"It's the water."

"Shut it!"

They froze. With my head against the road, I heard it. Horses. Not one. Not Lucy. A few. I couldn't guess how many. More than three.

"What did I tell you? A patrol."

"Congratulations, you're bloody right."

"Run or you'll bloody die!"

Their hands left me and they were gone. I rolled to my side and tried to sit up. Whatever patrol was coming, be they Saxons or Britons, I did not want to be wretched in their sight. I wanted to stand and accept my fate.

The horses emerged at a walk from the dark southeast road, the direction toward which I had been heading. There were five of them, all strong, able men, all armed and armored. At their lead was an impressive warrior, a savior or a nightmare. They reined their horses to a stop a few feet from me.

"Mistress Casey," said Lyonel. "I am delighted to see you."

FORTY FOUR

I didn't much like it when Lyonel sent his fellow soldiers galloping across the plains after the highway robbers. Not that I liked the highway robbers, but I was afraid to be alone with Lyonel. Seated in front of him on his horse, enfolded in his powerful arms, I wanted to feel safe, but I would have preferred crawling to Poste Perdu.

Once we'd passed the grove at the crossroads marker, the torches of Poste Perdu flickered into distant view. I tried to gauge that distance and thought it two or three miles at most, and my heart quickened with hope. I would get there in time. But Lyonel's horse walked at an even pace. Because I ached to give Lancelot my message for Guinevere's sake, I dared to ask.

"Lyonel, if you please, may we go faster?"

"My only wish is for your comfort, my lady."

"As fast as you can then, please."

To my surprise, he obeyed. He crushed me to him, which pulverized my arm but was necessary because there was no other seat belt but him. Then he dug his heels into his horse's flanks and we took off at a run.

Without further conversation, we soon arrived at Poste Perdu and entered the same gate through which we'd left with troops barely a month before. The guards, recognizing Lyonel, let us pass. Beyond the gate, stucco buildings cast sagging shadows on streets of dried mud. I was relieved to see people still about. A dice game gathered an audience at the fountain, and men loitered in the alleyways. That meant it was early enough.

Lyonel eased his grip on me. "I will take you to Lancelot. Will that please you, my lady?"

"Thank you, yes. I have an urgent message for him."

"Then we must hurry."

Lyonel clucked the horse to a canter. A run would have been too reckless in the fort's narrow passages. We stopped outside the courtyard of the central building, Lancelot's headquarters. Lyonel leapt down as nimbly as a smaller man might do, and reached up to help me dismount. I had not seen the chivalrous side of him before. Unwavering in propriety, he took my hand, gently, and led me inside. While we waited for the servant boy to fetch the commander, Lyonel found a chair for me, placed it beside the cold fire pit, and helped me to sit. I was completely fooled.

FORTY FIVE

Lancelot stepped in through the archway and stopped. In the flicker of light from the single torch on the wall, his curls glowed with gold and hid his eyes in their shadows. "You seek your death here," he said.

The servant boy peered in behind Lancelot, but ducked out again when he heard that.

Lancelot advanced into the room. With a little help from Lyonel, I surprised myself by falling out of my chair and throwing myself at Lancelot's feet. It took a second to catch my breath. "I've come to tell you—"

"I do not need to hear what you have to say. You force me to carry out my promise." Lancelot waved an arm at Lyonel. "Take her."

Lyonel knelt down, bathing me with hot breath. The scar on his cheek glowed red. He smiled.

I ignored him. "Lancelot. We waste time talking."

"We do. Remove her."

Lyonel lunged. Clamping one huge hand over my mouth, he encircled my waist with the other. Thus burdened, he stood and carried me out the door.

I heard Lancelot call after us, "Return to me when you have finished."

Lyonel did not answer but gripped me tighter. I kicked and struggled. I might as well have been a kitten or a mouse. His grip was so powerful it struck me that Lancelot hadn't been the only one at Cadebir strong enough to kill with his bare hands. It must have been Lyonel who killed poor, awkward Pawly—Lyonel, who now carried me under his arm, not as Lancelot had done in the woods, as though I were a bundle to be moved, but in his own brutal way, as though I were a sack of refuse to be done away with.

Knowing this was his plan, I flailed. Men and women still loitered in the streets but no one tried to help me. No one stopped Lyonel as he carried me down darker and emptier alleys and finally threw me to the cement floor of a forgotten shed.

"You are mine now."

I was. I knew that. He was too strong. I couldn't fight him to save myself. But I had to save Guinevere.

"Lyonel—"

"Be quiet."

"Please give my message to Lancelot."

"No one cares about your message."

He slapped a hand over my mouth and shoved me onto my back. I tried to stand and even got to my knees but he threw me to the floor again, so hard I whirled and landed on my stomach on what felt like a stack of sharp rocks. I tried to push myself up with my good arm, but Lyonel was on my back, clawing at my clothes.

He was heavy. I felt like one of the dilapidated buildings of Poste Perdu had fallen on me and I couldn't crawl out from under his smothering presence. I tried to kick, but I could not shove him off, nor could I roll away or free myself.

His hands crawled up inside my sweater and he growled, his lips on my ear, his breath brown with ale, sour meat and stale time. "I have a message for *you*."

As Lyonel pressed me against the piled rocks, something small and annoying pressed back, jabbing my hipbone. I'd forgotten about the hidden Velcro pocket of my cargo pants. While Lyonel's paws roamed, I inched my good hand under my hip. My fingers recognized the key from the Langhorne B&B, still attached to the plastic flashlight with the *Gone!* lightning logo. I could grasp it, just barely. I held it tight.

With a rough push, Lyonel rolled me onto my back to face him. "Wizard," he said, "I will show you magic."

He grabbed my wrists and pushed my arms against the floor. I aimed the flashlight for his eyes and pressed the button. That little flashlight actually flashed.

Lyonel shouted and fell away. I pressed the button again, gleeful at his fear, terrified in my glee. "Witch!" he hissed, "witch!" He stood, his eyes wide, and backed away until he stumbled into the opposite wall. His eyes never leaving me, he felt his way along the wall until he found the door and ran out.

I sat panting, tears streaming down my face, grateful that in the Dark Ages people believed in sorcery and feared it, and that across the centuries, the magic of that crummy little flashlight had held its spell.

My left arm didn't work anymore, but I could walk. With my right hand, I pushed myself to my feet by bracing against what I had thought were rocks but turned out to be cement bricks.

I stepped out onto the small threshold and waited, allowing my senses to orient. A path lay at my feet. Across it, a high, cement wall rose to meet the night. The full moon shone above, not low in the sky but not straight over my head, either. I'm no navigator but at least I know things rise in the east and set in the west.

Lancelot's headquarters were behind me then, at the fort's center. The gate was behind me, too, south and east. If I turned left, the path would eventually lead me there.

I remembered another gate. One morning, from the floor of my cell, I had watched as Gareth and Agravain greeted Medraut and Pawly there. The latter two had come to Poste Perdu via a road from Beran Byrig. Beyond that, to the north, lay Saxon territory. If I stepped off the threshold and turned right, the path would take me along the wall to the north side of the fort. I could leave.

Lyonel would have killed me like a cat kills a mouse, toying with me, taking his time, for fun. Lancelot would kill me only if he had to. He wouldn't enjoy it. He was cruel only when necessary. I counted on that. Either way, I'd be dead. And if I left, so would Guinevere.

I stepped onto the path and immediately ducked back into the hut when a guard paced toward me, high above on the wall. It wasn't going to be a simple matter of strolling along the road until I found Lancelot's courtyard. So I used my TV training. After the guard passed I crept to the edge of the threshold and stepped down when the coast was clear, then darted behind the next building and crouched low, avoiding windows, as I'd once done in a guest spot on a cop show.

The far reaches of the fort were quiet. Narrow streets and small buildings provided things to hide behind when the occasional pedestrian came my way. The fort's center was busier, with strolling men and women, perhaps on their way home after eating and drinking as they might have done at Cadebir. Every inch of me ached but I waited, knowing each second of hurry was time saved for Guinevere and time lost for me. I hid behind storage barrels, huts, and walls, and once even in a horse trough, until at last, dripping and exhausted, I crawled into Lancelot's dark courtyard. At first I didn't know where I was because I'd entered through a rear archway. But as I crawled around the side of the building and saw Lyonel stride out the door in a spill of light, I saw that I was beneath the overgrown vines and collapsing roof of the veranda.

I ducked back into the shadows.

Lyonel's footsteps receded. I dared another peek. He exited the courtyard and closed the gate behind him. I pulled myself up, sidled to the villa's door, and peered in.

I didn't expect to see Lancelot kneeling on the cold, cement floor in a spill of torchlight. I didn't expect his eyes to be closed or his hands to be folded in prayer. I didn't expect to see tears streaming down his face.

For a second I thought I should not invade his privacy. But my message was more urgent than his prayer.

"Lancelot," I whispered.

His eyes opened, then widened. "You are dead."

"Not yet," I said. "But if I'm to die by your promise I will have my death by your hands."

"Lyonel killed you."

"Did he tell you that? It doesn't matter. You've got to go back to Cadebir. They're going to burn Guinevere."

"I know the penalty. My men prepare for battle—"

"She burns at dawn."

He didn't answer right away, but only gaped at me, wide-eyed, as if I were a ghost. "You lie." He got to his feet.

"I'll go with you, but you have to go now. Arthur says there's nothing he can do."

"So he sends a woman?"

"He didn't send me. I came."

"But you wear his ring."

It was my turn to gape. Guin had asked me to give her ring to Arthur, but I'd forgotten. Tears welled in my eyes. "It's Guinevere's."

"Attendez." Lancelot circled the pit and crossed the empty room to face me, his sheath clanking against his belt as he strode. He lifted my right hand in his warm grip and examined the ring. With my hand in the hand of my killer, suddenly I was not afraid.

As he released my fingers, Lancelot's eyes hardened. He unsheathed his knife and raised it. "Lyonel is my strongest man," he said. "What did you do to him?"

"It was just a trick." No time to explain flashlights.

He appraised me with respect, albeit without fondness. "Magic?"

Though he was reluctant to do so Lancelot would kill me, because I had crossed him and because he had promised. Being anxious to get on with saving Guinevere only increased his anxiety, and mine. He deserved the truth. I breathed, trying and failing to still the pounding of my heart. "I lied to Arthur. I don't have magic."

His brow furrowed as he chewed on that. We faced each other. I still held my hand high, with Guinevere's ring on my little finger. Close enough to stab me, Lancelot held his knife aloft. We had both lied to Arthur. We had both lived inside our lies, and we both knew how bad that felt because we both loved the king.

"But how did you know about Galahad?"

"I read about him, and you. All of you. In a book."

"What book? There is no book."

"I read the book in the future."

He frowned, but he listened.

"I wish I could explain it but I don't understand how it happened. I'm not—"

I stopped for a breath. I would not cry as I faced Lancelot. I wouldn't beg, either, not even for my life. I wanted my dignity, even at that expense. I let my hand fall to my side. "I'm not supposed to be here. I came here from the future. It was an accident. I'm not important there, but I want to go back."

"But that *is* magic," he whispered.

I didn't believe in magic. All the elements of the spell were out of my reach—the car, the strange man who drove it, the lightning, and now Lucy. I had come all that way for something. Maybe it was death. Lost in a past that wasn't mine, I had no place to go where death wouldn't seek me. I could leave by the north gate and find death at the hands of the Saxons. I might escape by the southeast gate, run out onto the plains and find death in the clumsy paws of highway robbers. Or I could accept it at the expert hands of Lancelot.

"Lancelot. The book says you're going to save Guinevere, but you have to hurry."

The firelight flickered. He tapped his knife against his palm and shoved it into the sheath at his belt. "I need soldiers. I do not need you. You are free to go." It meant, "Don't stay." He turned his back, stepped past the fire pit and took the torch from its sconce.

I didn't faint or fall. I continued to breathe. "Lance," I said, wanting to give him one thing more, because honesty had saved me and I was glad to be saved.

He stopped.

"In all of history and legend, only one warrior is more powerful than you are."

"Who is that?" he asked, turning to me.

"Your son, Galahad."

Our eyes locked for a moment's truce, acknowledgement of our common shame and our common goal. Then he dashed out the door, shouting, "To horses!"

Poste Perdu responded with the clamor of metal and a thousand pounding footsteps, all rushing for the gate.

FORTY SIX

The full moon had gone into hiding. Lancelot and his army galloped west to rescue Guinevere. Regardless of speed or my intervention, legend told of their success. But I had learned history wasn't necessarily the same. I knew only that Lancelot had better ride fast, and I had done right to come.

The guards at the north gate ignored me as though I were invisible. A wall torch struggled against the rising wind, spitting sparks at the very power that threatened to snuff it. From the stone archway, the road led out to infinite, lumpen darkness. No light broke the eastern horizon. There was time—time to save Guinevere, at least, if not the Britons. I had time, too. Forever itself lay before me, a tempestuous ocean, empty of boats.

The dirt track led north. I made it about a hundred yards before the rain came. At first it was only a sprinkle and I pulled up my hood. Lightning ahead showed soot-black clouds packing for a rumble in the sky, with the full moon cowering behind them.

My shoulder was past throbbing. Throbbing connotes ebb and flow, up and down, a coming and going of pain. There was no ebb, no going of hurt, only flowing, increasing pain until the only place it could go was numbness.

Heedless of my tiny progress beneath them, the skies at last poured forth. The plains afforded no protection from the abuses the storm chose to throw. At first those were only rain upon rain, cold and repetitive as icy fingernails tap-tapping the Formica counter in a Midwestern winter kitchen. Like the pain in my shoulder there was only build, until wind drove the rain at my face and chest, and I walked against a freezing wall of wet.

I considered no choices. I had made my choice and all others were closed to me. I watched the ground and plodded on. The dirt track soon became mud. It filled my boots with extra weight, sucking obscenely at every step. But a step or a slog made no difference to me. I was going nowhere and I was in no hurry to get there.

In minutes, or hours, the track ended at a road. I hadn't looked up in a long while so when the orderly stones appeared at my feet I stopped, not knowing what to do about them. The choice of left or right was of no matter. I had infinite time to decide so I did not decide.

My father would have been ecstatic to see a real Roman road in such pristine form. As he would have done and as I had not yet had an opportunity to do, I knelt to examine the stones. Wild rain splashed on rock, then, turning tame, let itself be guided into gullies along the road's edges to drain from the surface. It was Roman engineering, at work long after the engineers had gone. Yet the road would be buried under civilization in a few hundred years. Nothing lasts forever, not even stone.

I picked up a gray-white rock. Arthur had an "extra muscle," he called it, to reach back and touch his ancestors. My father existed neither back in time nor forward. There I held him in the Roman stone, across unbridgeable time. I knew in my heart that I could not have saved my father. Nor could my mother have saved him. Only he could have saved himself.

I could not have saved Arthur, either. He had won wars and led armies long before I showed up. I had made too much of myself, taken too much on. I had done Arthur wrong but I had not ruined him; the larger world around him bore that burden regardless of me, even regardless of Arthur. He had asked honesty of me, and there I had failed him. That responsibility I accepted.

I don't know how long I sat hugging the rock to my chest. The rain did not let up but I felt no need to shelter from it. Gradually, dawn glistened on the splashing gullies. Clouds and rain could not disguise day, however sunless. In the west the light would soon break over Cadebir. Even slowed by the storm, Lancelot and his men would be there by now, fighting to save Guinevere. I pushed myself up to stand, watching rain splash into the channels and drain away like memory. The stone in my hand was as heavy as a heart. No road could take me back to repair my mistakes. Some mistakes were not mine to fix. "Bless them," I whispered to the stone. With my good arm, I threw it as far as I could, out onto the plain.

The Giant's Ring loomed there in the downpour, across a bleak meadow. I hadn't seen it in the dark, standing staunch against the storm. My first impression of the stones had been of hulking, downtrodden animals. But in the wind and rain, with no fence to cage them, the stones appeared more like great wizards who chose to congregate there, standing strong together and waiting to welcome me.

I sought the land bridge and found it not far up the road. When our war party had loitered there, King Arthur and his friends had taken their time crossing the bridge, their heads bent in contemplation. Had Arthur reached across the centuries and touched his ancestors then? Had he considered time as he walked among the stones rubbing his square, stubbled chin? If there were a place in the world where reaching back was possible, it was Stonehenge. Could it be a place for reaching forward?

Soaked past cold, my sodden boots sank in the puddles. Water splashed in the ditch below the land bridge. I had no need for hurry. At the end of the bridge I came to a single, giant stone that lay in the grass. It was rough to the touch. Drawing my fingers along its length, I crossed over to hallowed ground.

The standing stones faced each other in pairs, some with a third slab across their tops for a roof, making rocky gazebos in an ethereal park. Like any animal would, I scrambled through the weeds to take shelter beneath the nearest one and sank to the ground, closing my eyes against the shivers that rattled me. Now I could go home.

I had once feared death in the Dark Ages because it meant I would never be born, never be known. Ha! Ridiculous. What others knew of me didn't make me important. It was what I knew of myself that mattered. I had done something worthwhile at last. I had loved my friends. I had given everything for them. They wouldn't know and neither would history. But I knew, and I could rest.

FORTY SEVEN

Something soft nibbled my ear, setting off a pounding in my head, and a tingling static that shook my body. The thing nibbled again and the shaking and pounding stopped. I opened my eyes. I lay, fetal and numb, in a rain-filled puddle. Lucy's big face hovered over me. She nickered sweet and low.

"Lucy." My lips formed her name but my lungs gave no breath to sound.

Lucy nickered again and nudged my thigh with her nose.

"I can't get up." I didn't want to try.

Lucy insisted, nibbling at my legs and snorting. With her saddle still strapped on her back, she was missing half a rein. The other one dragged on the ground, threatening to trip her. She was soaked and muddy but otherwise unscathed.

"You're so beautiful."

Lucy nudged my foot and tossed her head, as if she had something to say.

I still had one good arm. I used it to push myself up to sit, and leaned against the stone. The rain would not stop. My last meal had been the night before. The constant pain exhausted me. I had completed my mission with nowhere to go.

Lucy didn't seem to mind the rain. Together we watched as the wind rose. It threw its weight around and beat down the grass. When thunder shook with the seismic volume of an earthquake, the lightning that followed came so close it blinded me. In its split-second after-light I saw what Lucy was trying to tell me.

Myrddin had been at the Giant's Ring.

Across the circle, atop the stone formations where the tops were as flat as tables, stood a legion of clumsy, clay jars—a little army poised at attention.

Rain at the full moon. Myrddin must have waited for me and finally given up. But he had come.

The stone's surface felt smoother than I expected, but rough enough for gripping. I pulled myself up, stiff with unfolding surrender. Lucy snorted and tossed her head, glad to see me obey her. I led her into the open by her single rein, seeking a boost, stumbling in the weeds to find a stone from which to mount. But even the fallen stones were giants too huge to climb. With thunder and lightning crackling around us, at last I found a smaller stone I could crawl onto. From there I finally managed to throw myself across the wet saddle and pull until I was home on Lucy's back.

I had not wanted to leave Cadebir. I still didn't. But I had to go. One more deep breath filled me with the sorrow and gratitude of a last look around a strange and feral place. I drew Myrddin's knife from my belt. I would be ready when lightning struck.

The sky emitted a growl from its thunderous throat. The growl became a rumble, then a roar. Lucy reared and neighed. When the lightning came it shattered sight into a thousand pieces, like a mirror smashed against a wall. I threw Myrddin's knife at the batteries, thinking not of my bad aim in junior high sports but of my success with a fireball on the promontory. For a second I regretted throwing; if I missed I might yet need Myrddin's knife to protect myself. But if I missed, no weapon would help me.

The little knife flew through the air and hit the batteries at the moment the thunder exploded. Lucy reared again and because I wasn't holding on I fell. I scrambled for her single rein, unable to find it in my chaotic tumble. I couldn't lose Lucy again. I couldn't get home without her and I couldn't be without her in the Dark Ages. She and I were refugees from the same paved roads, the same streetlights, the same comforts, the same smells, the same familiar, inexplicably lost century.

I tripped and fell backward in the high grass. Lucy's big, gray nose loomed above me. A flash of lightning revealed her dangling rein. I reached for it.

FORTY EIGHT

"...shoulder's dislocated rather badly. How're the scans?"

"Normal."

"Lucky."

English. The British kind. One male, one female. Strong smell of antiseptic.

A finger lifted my eyelid. A light beamed directly into my eye. I jerked back.

"Oh, hello!" A white-haired man hovered behind the bright orb, his face mere inches from mine. He clicked off the light and sat back, revealing a dour nurse behind him.

"I'm Dr. Rattish," said the man. "Do you know who you are?"

"Mmm. Yeah."

"Tell me your name." He tucked the flashlight into the pocket of his lab coat.

"Cassandra." My throat was dry, my head hurt and my ears would not stop ringing.

"Do you know where you are?"

"Uh...hospital?"

"Right you are. In hospital at Salisbury. How many fingers?" His dry, wrinkly hand snapped out of the end of his lab coat sleeve like the head of a tortoise.

The fluorescents forced me to squint. "Two."

"Excellent. Now count backwards for me, from ten."

I did, mumbling.

"That's fine. You must not move your left arm and shoulder for now. When the painkiller wears off, ring for the nurse."

The nurse frowned.

"You've a concussion which we shall monitor," said Dr. Rattish, "but your signs are good. We'll keep you tonight for observation and if you're well enough tomorrow, you may go home."

Wherever that was. "What happened?"

"The police are hoping you can tell them. You've gone missing a month. Do you know where you've been?"

I knew. "No."

"Well. You haven't been unconscious for thirty days. That's not possible. If the memory doesn't return, you may want to speak to a psychologist. Oh!" He jabbed his hand into his pocket and pulled out a white business card, which he laid on the tray table beside the bed. "There's a lawyer wants you to ring him. But rest before litigation, if you please."

"Lucy?"

"I'm sure I don't know her. You may telephone your friends tomorrow. Rest now." The last bit he said as the door swung closed behind him, the nurse at his heels.

Next to the business card stood a plastic sippy cup with a straw. Glad I hadn't blurted out some insanity to the doctor ("I went to Camelot!"), I was more thirsty than curious. Water, in its controlled form, was a relief.

Missing a month.

My memory had the purity of reality, but although Arthur had spoken of reaching back through time one doesn't really do that, one only wishes one could. I'd had a concussion, not an experience. An injury, not a memory.

I tried to roll onto my side and became twisted in the sheets, frustrated by the pillow. I ended up on my back as before, with tears draining into my ears.

None of it had happened.

I pushed myself to sitting, a one-armed-struggle, and plucked up the business card. Its embossed, gray lettering said "A. D. Bellorham, Esq." Ambulance-chaser. I flipped the card to the table and missed. The card fell to the floor. With the flipping motion I caught sight of Guinevere's tarnished ring on my little finger, with the shape of Stonehenge etched on its surface.

FORTY NINE

Constable Norman Davies stank of cigarettes. His mud-brown hair was parted in the middle, as was the thick mustache that sheltered most of his mouth like the thatched eaves of an English cottage. I wondered how he smoked under there without igniting himself. Davies ushered me through the hospital door into a morning so bright I had to shield my eyes.

"Lovely after all that rain, innit? It was really chuckin'it down."

The constable's petite, brightly-checkered police car waited conveniently in the circular driveway. I was thankful we didn't have to walk far. Wherever I'd been, not everything had survived the ordeal and I didn't much relish being seen. My fanny pack was no longer black but a faded charcoal color; I carried it bundled in my hand because the threads were gone where Lynet had sewn the belt—if indeed she had sewn it. The pockets of my cargo pants hung open like astonished mouths where I remembered, or imagined, Lynet had repaired them. My bandaged feet would not fit my ravaged, silly boots, so the constable carried the boots and I wore sillier hospital booties. The only thing on me that wasn't ruined was my nice, new sling.

Davies helped me into the front seat. Good. I was not to be caged in the back like a perp on a cop show. The car didn't stink. Obviously Davies didn't smoke in there.

"S'not far. I'll have you there by nine."

I held my hospital discharge papers in my lap. They included myriad instructions: no driving; watch for dizziness, nausea and memory problems; come back in two weeks; sooner if trouble occurred.

The compact leaped forward with a jerk and the papers flew from my lap. We sped out of the parking lot. Davies managed wide avenues and cobbled alleyways with equal expertise. After living out of time for a month the speed was shocking, and Salisbury's streets felt claustrophobic and too smooth. It was my bad luck to be seated on the left side of the car because I couldn't use my left hand to hold onto the door handle. Instead I grabbed the dashboard with my right, grappling with the unsettling but related concepts of returning to the world, possible amnesia and driving on the wrong side of the road.

We merged onto a highway charmingly dubbed "A345," which led north out of town. I felt less closed in, but more disconcerted as we gained highway speed.

Davies pointed to a flat-topped hill. "Old Sarum."

"I should visit while I'm here."

"Should, yes."

I stared ahead and tried to relax. "Dr. Rattish said you have questions."

"Not without your lawyer present, miss."

"I don't have a lawyer."

"Mr. Bellorham's representing you."

The business card, probably still on the floor in my hospital room. "Did I commit a crime?"

"Well, er. We haven't sorted that out."

Davies didn't say any more. That was a good thing. During the half-hour drive to Small Common I had shock, relief, heartache and painkillers to sort through, and conversation was more than I could handle. When we arrived at the southern edge of the village I barely got a glimpse as we flew by the livery stable. Horses leaned their long necks out of its windows, but I didn't see Lucy among them. By the time we rolled onto the gravel drive of the brick B&B with the familiar, sideways lean I was shaken by tarmac and speed, and the constable was tapping the steering wheel, anxious for his next cigarette.

"Ajay's expecting you," he said. "Bellorham will pick you up at noon."

"Have a shower, love. I'll put on some tea." Ajay flashed his fluorescent smile but his shock at the sight of me showed in his eyes. He handed me a clean towel and ushered me up a single flight of stairs, then left me alone. The perfect innkeeper, he had thought to assemble my shopping bags in a tidy room on the same floor as the bathroom. I loved him for it. I ransacked my bags for shower supplies. Then I shuffled down the hall, locked myself in the bathroom and flipped the switch. Light. Just like that.

And a mirror.

The woman looking back at me across the bathroom sink had careless, wavy hair. A few gray hairs gleefully interspersed themselves with brown roots that emerged from fading, dyed blonde. Her suntanned skin stretched taut over freckled cheekbones and she had a dim, yellowed bruise on her forehead that was almost healed. Unplucked eyebrows lifted high over blue eyes, reflecting surprise. Then the corners of those eyes wrinkled in a soft smile of recognition. I liked her.

The bathroom was plain and clean, clean, clean. The walls were painted blue. White lace curtains hung from the sunny window. The white bath mat had been freshly laundered. I stepped around it to avoid getting it dirty.

I turned the shower on as hot as I could stand it and took my toothbrush in with me. Being one-armed, drugged, and with the added difficulty of having to keep the left arm dry was complicated, but I was determined. I remembered King Arthur saying, "You seem to like bathing." I laughed out loud then remembered to stifle the laugh. Then I remembered no one had said it.

It wasn't as though I hadn't washed at all in the last thirty days. I had dangled my feet in the well on many days, and after steeling myself had even splashed my face in its green waters. Myrddin kept rain barrels where I often dipped my hair and, if no one was around, scooped a handful to splash in my armpits. It had been almost a month, but I'd had a decent bath in the workroom behind the kitchen, given by two souls whose kindness I missed. And I had rinsed myself in a dark stream in the woods one night, hopeful of a touch I never knew.

I had almost become accustomed to the filth—almost—but sense memory of clean lay latent in my toes and my teeth. As soap revealed my suntan; as I massaged the goop of suds beneath my breasts and behind my knees; as I scrubbed my scalp with shampoo and rinsed, then lathered again like the label says to do but I had rarely done before; and as I brushed my teeth (Davies and Ajay had been too kind to mention my breath or the mixture of scents emanating from my armpits) I reveled in my return to the real world.

Yet I could not let go of Cadebir.

I had no desire to return to Los Angeles. Cadebir wasn't possible, but I had a hole in me the size of a hill fort. I twisted the ring on my pinkie and wished for home.

What rushed down the drain was merely a month's grime. Time, memory, pain—none of that would wash away. Even if it was crazy, it was part of me. It was mine.

"You were zonked, remember?" Ajay sipped his tea while I spread jam on my scone. "I was so swamped I didn't report you missing 'til the next morning. Sorry. Tourist season." He winced. "Davies was already searching for you by then."

"How did he know?"

"Bellorham."

I set down the scone without biting. "Who is this Bellorham guy?"

"He was driving the car that almost hit you."

"Conflict of interest. He's supposed to be my lawyer."

"He was quite upset. Everyone was."

I threw up my hands—hand.

"It's a tiny village, dearie. More tea?"

"No thanks." I stood to go.

Ajay rested his chin on his hands and gazed at me. "Are you going to tell me where you were all that time?"

"I'd better talk to my lawyer first," I said. I had questions of my own.

Bellorham was due in a few minutes. I gathered my nerve and called my mother from the phone in the hall. She didn't answer.

"It's Evelyn," said her cheerful outgoing message. "You know what to do, so do it."

I took a deep breath.

"Hi Mom. It's Casey. I know, I know, it's not a holiday, but guess what? I'm in England. I actually took a vacation. Um...listen, I just wanted to say hello. I'll try you again soon." I hung up, relieved and shaking slightly.

At 11:55, having dented the pain in both head and arm with Dr. Rattish's prescription painkiller, I waited on the Langhorne's front porch. I had left both purse and fanny pack behind. Everything I needed fit in my pockets. My muscles were stiff but my jeans were loose. I felt lean and tough and ready to stand up to whatever Bellorham had to say.

The daylight made me squint, probably an effect of the concussion, so my sunglasses came in handy. I could have done without the bra, but the thrill of clean underpants was no small thing. My feet burned from the abuse of my stylish, ruined boots, which I wore without zipping them.

It hardly mattered because the soles flopped loose, but Small Common didn't have a shoe store and I was damned if I'd wear hospital booties to meet a lawyer.

From the porch I could see thatched roofs across the way, reminders that what Small Common lacked in commerce it made up for in charm. It might be the perfect hideout for a green-thumbed widow, a novelist with a day-job in Salisbury or an errant actor who needed a new path.

Tires crunched on gravel. A black Mercedes-Benz sedan—not new, not old—rolled to a stop on the driveway. I ran my fingers through my newly defiant hair.

A dark-haired man climbed out of the driver's side. I took one step down the porch stairs and stopped. The man approached and offered his business card.

"Hello, I'm Arthur," he said.

He was.

FIFTY

I stared.

"Perhaps you have one already." He even had the gravel voice.

"Sorry. No. Please." I held out my hand.

He smiled and gave me the card. "I'm glad to meet you, Cassandra." He had whiter, straighter teeth than the king's, which was to be expected in a century with dentists. "Extremely glad. Relieved, actually." He laughed in a soft, embarrassed way, as though maybe he shouldn't have said that. He had gray eyes.

"You mean the accident." I hardly heard myself.

"Well. Yes. Erm." He cleared his throat. "Have you had lunch?"

Bellorham had a sturdy build, like the king's. He was clean cut, like a lawyer should be, but not overly so. He wore his brown hair just long enough to pull it behind his ears. A country lawyer, I assumed. Without whiskers to soften it, the corner of his jaw was accentuated. Instead of a tunic he wore a white shirt with the sleeves rolled up. Whatever battles he may have fought had not scarred his arms.

He ushered me down the steps and held the car door for me. Such gentlemen, the Brits.

"I'm certain we can put things right without much trouble," he said, as he backed the car out of Ajay's small, gravel lot. "There was no damage to the monument and English Heritage doesn't want publicity. If the world knows how you got inside the fence then everyone'll want to have a go at it. And of course they're afraid you'll sue." He glanced at me, then back at the street. "You're not going to sue, are you?"

"English Heritage?"

"Stonehenge is one of their properties."

"Why would I sue?"

"Some people think that's what Americans do."

If I hadn't been in shock I'd have laughed. I tried smiling.

"You must tell me if you don't feel well," he said.

Not the reaction I was hoping for.

"I'll be happy to drive you to Salisbury if you need to see Rattish again."

"Thanks. No, I'm okay."

We pulled up in front of the pub and he hurried around to help me out of the car. I could have managed myself. We could have walked to the pub, for that matter.

An unlettered, painted sign, a picture of a turkey and a cat, hung above the door. Inside the pub a carved, wooden bar, leather booths and a stone fireplace (unlit for summer) accommodated a few regulars.

"I recommend the fish and chips," said Bellorham. "It's the real thing, not that greasy stuff they sell in the tourist spots. Hello, Tom."

The red-faced innkeeper ambled over to us from the far end of the bar.

"Welcome to Two Toms, miss. Good to see you're feeling better. Fish and chips?"

"Two," said Bellorham. He ordered a pint for himself and a sparkling water for me. The regulars tracked our progress across the room and we took a booth in the farthest corner by the window. One man said, "Hello, miss."

I welcomed the engulfing coziness of brown leather seats. "I guess people notice strangers in a town this small," I said to Bellorham as we settled in.

"We're only just a village. And you're a bit of a celebrity."

"Oh no," I blushed, "I'm not famous."

"You were a missing person. We've all been concerned. Especially me."

"Oh." Of course they hadn't seen my commercials. "Because you were driving."

"Yes." He leaned across the table and whispered. "And because it was strange. I didn't hit you. Did I?"

"I don't think so."

He gave a satisfied nod. "I did brake, you know, as hard as I could. But it was raining. The horse slid on the pavement. You flew into the bushes and the horse...seemed to fly after you. I got out to help and you were...gone."

He waited for my reaction with eyebrows raised.

"Gone?"

"Completely disappeared." He slapped the table. "The vision has not ceased to plague me."

It happened. He saw it happen. He saw me leave.

He tilted his head to intercept my gaze. "What is it?"

"Maybe you imagined it."

"I did nothing of the sort. The horse practically left skid marks."

"That's wild."

"Yes it is," said Arthur, watching me.

I turned away and gazed out the window, not knowing what else to do. People came and went from the half-timbered buildings of Small Common's one block downtown. They carried bags, swept sidewalks or stopped to chat. Between the shops, shady alleys beckoned to secret hiding places overflowing with flowered vines.

"I like Small Common," I said.

"It must seem provincial compared to Hollywood."

"Not necessarily a bad thing." I touched the rippled window glass and wondered about other eyes that had gazed through it in other years.

"That ring is most unusual," said Arthur. "Where'd you get it?"

"Um."

"I have one much like it."

He placed his hands on the table. They were just like the king's, only cleaner and without calluses. He didn't wear a wedding ring. On the fourth finger of his right hand he wore a ring like King Arthur's, the one that matched Guinevere's. It could have been the same ring, black from tarnish and age.

Tom arrived with our fish and chips. "Best in town," he said, placing the plates before us before heading back to the bar.

"Easy to say when you're the only pub," said Arthur to Tom's back.

I stared at the food, taking in the aroma of fried fish and hot potatoes.

"Go on. Aren't you hungry?"

I remembered I was famished. The fork felt strange in my hand. The fish was delicious and the green, lumpy stuff on my plate was interesting.

Inexplicably, Arthur poured vinegar on his meal. "The ring's been in my family for as long as anyone remembers. I've never seen another one 'til yours." He wiped his hands with his napkin, pulled his bifocals from his shirt pocket and lifted my hand to examine Guinevere's ring. "Yours is exactly the same only smaller, as though they were made to be companions. Sorry." He returned my hand to where he'd found it. "I assume you bought it in England?"

I swallowed. "It was sort of a gift."

"Sort of? From whom?"

I sat there with my ears ringing, wanting to tell him, but not wanting to tell him, how I got Guinevere's ring.

Arthur shook his head. "That was prying. Sorry."

"No."

"It was. Mind you, not all my questions are prying, but that one was."

He picked up his glass and, resisting the urge to ask more questions, dabbed his napkin at the puddle it left behind. I wasn't sure if I could trust him with my story and even if I could, I didn't know how to begin. Is there a good way to tell someone you went back in time without letting him think you're nuts? I took another bite of fish. I hadn't had much salt in a while and my mouth watered indecently. I gulped my water and splashed a little onto my shirt. I couldn't find my napkin.

"This must be difficult," Arthur said, breaking the silence. "Your holiday marred by an accident and now all these questions." He toyed with his—King Arthur's—ring. "At least I assume you're on holiday. Or do you intend to stay?"

"I haven't thought that far ahead."

"You must have come to Small Common for a reason. As opposed to London, for example."

To lose myself. "It's funny. I meant to visit King Arthur sites."

"Why is that funny?"

"I guess I got sidetracked."

"Well, I'm your man. I'm his namesake."

"Of course you are."

"Where would you like to go?"

Having the pleasure of Arthur's company beyond lunch was an appealing prospect. "Is there a hill?"

"Lots of hills."

"Big one. Flat."

"That would be Cadbury Castle."

My breath went shallow. "That's it."

"It's said to have been Camelot."

"There was no Camelot."

"Not much of a King Arthur fan, are you? All facts and no fantasy."

"I'm interested in the history, in what really happened."

"Fine. But we must stop at the stables first. They've agreed not to press charges if you settle the rental fee and pay for the farrier."

"What charges?"

His eyebrows went up. "Horse theft, my lady."

"Oh."

He leaned forward, with an expression of curiosity rather than accusation, and whispered again, "How *did* you get the horse inside the fence at Stonehenge?"

"I don't remember." I wasn't going to tell him there was no fence when I got there.

He was sympathetic. "Is it a total blank?"

"I rented Lucy. It started to rain. Your car came along, I remember that. Then lightning. I think that's what frightened Lucy. Then I don't remember anything 'til the hospital." My voice wavered on the lie.

Bellorham leaned back against the leather seat. His upper lip curled with a hint of mischief. "A month is a long time," he said. "It'll come back to you."

Lucy thrust her long, gray neck out of the stable window and neighed.

I hopped from the car and limped over to kiss her velvet muzzle. She knew me, all right, and I knew by the way she nibbled my hair that she was happy to see me. I wished she could talk. I wondered if she was as confused as I was and if she missed Llamrai as much as I missed my friends.

"You've bonded with that horse, haven't you?" said Arthur.

"Yeah."

"It's as though you've been through a trauma with her."

"Maybe I have."

The livery owner was happy to see me but for different reasons than everyone else's. I paid with a credit card, which suited him. Outside I kissed Lucy again and promised to visit her, knowing I'd keep the promise.

Arthur and I settled into his car once more. We turned south onto Old Wigley Road, the same winding road Lucy and I had taken a month before. "There's where my car almost hit you," said Arthur, as we approached an intersection where a gravel road met up with the paving alongside a row of bushes. There was indeed a gap in the bushes. I craned my neck to look back as we passed. On one side of the bushes, a gravel road. On the other side, a plowed field.

I tried to recognize landmarks but everything goes by faster in a car than it does on horseback. The sixth century woods where I'd landed must have been just past the bushes in that field. Britons and Saxons had fought and died there. King Arthur had stood on that very ground. Barns and hedgerows tamed it now and I couldn't be sure.

We stopped in the town of Warminster because Warminster had a shoe store and "You can't climb a hill in those sorry excuses for footwear." I was in a hurry to see Cadebir so I bought the first pair of comfortable walking shoes that fit. Arthur said he'd never known a woman to buy shoes in such haste, and I said I hadn't either.

Cadbury Hill dominated the landscape more like a sagging, green layer cake than the proud battleship it had once appeared to be. Where the ramparts had been imposing long ago, they were now overgrown with trees and grass. But it was Cadebir, and the sight of it in the distance simultaneously inflated and punctured me.

Other than the location it occupied at the foot of Cadbury Hill, the town of South Cadbury didn't resemble Cadebir Town in the least. The village marketed its English charm, not to Disneyland proportions, but with plenty of tourist accommodations and an inn called The Camelot. No soldier lurked, no chimney smoked. Tourists in running shoes and shorts roamed the streets snapping pictures of pubs, old churches, and cottage gardens.

Arthur parked beyond a church at the south end of town. We followed a shaded path up a mild slope and climbed some steps to a gate in a stone wall, where a sign declared we were about to enter "Castle Lane Leading to Camelot Fort." Castle Lane led straight up the hill without zig-zagging. Nor was it as steep as I remembered. Fifteen hundred years of marching feet and erosion had cut it deep. Trees towered above us and we walked in their canyon of roots.

Minutes before, I'd been eager; now I dragged my feet in my new walking shoes, afraid to arrive at the top, afraid of how different the hill fort would be. My heart bounced like a ball in a box, picking up momentum every time it hit the sides. I stopped to breathe away the dizziness. Arthur held my arm.

"Maybe this wasn't a good idea."

"I just need a minute."

I tried to focus on him. The irony that I approached Cadebir fort with a possible descendant of Arthur himself was not lost on me. But this man wasn't King Arthur. He looked the same, but something about him was fundamentally different from the king I had loved. I wondered if Bellorham felt connected to the place or if I just wanted him to.

The top wasn't far. When we crested it, Arthur waited, sensing I needed to take it in.

Everything was gone.

Nothing remained of the gate where I'd first entered the fort, or if it did, the guard house rested under years of earth. No hall, no barn, no barracks, no wall. Summer's sweet air replaced the smoke of the smithy.

Yet traces remained if I allowed myself to see them. The once dusty path that led up to the promontory had given over to wild, green grass on a mild slope. Even the wall could be imagined in the gentle berm around the hilltop. A few people walked the perimeter, looking out over the countryside and taking pictures. A big, white dog followed along behind a young couple holding hands.

"We can see the ramparts best on the south side," said Arthur. "Too many trees on the north. Watch your step."

He touched my good arm to guide me along the top of the berm, clockwise toward the south. My friends and I had made a habit of walking in the other direction. The smooth ground along the east side remained even where the breach had been, only two nights before. Where once there had been a copse, few trees grew; we strolled past it to the south wall and stood with the pasture at our backs.

"There," said Arthur. "The locals brag about this view."

The southern ramparts were in good shape, their tiers more defined than those we'd seen on our approach from the north. Arthur walked on and I followed slowly until I had to stop. Squinting, I looked out across the years. Guinevere and I had stood near this spot when, in our first private conversation, she'd told me that everything I could see, including herself, belonged to King Arthur. A country village sprouted where the road to her childhood home had once cut through the king's southwestern territory.

"You're not impressed?"

Arthur stood watching me, tossing a small rock from palm to palm. I hadn't spoken since we'd arrived on the hilltop. If I opened my mouth I'd cry. "Mmhmm."

"Such unbridled enthusiasm," he teased. "I think you should rest. Not much shade here, I'm afraid. I'll help you down."

He started down the berm and reached after to help me. I gave him my hand, stepping carefully down the slippery grass of the inside slope.

"There's a bench just over here."

My weariness surprised me. Perhaps the concussion had weakened me, or maybe I was worn out from the ordeal of two days before—if it had happened. I twisted Guinevere's ring on my finger to be sure it was still there.

"We'll sit here until you're rested. Perhaps this trip could have waited a day or two. That is, if you're staying."

"I have to stay, don't I?" I said, taking a seat on the bench.

"Why so?"

"To answer charges, I guess."

"I don't mind telling you I'm a very good lawyer," said Arthur, sitting beside me. "I wouldn't be surprised if we can take care of it all through email and a few memos."

That was a relief. "I should mention I'm unemployed."

"There's no fee."

"So, you're not a real lawyer?"

He laughed loud and full. "No—I mean yes. But I feel responsible." He tossed the rock into the grass and placed his hands on his hips as if to scold. "And damn it, I want to know how you got that horse inside Stonehenge." He was flirting.

"Are you married?" I had never asked such a forward question. I'd never cared before. It embarrassed me immediately but I had to know before I flirted back.

He was undaunted. "Not anymore. She cheated. Rather put me off. You?"

"Single, so far."

"Remarkable." He grinned.

I grinned back.

What was it that made him so different from the king besides the clothes, the haircut and the shave? He was physically the same, but this man was not King Arthur. I liked him enough to know I wanted at least to be his friend. I wouldn't lie to him—that much I'd learned—but I couldn't bring myself to tell him how Lucy and I had gotten inside that fence. I lowered my eyes. He didn't push it.

"Rested? Come on then, there's more." We stood. He didn't seem to think it at all strange to take my hand to lead me. It made me self-conscious.

"There was a dig in the late '60s. Some archaeologists tore the place up. They found a massive gate over here."

The southwest gate had indeed been impressive. Now it appeared as a depression in the berm, with a view out over the village to the south. A path wandered down the hill where once the wider road had led to Guinevere's childhood home. Trees overgrew the western slope, but where dense woods had once sheltered Myrddin's compound, a plowed field lay open to the sky as if a thick, unknowable forest had never existed there. Myrddin might never have existed, either, to scold me or teach me or help me back across the Gap, or to wonder if his batteries had saved my life.

"The bulk of the dig happened up there." Arthur released my hand to hike to the higher ground of the promontory. I remembered the rise as loftier. Arthur climbed to the plateau, folded his arms across his chest and watched my slow approach. An afternoon breeze lifted his hair from his temples. "Somewhere up here they found remnants of a great hall. I'm not sure exactly where, but it was toward this end of the hill. They didn't dig everywhere."

He was standing where King Arthur had stood beside his desk two days before. I shuffled through the grass in the hall where Agravain had leapt for Medraut's throat, a battle had ignited and lives, once interwoven, had begun to unravel. Two days before there'd been a kitchen, barracks, a barn and an imposing wall. Below, army camps had carpeted the plains. Two days before my friends had lived there, and an Arthur I'd loved who didn't love me. Two days before I'd cowered in my hut, right over there. I had crouched in the dark and made a fake Casey. I'd left her behind and run away, because I'd had to.

Arthur was talking.

"...essentially, though, it was their horsemanship that enabled them to resist the Saxons as long as they did."

"Stirrups."

"It's possible. But there's no proof they had them."

"They had them."

"What's your source?"

"My...?"

"How do you know they had stirrups?"

My chin quivered. "I guess I don't." I blinked back a tear, but it was too late.

"Cassandra, I'm sorry."

I tried unsuccessfully to stifle a sob. The wind was picking up. I should have brought a sweater.

Careful of my sling, Arthur put his arm around me. "It's only stirrups."

"Not exactly." And just like that I was weeping in his arms.

I missed King Arthur and Guinevere. I missed Cai's officiousness, Heulwen's spicy food and the timber walls of Cadebir's small world. I wished for idyllic days that never were, with King Arthur at Ynys Witrin. Even the smells of smoke and dung had become dear and I wanted them back.

But mostly I wept for time: time gone, time done that can't be undone, time we can't reach down through to touch those we've loved and lost.

Like a magician pulling a dove from his sleeve, Arthur produced a packet of tissues from his pocket. I'd been on a month-long quest for tissues and there they were. I laughed through my tears. "Thank you." Calming myself, I pulled one from the packet and turned away to blow my nose. The part of my body closest to Arthur was warm. When I caught my breath I said, "You must think I'm crazy."

"I do, quite."

I laughed again, which made me cry again.

The hint of glee had returned to curl his upper lip. I knew then what it was about him that was so fundamentally different from King Arthur. The king was melancholy. This Arthur was a happy man.

"Breakthrough?" he asked.

"Maybe." I smiled, sniffling. When I could breathe evenly we walked again. "I don't think any of this was your fault."

"Perhaps. But even so, you might let me help."

"Do I really need a lawyer?"

"Probably not."

We'd found our way to the north side of the hill. Miles of farms and fields stretched away through what had once been misty marshes. In the distance the sun was setting on a familiar shape.

"That's Glastonbury Tor," said Arthur. I'll take you there when you're feeling better. If you're staying a while, that is."

"The Tor," I repeated to myself. Its contours had softened and the lake was gone, but with the exception of a small tower on its top, from the distance it was essentially the same.

It had happened. It didn't matter if other people thought so. It had happened to me and I knew it. It was mine.

I had left nothing of value in Los Angeles. The only real friends I'd ever had, imaginary or not, were out of reach. On the northern ramparts of Cadbury Castle, I stood beside my new chance. "I'm staying."

Arthur squeezed my hand, the one that wore Guinevere's ring.

"You haven't told me how you and Lucy got inside that fence."

Myrddin had said, "If you should ever get a chance to start again, do begin with the truth next time."

Arthur had already said he thought I was crazy.

"This ring," I said, showing him my hand, "I think it belongs to your family. I promised someone I'd deliver it."

The sun gilded the Tor, glinting off the little tower, and the ring.

"I'm listening," said Arthur.

I breathed in the fresh, August air. "When I disappeared," I said, "I found myself here."

And I took it from there.

THE END

Acknowledgements

Maybe some people can create a book on their own, but I've had a good deal of help.

Colleen Dunn Bates, Tracy Connor, Donnie Dale, Gretchen Genz Davidson, Barbara Ellis, Margaret Finnegan, Reedy Gibbs and Susan Savitt Schwartz all read early drafts and offered valuable notes.

I wrote *Camelot & Vine* in California, but I had on-the-ground reconnaissance in England. Tom and Thicha Ellis checked out the approach to Cadbury Hill to make sure my description was correct. Karl Evans scouted Cadbury Hill itself, and even drew me a map.

Followers of my blog, Pasadena Daily Photo, inspire and encourage me every day. I'm also grateful for the support of my writers group: Janet Aird, Karin Bugge, Linda Dove, Margaret Finnegan, Paula Johnson, Karen E. Klein and Desirée Zamorano. If not for Paula Johnson I'd still be calling the book *Actress Meets King/has Adventure (Working Title)*. Not only did Paula come up with the title, she also designed my website, PetreaBurchard.com.

Thanks go to Tim Weske and the crew at SwordPlayLA.com for demonstrating a real sword fight. My bits of Latin came from Greg Bell. My French was repaired by Katie Murphy and her cousin-in-law, Jacques-Arthur Weil. I owe more thanks than I can count to Barbara Ellis for steering me on history and lore, and for sorting out my British. (One says "trousers," not "pants." I knew that.)

The book was proofread by Margaret Finnegan, Barbara Ellis, and John Sandel. I can't thank them enough, nor can I imagine we missed anything.

I cannot overstate the value of Kate Wong. She designed the book, from its smart interior to its gorgeous cover. I'm blessed to have worked with her early in her career. She will soon be out of my league.

I have the best husband ever (it's a proven fact). Thank you, John Sandel, for everything—and I do mean everything.

About the Author

Petrea Burchard is notorious as the first English voice of Ryoko, the sexy space pirate in the animé classic, *Tenchi Muyo!* Her acting career moved from Chicago to Hollywood via stage, television, film, and voice-over.

Petrea's writing career began with her humor column about the actor's life, *Act As If*, at NowCasting.com. Her articles, essays and short fiction have appeared in print and online. *Camelot & Vine* is her first novel.

petreaburchard.com